ENCHANTED

ALETHEA KONTIS

HARCOURT
Houghton Mifflin Harcourt
Boston | New York | 2012

Harcourt is an imprint of
Houghton Mifflin Harcourt Publishing Company.

www.hmhbooks.com

Text set in 12.5-point Perpetua Std

Design by Christine Kettner

LIBRARY OF CONGRESS CATALOGING-IN-PUBLICATION DATA
Kontis, Alethea.
Enchanted / Alethea Kontis.
p. cm.
ISBN 978-0-547-64570-4
[1. Fairy tales.] I. Title.
PZ8.K833En 2012
[Fic]—dc23
2011027317

Manufactured in the United States of America
DOC 10 9 8 7 6 5 4 3 2 1
4500349381

For my father,

who first read the fairy tales to me,

for my mother,

who told me to write her a new one,

and for my little sister, who was—

and always will be—

ungrateful.

May we all be doomed to a happy life.

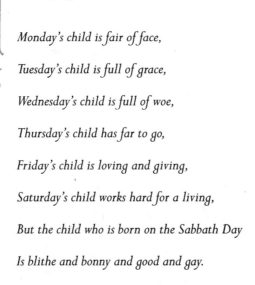

Monday's child is fair of face,

Tuesday's child is full of grace,

Wednesday's child is full of woe,

Thursday's child has far to go,

Friday's child is loving and giving,

Saturday's child works hard for a living,

But the child who is born on the Sabbath Day

Is blithe and bonny and good and gay.

1

Fool's Gold and Fairy Stones

MY NAME IS SUNDAY WOODCUTTER, and I am doomed to a happy life.

I am the seventh daughter of Jack and Seven Woodcutter, Jack a seventh son and Seven a seventh daughter herself. Papa's dream was to give birth to the charmed, all-powerful Seventh Son of a Seventh Son. Mama told him seven girls or seven boys, whichever came first. Jack Junior was first. Papa was elated. His dream died the morning I popped out, blithe and bonny and good and gay, seven daughters later.

Fortunately, coming first did not stop Jack Junior from being a wunderkind. I never knew my eldest sibling, but I know his legend. All of Arilland's children grew up in Jack's shadow, his younger siblings more than most. I have never known a time when I wasn't surrounded by the overdramatic songs and stories of Jack Junior's exploits. A good *number of new ones continue to spring up about the countryside to this very day. I have heard them all. (Well, all but the Forbidden Tale. I'm not old enough for that one yet.)*

But I know the most important tale: the tale of his demise, while he served in the King's Royal Guard. One day, in a fit of pique or passion (depending on the bard), he killed Prince Rumbold's prized pup. As punishment, the prince's evil fairy godmother witched Jack Junior into a mutt and forced him to take the pup's place. He was never heard from again.

They say my family was never the same after that. I wish I could know my father as tales portray him then: loud, confident, and opinionated. Now he is simply a strong, quiet man, content with his place in life. It is no secret that Papa harbors no loyalty to the royal family of Arilland, but he would not say a word against them.

My second-eldest brother's name is Peter. My third brother is Trix. Trix was a foundling child whom Papa discovered in the limbs of a tree at the edge of the Wood one winter's workday before I was born. The way Mama tells it, Trix was a son she didn't have to give birth to, and he made Papa happy. She already had too many children to feed, what was one more?

My sisters and I—

"What are you doing?"

Sunday's head snapped up from her journal. She had chosen this spot for its solitude, followed the half-hidden path through the underbrush to the decaying rocks of the abandoned well, sure that she had escaped her family. And yet, the voice that had interrupted her thoughts was not familiar to her. Her eyes took a moment to adjust, slowly focusing on the mottled shadows the afternoon sun cast through dancing leaves.

"I'm sorry?" She posed the polite query to her unknown visitor in an effort to make him reveal himself, be he real or imagined, dead or alive, fairy or—

"I said, 'What are you doing?'"

—frog.

Sunday forced her gaping mouth closed. Caught off-guard, she sputtered the truth: "I'm telling myself stories."

The frog considered her answer. He balanced himself on his spotted hind legs and blinked at her with his bulbous eyes. "Why? Do you have no one to whom you can tell them?"

Apart from his interruption, he maintained an air of polite decorum. *He's smart, too,* Sunday thought. *He must have been a human before being cursed.* Animals of the Wood only ever spoke in wise riddles and almost-truths.

"I have quite a large family, actually, with lots of stories. Only . . ."

"Only what?"

"Only no one wants to hear them."

"I do," said the frog. "Read me your story, the story you have just written there, and I will listen."

She liked this frog. Sunday smiled, but slowly closed her book. "You don't want to hear this story."

"Why not?"

"It's not very interesting."

"What's it about?"

"It's about me. That's why none of my family wants to hear it. They already know all about me."

The frog stretched out on his sun-dappled rock as if he were settling into a chaise lounge. She could tell from his body language—so much more human than frog—there would be no turning him down. "I don't know anything about you," he said. "You may begin your story."

It was completely absurd. Absurd that Sunday was in the middle of the Wood talking to a frog. Absurd that he wanted to learn about her. Absurd that he would care. It was so absurd that she opened her journal and started reading from the top of the page.

"'My name is Sunday Woodcutter—'"

"Grumble," croaked the frog.

"If you're going to grumble through the whole thing, why did you ask me to read it in the first place?"

"You said your name was Sunday Woodcutter," said the frog. "My name is Grumble."

"Oh." Her face felt hot. Sunday wondered briefly if frogs could tell that a human was blushing or if they were one of the many colorblind denizens of the forest. She bowed her head slightly. "It's very nice to meet you, Grumble."

"At your service," said Grumble. "Please, carry on with your story."

It was awkward, as Sunday had never read her musings aloud to anyone. She cleared her throat several times. More than once she had to stop after a sentence she had quickly stumbled through and start again more slowly. Her voice seemed overloud and the words felt foreign and sometimes wrong; she resisted the urge to scratch them out or change them as she went along. She was worried that this frog-who-used-to-be-a-man would hear her words and think she was silly. He would want nothing more to do with her. He would thank her for her time, and she would never see him again. Had her young life come to this? Was she so desperate for intelligent conversation that she was willing to bare her soul to a complete stranger?

Sunday realized, as she continued to read, that it didn't matter. She would have Grumble know her for who she was.

For as long as she had sat under the tree writing, she thought the reading of it would have taken longer, but Sunday came to the end in no time at all. "I had meant to go on about my sisters," she apologized, "but . . ."

The frog was strangely silent. He stared off into the Wood.

Sunday turned her face to the sun. She was afraid of his next words. If he didn't like the writing, then he didn't like her, and everything she had done in her whole life would be for nothing. Which was silly, but she was silly, and absurd, and sometimes ungrateful, but she promised the gods that she would not be ungrateful now, no matter what the frog said. If he said anything at all. And then, finally:

"I remember a snowy winter's night. It was so cold outside that your fingertips burned if you put them on the window-pane. I tried it only once." He let out a long croak. "I remember a warm, crackling fire on a hearth so large I could have stood up in it twice. There was a puppy there, smothering me with love, as puppies are wont to do. I was his whole world. He needed me and I felt like . . . like I had a purpose. I remember being happy then. Maybe the happiest I've been in my whole life." The frog closed his eyes and bowed his head. "I don't remember much of my life before. But now, just now, I remember that. Thank you."

Sunday clasped her shaking fingers together and swallowed the lump in her throat. He was definitely a man in a frog's body, and he was sad. She couldn't think what in her words had moved him so, but that wasn't the point. She had touched him. Not just him as a frog but the man he used to be. A more gracious reply Sunday could never have imagined. "I am honored," she said, for she was.

"And then I interrupted you." Grumble snapped out of his dreamlike tone into a more playful one. "Forgive me. As you can imagine, I don't get many visitors. You honor *me* by indulging me with your words, kind lady. Do you write often?"

"Yes. Every morning and every night and every moment I can sneak in between."

"And do you always write about your family?"

Sunday flipped the pages of her never-ending journal— her nameday gift from Fairy Godmother Joy—past her thumb. It was a nervous habit she'd had all her life. "I am afraid to write anything else."

"Why is that?"

Maybe it was because the honesty was intoxicatingly freeing or because he was a frog and not a man, but she felt strangely comfortable with Grumble. She had already told him so much about her life, more than anyone had ever before cared to know. Why should she stop now? "Things I write . . . well . . . they have a tendency to come true. And not in the best way."

"For instance?"

"I didn't want to gather the eggs one morning, so I wrote down that I didn't have to. That night, a weasel got into the henhouse. No one got eggs that morning. Another time, I did not want to go with the family to market."

"Did the wagon break a wheel?"

"I got sick with the flu and was in bed for a week," she said with a smile. "'Regret' is not a strong enough word."

"I imagine not," said Grumble.

"And now you're wondering what would happen if I wrote that you were free of your spell."

"The thought had crossed my mind."

"You might not come back as a man but as a mouse or a mule or a tiger who'd eat me alive. You might come back as a man but not the man you were. You might be missing something vital, like an arm or a leg or—"

"My mind?" Grumble joked.

"—breath," Sunday answered seriously.

"Ah. We must always be careful what we wish for."

"Exactly. If I write only about events that have already come to pass, there is no danger of my accidentally altering the future. No one but the gods should have power over such things."

"A very practical decision."

"Yes." She sighed. "Very practical and very boring. Very just like me."

"On the contrary. I found your brief essay quite intriguing."

"Really?" He was just saying that to be nice. And then she remembered he was a frog. Funny how she kept forgetting.

"Will you read to me again tomorrow?"

If her ridiculously large smile didn't scare him off, surely nothing she wrote could. "I would love to."

"And would you . . . be my friend?" he asked tenuously.

The request was charming and humble. "Only if you will be mine in return."

Grumble's mouth opened wide into what Sunday took to be a froggy grin. "And . . . if I may be so bold, Miss Woodcutter—"

"Please, call me Sunday."

"Sunday . . . do you think you could find it in your heart to . . . kiss me?"

She had wondered how long it would take before he got around to asking. A maiden's kiss was the usual remedy for his particular enchantment. Normally Sunday would have declined without a thought. But he had been so polite, and she was surely the only maiden he would come across for a very long time. It was the least she could do.

His skin was bumpy and slightly damp, but she tried not to think about it. After she kissed him, she straightened up quickly and backed away. She wasn't sure what to expect. A shower of sparks? Some sort of explosion? Either way, she wanted to stand clear of whatever was involved in turning a frog back into a man.

Sunday waited.

And waited.

Nothing happened.

They stared at each other for a long time afterward.

"I don't have to come back, you know, in case you were offering just to be courteous."

"Oh no," he said quickly. "I look forward to hearing about your sisters. Please, do come back tomorrow."

"Then I will, after I finish my chores. But I should go now, before it gets dark. Mama will be expecting me to help with dinner." She stood and brushed what dirt she could off her skirt. "Good night, Grumble."

"Until tomorrow, Sunday."

ellee

"Sunday, where have you been?"

Mama was a woman of few words, and those she was begrudgingly willing to part with could sting enough to make eyes water. She took one look at Sunday's skirt and answered her own question. "Dawdling in the Wood again. Well, I'm glad you decided to come back before the bugaboos made off with you. I'll thank you to take that spoon from your brother and get to stirring the pot. He's been at it long enough."

"Yes, Mama." Sunday removed the kerchief from her hair and slid her book into the pocket of her pinafore.

"Thanks, Sunday!" Trix happily handed over the spoon and scampered off to meet Papa, Peter, and Saturday at the edge of the Wood, at the end of their workday, just like he always did.

For all that he was two years her senior, Trix looked and acted like he had stopped aging at twelve. His fey blood kept him from growing at the same rate as his foster siblings—ultimately, he'd outlive them all. His blood was also the reason he was allowed to tend the cows but never milk them. Trix had a way with animals, but milk from his bucket was always sour. And if Trix stirred a pot for too long, the stew would be . . . different. The outcome was never the same. The first time, the stew tasted of the finest venison, with seasoned potatoes and wild mushrooms. The second time, it stank of vinegar. Mama never let Trix stir the pot for too long after that. She said the family didn't have enough food to go gambling it away, no matter how delicious the end result might be. Mama only ever bet on a sure thing.

Sunday worked the spoon absent-mindedly as she dreamt, scraping the bottom after every three turns. Mama checked on the bread in the oven. Friday set the table.

Most of Friday's dark hair was caught up into a knot, but several curls escaped, much like the halo of iron gray snakes around Mama's head. Friday had been mending—the straight pins in a row down the length of her sleeve gave her away—and she was wearing one of the patchwork skirts Sunday loved so much. Friday was deft with her needle, her own nameday gift from Fairy Godmother Joy. The fabric stallkeepers at the market gave their rags and remnants to the church in lieu of their tithe, and the church in turn gave them to Friday, along with measurements of any newly orphaned children and what articles of clothing they needed most. In return Friday kept whatever small pieces were left. Eventually, those pieces made up Friday's multicolored skirts. They were Sunday's favorite not just because they were so beautiful and lively, but because they were the result of many long hours spent toiling for the love of children her sister might never know.

"Go fetch Wednesday down from the tower," Mama told Friday as she set down the last fork. "Your father will be home any second."

Papa walked in the door as if on command, followed by a very weary Peter and a flushed and bright-eyed Saturday. Sunday imagined that on the verge of death, her workaholic sister would still be flushed and bright-eyed.

"Evening, my darlin'," Papa said as he hung his hat. "Fair weather today, so there was work aplenty. Wasn't much we left undone."

"Good, good," Mama said. "Go on, then, wash yourselves for dinner." Peter was too exhausted to argue. Saturday kissed her father on the cheek and scampered after her brother.

"Hello, my Sunday." Papa picked her up in his strong arms and spun her around. She hugged him tightly, breathing in his familiar scent of sweat and sap and fresh Wood air. "Any new stories today?"

"I wrote a little," she told him. "I mean to do more tonight."

"Words have power. You be careful."

"Yes, Mama." She couldn't ever mention her writing without this admonishment from her mother. Sunday tried not to be disrespectful and roll her eyes. Instead, she concentrated on Papa as he slowly lowered his large body into the chair at the head of the table. "What of your day, Papa? Did you find any new stories to tell?"

He sighed and rubbed his shoulder, which worried Sunday. Storyless days happened, when the weather was foul or the work had been troublesome. Most days, however, he brought her a little something: a tale or a trinket. His eyes would get bright, and there would be mischief and laughter in his voice. For that brief moment, Papa was happy, and he was all hers. Not that anything could dim the happiness that still shone inside her from making a new friend, but a story from Papa would have been the perfect ending to a perfect day.

Papa sat back and rested his hands on the table. He looked at Sunday thoughtfully, for a long time. And then he smiled. Sunday caught it and grinned right back at him, for in that smile was a story.

"We went deep into the Wood today." He leaned forward to whisper the words to her, as if they were a secret between the two of them. "Deep into the Wood, where the trees are so tall and the leaves are so thick that no sunlight touches the dark ground."

"Were you scared?" Sunday whispered back.

"A little," he admitted. "I told Peter and Saturday to stay at the edge of the Wood."

"You told Saturday to do something and she obeyed?" The

only orders Sunday had ever seen her sister obey were Mama's. Everyone always did what Mama said. Every time.

"Well, no," admitted Papa. "I gave her a very large task and told her she could join me when she'd finished."

"Did she finish?"

"Not yet. It was a very, very large task."

"You are a clever Papa."

"I am a Papa with much experience keeping his mischievous children out of harm's way," he said. "The edge is the safest, but deep in the Wood is where one finds the best trees. The old trees. I never take more than one at a time, and I always wait several moons before I take another one. The lumber from that tree will always fetch the highest price. It will be the most beautiful, and it will last forever. No mortal fire can burn Elder Wood."

"Did you take an Elder Wood tree today?"

"I did. I asked the gods' permission and begged the tree's forgiveness before I forced it to give its life. And since no one was around, I did not yell 'timber' before its fall."

Sunday gasped. Anyone who had ever lived near the Wood knew the importance of yelling to announce a treefall. Silence had dangerous consequences.

"The tree came down with a spectacular crash! And when the Wood became silent again, I heard a yelping."

"Did you hurt someone?" She was afraid to know the answer. It was clear that Mama wasn't worried; she continued to busy herself in the kitchen as if she hadn't heard a word of Papa's tale.

"Very nearly. It took me a long time to get to the other

side of the tree. When I did, I found a leprechaun hopping around."

"A leprechaun? Wasn't that lucky," Sunday remarked skeptically.

"Luckier for him! He was still alive to be hopping around," Papa said. "Trapped by his beard, he was, and mighty put out about it, too." Sunday laughed.

"I hope you asked for his gold," Mama's voice echoed from inside the oven as she retrieved the bread.

"Of course I did, woman! What kind of man do you take me for?"

"A fool, most days," Mama murmured. She wiped her hands on her apron and picked up a knife to cut the loaf. "Go on, finish your story."

"Thank you, wife." Papa leaned forward again and took up his storytelling tone once more. "The leprechaun pleaded with me to set him free."

"And did you?"

"I asked for his gold first." Papa glanced at Mama, but she did not show that she had heard his comment. "He promised it all to me. Told me if I used my ax to chop him free he would lead me to it." Mama clucked her tongue. She was listening. "Of course I didn't believe him," Papa said loudly. "I said I wanted proof. He told me he had three gold coins in his pocket. He would give them to me as a down payment, so if he ran away, I wouldn't be left with nothing for my trouble."

"And you took the gold?"

"I did indeed. Three solid pieces of bright gold, they were.

I put them in my pocket." He patted his hip. "Then I cut the leprechaun free. And do you know what he did?"

"What?"

"He complained! Cheeky little bugger. Said I had made a wreck of his charming beard and that it would never grow back the same! I pointed out that I was a woodsman, not a barber. The vain imp! Should have been grateful just to be alive!" Sunday giggled helplessly at the thought of burly Papa as a hairdresser. "He would have none of it. Told me that since I had ruined his good looks I didn't deserve any of his gold. He wiggled his nose and vanished right there in front of my eyes."

"But you still had the three gold pieces?"

"I did indeed, so I don't feel cheated in the slightest. I brought them home for you." Sunday's heart leapt for joy as he reached into his pocket. Whatever treasure Papa had brought would certainly go to the family, but it meant the world that he made a show of giving it to her. Mama acted as if she weren't paying any attention, but she had stopped cutting the bread mid-slice.

"I'm afraid they're a little worse for the wear." Papa opened his hand and dropped the contents onto the table.

"Bah!" Mama scoffed when she saw. "Fool's gold and fairy stones. Such has been this family's lot in life. I should have known."

Sunday's treasure was three small stones. One was smooth and deep ocean blue run with lines of stark white, one was splotchy green like moss trapped in pale amber, and one was sharp-edged and milky pink. Fool's gold or not, these stones were hers to keep, a thousand times more valuable to her than any gold ever could be. Inside these stones Papa's story would live forever; Sunday would remember the tale every time she saw them. It was just as she'd hoped: the perfect end to a perfect day.

"They're beautiful," Sunday said over the shiny stones.

"They're yours if you want them."

Sunday threw herself into Papa's arms and hugged him again.

Mama set the platter of bread firmly on the table beside them. "Enough nonsense now. Sunday, mind the stew. Jack, bank the fire and call your children. It's time for supper."

2

Conversing with Fairies

*MY SISTERS AND I are the products of a woman
with as little creativity as her mother before her, and
so our naming was as clever in its simplicity as it was damning in its
curses. Second born to my mother were the twins, thus securing a female
majority in the household that was never again in jeopardy. Monday
was indeed fair of face, but Tuesday was the dancer.*

*Stories describe Tuesday as a slip of a young girl, a moth at the
flame, a reed in the wind, a vision of constant movement whose grace
the stars and sunsets envied. Ever the Life of the Party, Tuesday garnered
invitations for every occasion from Royal Balls to County Fairs (from
which Monday always returned home as the belle).*

*Mama enjoyed the popularity but, true to form, complained about
travel expenses and the cost of keeping her active daughter in shoes,*

which she reputedly remarked was more than enough for twelve dancing princesses. It seemed a godsend when an elfin shoemaker gave Tuesday a pair of scarlet slippers that would never wear out. Mama had her doubts, but she hoped he was right. And so he was, for Tuesday could not dance those shoes to death.

They danced her to death instead.

Tuesday died less than a year post-Jack (my family's history is broken up into pre— or post—Jack Junior events). There was immense sadness in the wake of her passing, but no one mourned more than Monday. Worse yet, Monday's grief apparently amplified her fair beauty. She held her tongue to keep others' from wagging, but her silence only added to the intrigue. Songs called her the most beautiful woman in the land. Monday hated every minute. She ventured outside only to walk the many miles to the cemetery on the hill and place flowers on her twin's grave. Every Tuesday she went, rain or shine, sleet or snow, despite our parents' wishes.

One sickly green morning, heedless of the weather as she always was, Monday was caught in a storm sent from the bowels of Hell itself. Tossed in the merciless wind, pelted by walls of rain, and battered by fists of ice, Monday lost her way in the Wood and found herself at the doorstep of a hunting cabin. Inside were two princes on holiday——one dark and one fair——who had chosen to celebrate the storm as most men choose to celebrate everything.

As they toasted each other for the umpteenth time, the fair prince congratulated himself on his recent success at finding the perfect wife. He had given the girl a test, and she had spun three rooms full of straw into gold for him! The dark prince, upon hearing the tale, drunkenly announced that his wife would be so beautiful, so delicate, that she *would not be able to sleep comfortably with a pea under the mattresses. And then Monday arrived—a bedraggled, tempest-tossed wretch on the stoop, begging asylum. They begrudgingly offered her a room and slipped a pea under the mattress there. The next morning, when my lovely sister greeted her hosts with a rash of fresh bruises, the dark prince fell to his knees and asked for her hand in marriage.*

We owe our current livelihood to Monday. Her bride gift was a tower at the edge of the Wood that had no door—

"No door?" Grumble croaked.

"It has only one high window, on the uppermost floor. The property had been handed down in some royal female line for generations, but it was never used, since there was no practical way of getting inside it," said Sunday. "If it was ever part of a castle, the rest has long since crumbled. Not that we cared; at the time we were crawling over ourselves like rats in our little cottage. So Papa knocked a door in the tower and built the rest of our house around its base. We call it the 'towerhouse.'"

"What once was a 'dower house.' Very clever."

Sunday groaned. "Yes, I think Papa came up with that one. Unfortunately, it looks nothing like a castle. More like . . . a shoe." Oh, the years of school-age ridicule that had borne.

"A shoe."

The way he said the word made Sunday giggle. Her cheeks ached; no friend before had made her laugh as much as Grumble. It was nice to be so happy, even for a few hours. "Between Tuesday's fate and our house, shoes are a recurring theme in my life."

"And what of your other sisters?"

Having come to the end of what she'd written about Monday, Sunday folded her journal across her stomach and stretched out in a patch of fading sunlight before answering his question. "Wednesday is the poet, all prosaic and lyrical."

"'Wednesday's child is full of woe,'" quoted Grumble. Of all things he might have forgotten, that childish nonsense rhyme about the days of the week wasn't one of them.

"I might suggest other things she's full of," said Sunday, trying to find a comfortable position on the moss-covered ground. The last frost of winter had come and gone, so they'd planted beans for hours that morning. Beans were always the first to go into the garden. The afternoon sun was warm on her weary bones, and the conversation with Grumble was easy and comfortable. No one else made Sunday feel quite so peaceful. She wished she could stay like this forever.

"Thursday ran off with the Pirate King when she was a little older than me, but she still sends us letters and gifts from time to time. She always knows when we'll be needing something. A package from Thursday is always a bit of an event at our house."

"'Thursday's child has far to go.'" Grumble hopped back into the well to rewet his drying skin. "Is Friday 'loving and giving,' then?" he asked when he returned.

"Friday is the best of us all. She spends most of her days at the church helping orphans and the elderly. At night she makes clothes for them after she's finished with the household mending. She performs miracles with cloth that should have worn out long ago; I often wonder what she could do if she had whatever material she wanted at her disposal. There are few who would not envy Friday's talent."

Grumble noticed what she had left unsaid. "And you are one of those few."

It was strange to have someone who listened to her so intently, who *cared* about her. Sunday liked the attention so much that it scared her a little. "If there is anything of Friday's I would wish to have, it would be her heart. Every task that Friday performs is done with love: pure, unconditional love with no malice, no strings attached."

"I find it very hard to believe you lack such compassion."

"I'm just as selfish as anyone else."

Thankfully, Grumble did not press her further. "And Saturday? Is she indeed a hard worker?"

"She works hard at being a pain in the neck, most days." The comment coaxed a chuckling burp from Grumble. "Saturday is best when she's kept busy. She goes into the Wood every morning and helps Papa and Peter with the cutting like a sturdy workhorse, but I think she takes after Thursday more than everyone realizes. I see it sometimes, that glint of a daydream in her eye. And mischief. Gods help us all if she's ever left idle."

"Which brings us to you, the doomed one."

The laugh that burst from Sunday's lips surprised her. It was a curious thing, having one's words thrown back like that. "'Blithe and bonny and good and gay.' Who could ever live up to that? It's not in any way realistic. I don't want to be happy and good and dull. I want to be *interesting*."

"I assure you, my bonny friend, you are very interesting. And you are a writer, like your sister before you?"

"Well, I'm not quite so melancholy gravy as Wednesday, Our Lady of Perpetual Shadow . . . but yes, a little. In my own way."

"You have a gift for words," said Grumble.

"A curse, more like. But perhaps it's good that I write only about the past. Mama says I spend too much time in little fantasy worlds and not enough in this one."

"If you did not indulge in fantasies, how else would you know if you were living an interesting life?"

"Thank you. I fully intend to argue that point with Mama next time she brings it up." Sunday looked at the sky. "Which, if not tonight, will be tomorrow morning at the earliest. I will report back to you, Sir Frog."

Either the gasping half-croaks that Grumble let out were a froggy laugh, or he was dying. Or both. "I can't remember when I've enjoyed a conversation more, my lady. But as I can't remember much of anything, it's possible that's not saying much."

"I will take it as a compliment."

"Please do." He blew out his bright yellow throat and then sighed. "Would that I were a man, Sunday. If I met you tomorrow, I would probably propose."

Lulled into comfort, Sunday answered from her heart before she had time to consult her brain. "If you met me tomorrow, I'd probably say yes." She sat up immediately. The pool of sunlight had faded and the twilight breeze was cool on her skin. "I should be getting back home before I am missed."

He didn't acknowledge her reply, but she could tell it had made him happy. She was feeling a little happy herself. "Will you come again tomorrow?" Grumble asked. "Please?"

"I will try." Her heart fluttered in her chest, and she was sure her face was red again. She ran her fingers through her hair, dislodging bits of twigs and grass and hiding her bashfulness from her new friend, yesterday a stranger and today so much more. The bond forming between them was strong and fast; her emotions seemed entirely too powerful for something that could never happen.

Was she falling in love with this frog? Did she even know what love was? Would that she had ever been courted by a man so that she might know if her feelings were true or fleeting. She wished that she had the power to turn Grumble back into a man so that she might discover for herself.

"Sunday?"

She ceased her tidying and forced her silly brain to stop its chatter. "Yes?"

"Will you kiss me before you go?"

It was as if he'd heard her thoughts. She wanted to try again, though it hadn't worked yesterday; there was no reason to suppose it would work today. Sunday felt terrible. But Grumble's little heart seemed to hold more hope than most people had in a lifetime. Why couldn't she summon that optimism so easily? At least magic would answer the question of whether her love (or whatever this was she felt) was true . . . She pulled her tidied hair from her face and leaned down to kiss his back once again.

Once again, nothing happened. Once again, she wasn't sure how to feel.

"Good night, Grumble."

"Good night, my Sunday."

eelle

Darkness hugged the world in hazy twilight, and Sunday's mind cartwheeled with silly thoughts, so her sister easily half scared the life right out of her. Perched atop the garden's rock wall, Saturday leapt out of the shadows like a huge wildcat. Sunday shrieked, and then narrowed her eyes at Saturday's anything-but-innocent smile. Sometimes she could be worse than Trix.

And odd. Saturday never had time for her lazy dreamer sister after a hard day's work. Sunday might have expected Mama at the gate, wooden spoon in hand to rap her on the knuckles for being late. Wednesday often wandered the garden at dusk, having stared at the sky so long she'd forgotten whether she was really in this world or another (it could go either way with Wednesday). All things considered, meeting Saturday meant there was a story somewhere, so Sunday was all ears.

"You missed them, Sunday! They were both so handsome, and they wore daggers in their boots, and they finished each other's sentences, which was a little odd, because one of them had the strangest accent. But odd in a good way, you know? A very good way." She said "very" as if the word might stretch all the way to the moon.

As usual, Saturday was starting her story in the wrong place. Sunday would have scolded her, but her sister's enthusiasm was terribly contagious. "Who?" Sunday asked, half because she knew Saturday wanted her to and half because she really wanted to know. "Who was here? Who did I miss?"

"Their names were Crow and Magpie. Magpie had the funny accent. Or was it Crow? Anyway, they've come and gone now and you've missed them, but they left us a trunk from Thursday." She took Sunday's hand and dragged her up the walk to the door. "We had to wait for you, and you've dawdled a painfully long time. So hurry!"

A full head taller than Sunday already and rippling with muscles beneath her boy's clothes, Saturday constantly underestimated her own brute strength. Sunday followed her just fast enough to keep her shoulder from being ripped out of its socket. Thursday never forgot a birthday or anniversary or nameday, but sending cards and presents at regular intervals wouldn't have left her and her husband any time for actual pirating and would put them under constant threat of various authorities. So now and again, at random intervals, a trunk or crate would arrive, teeming with gifts.

Sunday regretted missing the illustrious Crow and Magpie. She would have to ask someone about them later, but whom? Saturday would take forever, purposefully and annoyingly, but Sunday would pry information out of her eventually. Mama would no doubt describe them as dirty rotten scoundrels with eyes on the silver. Wednesday would put together an eloquent string of seemingly unconnected adjectives that one day, months later, would make perfect sense. Papa might do them justice if he wasn't too tired after the festivities.

Saturday burst through the door, dragging Sunday in her wake. All heads turned except Friday's; she was on her knees before the enormous trunk, her patchwork skirts a rainbow pool around her. Trix sat cross-legged on the lid; if anyone was going to open it, he would know about it first. Mama and Wednesday were perched on the couch. Peter slumped beside them, his heavy-lidded eyes trying their best to stay open. Papa stabbed the logs in the hearth with a poker, urging a bit more warmth out of them. Fresh, burning wood always reminded Sunday of Papa.

"Welcome home, little one. Hour got away from you while conversing with fairies again?"

Saturday came to an abrupt halt, and Sunday got a face full of cotton shirt. She shoved her giant sister forward. "They do have the best stories to tell," Sunday said to her father.

Papa put his hand over his heart. "Better than mine? You wound me! Now, shall we see what booty my daughter the Pirate Queen has sent us?" Trix hopped off the trunk. Papa turned the latch and threw the lid back with a crash that startled Peter awake. Friday gasped and covered her mouth with her hands.

Folded inside the trunk was the most frighteningly exquisite material Sunday had ever seen. It shimmered in the firelight like silver fairy wings. "I can't touch it," Friday whispered. "It's too beautiful."

Papa patted her on the head. "Give yourself a moment, darlin'." He reached over her to retrieve the folded parchment that lay atop the mesmerizing cloth. While he read Thursday's letter aloud, Sunday closed her eyes and pictured her feisty, fiery sister there in the room with them.

"*Dear beloved family,*

I hope my treasure box finds you all well—Crow and Magpie will report to me if they see otherwise. Or if they don't see some of you at all, since I suspect Sunday will have been wandering the Wood all day, as she always does once spring warms the ground enough.

This letter will make more sense if you've already seen your gifts, so go ahead and upend the trunk. Papa can finish reading once you've hit bottom. Yes, Friday, the fabric is for you, but if you don't touch it, how are you ever going to be able to make anything with it?"

Papa smiled, folded the letter, and put it in his pocket. Even oceans and continents away, Thursday knew her family all too well. Friday wiped her palms on her skirt and gingerly lifted the silver fairy fabric out of the trunk. Beneath that bolt was a scarlet one, then one of dusky rose. By the time she uncovered the layer of iridescent blue-gray, her eyes were brimming with tears.

"All my sisters will have dresses," Friday proclaimed. "The most beautiful dresses in the world!"

"Can't I have trousers instead?" whined Saturday.

"Dresses designed for damsels divine," Wednesday said dreamily.

"Woodcutters' daughters have no need for fancy dresses," Mama muttered.

"I want the silver one," called Sunday.

"There's got to be something else in that chest!" All the women in the room glared at Trix save Saturday, who crouched behind him, urging him on. Friday stuck out her tongue and lifted out a damask-covered box that had her name on a scrap of paper pinned to the top. She gasped as she opened this, too. "A proper seamstress's kit!"

Having had enough of what would ultimately become laundry, Trix shoved Friday out of the way and dove headfirst into the trunk. Papa stopped chuckling long enough to say, "Careful, son." As usual, it was too late.

"A bow!" Trix cried triumphantly. "And arrows! She's sent along some arrows for you too, Peter, but no bow. Too bad."

"A proper man-sized bow for Peter wouldn't have fit inside that trunk." Papa lifted Trix out of the chest with one strong arm. "You've had your treasures now, boy. Let your sisters have theirs."

"I will thank you to shoot those arrows outside," Mama said sternly. Trix was already trying on his quiver and prancing about trying to draw the bowstring.

Friday handed a no-longer-sleepy Peter the larger set of arrows. He pulled a long sheath from the quiver and examined the arrow intently. Peter had always been fascinated by how things were made.

"These books are surely for you, Wednesday." Friday lifted out four thick, leather-bound volumes and handed them one by one to Wednesday, whose smile got bigger and bigger as the pile in her lap grew. Sunday tried not to be envious; Wednesday always let her borrow books from her library at the top of the tower.

Mama was the just-gracious-enough recipient of a large marble rolling pin, and Papa spared Friday lifting out his new sharpening stone and a bag of dark seeds. Saturday and Sunday received small silk bags with their names written on scraps of thick paper and tied to the closing ribbons. Sunday's contained a wealth of shiny hairpins with tiny stars and insects and mythical creatures on them. Saturday's clutch contained a beautiful brush and mirror set. The brush had an elegant ebony handle, and the mirror was silver, with intricately carved roses that stood out in relief on the back and sides. Each piece had words etched into it that might have been French, but Saturday didn't leave the offending items visible long enough for Sunday to tell for sure. She shoved them both back into the silk bag and then sat on it. Despite Thursday's good intentions and omniscient magic spyglass, she still labored under the impression that Sunday was a baby . . . and that Saturday was a girl.

She had also apparently forgotten that the family was a sister short. Alone at the bottom of the trunk was one last long, thin, silk bag. The scrap of paper tied to this ribbon read MONDAY.

No one made a move to touch it.

Sunday was very young when she'd last seen her eldest sister, shortly after her marriage and before the Woodcutter family had moved into the towerhouse. Mama and Monday didn't speak at all; while Sunday didn't know the exact reason why, she could guess. Simply put, Mama was a very hard person to love. Her work ethic prescribed sweating and bleeding and earning one's riches rather than marrying into them and moving away at the first opportunity. Mama accepted Thursday's gifts because Thursday had always been stubborn and defiant, mishearing Mama's petty comments and scolding as professions of love. (The girls had learned a lot from Thursday about how to deal with their mother.) This gift for the outcast sister was just a further demonstration of that defiance. Odd and uncomfortable but definitely expected.

Monday was another story. She had traded her bride gift for her freedom and never contacted them again. The towerhouse had been the beginning and the end of Monday's generosity; Mama frowned upon charity just as she frowned upon everything else.

It was Wednesday who scooped the small bag out of the trunk. She put it in her pocket and, nice as you please, said, "Let's hear the rest of the letter now, Papa."

Sunday was as shocked by Wednesday's ability to string together a coherent sentence as she was by Monday's gift. As instructed, Papa retrieved the parchment from his pocket and resumed his reading.

"Every woman deserves something beautiful. My sisters are no exception. (Don't scowl, Saturday. You might even thank me one day.) Friday, please don't forget to make a dress for yourself. I know how you are. Peter, I knew you would prefer to carve your own bow. Use Trix's as a guide. Papa will help you.

*I love and miss you all and think about you every day.
Don't worry, Mama: I don't harbor the slightest notion of
giving up my perfect home on the seas, where the stars fall
straight into the water and the storms are so fierce that
afterward you remember what a divine privilege it is to be alive.
Dream of me, my beloved family, happy in my plundering and
adventuring, for when the waves rock me to sleep tonight, I will
be dreaming of you.*

    Give Monday my love.

    Your favorite daughter and sister, Thursday"

3
Gifts Like Words

GRUMBLE? Are you here?" Bucket in hand, Sunday carefully tiptoed around the crumbled pieces of the well. In the heat of the day, the rocks perspired more than Sunday herself, and she slipped. She threw her arms out in an effort to catch herself—she didn't want to squash the best friend she'd ever had! After tilting about madly for a moment, she regained her balance.

There was a deep, rumbling croak of froggy laughter to her left.

"Caught that, did you?"

"Yes," he answered. "Though I was afraid you wouldn't."

Sunday found a more level section of ground and plopped down on it. "Grace was a different sister, remember?"

"So true, so true." He hopped closer. "You're early. No chores today?"

"I wish! I'm supposed to be taking Trix to market to sell the cow; the chores that didn't get done this morning will still be there when we get home. Tomorrow I'm off to church to help Friday, which means even more chores later. Chores, chores. Sometimes I think all I do is chores."

"Will your brother be all right by himself?"

"He knows exactly where to go, to whom he's supposed to sell the cow, and what price he's to fetch. He'll be fine." The last part was more prayer than statement. Sunday had outlined every detail with Trix, three times over, but Trix was a force of nature. She refused to think about all the things that could go wrong, so she changed the subject. "I brought you a present." She held out the small bucket.

"I . . ."

Grumble clearly had no idea what to thank her for, and she laughed. "We talk for so long that you get dehydrated. This way"—she leaned over the side of the well and dropped the bucket in the water, scooping it full to the brim—"you won't have to excuse yourself to take a swim." She nestled the bucket between two oversized rocks. "See? You don't have to go to the well, for I've brought the well to you."

"I have never known such kindness," he said.

"Of course you have," she assured him. "You just don't remember."

He didn't contradict her.

The giving and receiving of gifts had always been important in Sunday's family. Gifts, like words, carried with them a great deal of power. They bestowed good fortune just as power-fully as they could curse; they could bind people together or tear them apart. The bucket was merely a token of how deeply Sunday valued Grumble's friendship, but she was glad to see that it meant as much to him as it did to her. If she couldn't wish him human again, she could at least wish him happy.

Sunday ran her thumb across the pages of her book. "I didn't have a lot of time to write last night, but you will enjoy the reason." Grumble hopped to a large rock beside his new wooden wading pool and settled in as Sunday told him of Thursday's amazing trunk, her pirate husband, and the magic spyglass that could see the past, present, and future from leagues away—her fairy godmother's nameday gift.

Sunday didn't skim over any detail. Grumble laughed at her reenactment of Trix's intentions to steal from the rich and give to the poor, and he worried over the puzzle of Thursday's gift for Monday. When she was done, he urged her for more, so she opened her book and read to him what little she had writ-ten about her siblings and each of their nameday gifts from Fairy Godmother Joy.

With every word she spoke, Sunday felt more comfortable. It was as if she had known Grumble all her life, only to him all her stories were new. She hoped they could be friends forever and was wistful they could not be more. Between all the stories she had left to tell and all the adventures she was sure were yet to come, they would always have something to talk about. Always.

But she knew that could never be; their friendship would last only as long as Grumble retained his memories. If he stayed a frog, she knew from Papa's tales that he would eventually forget he had ever been a man. He would not be able to hear her stories. He would lose the power of speech. Eventually, he would not know Sunday at all. Inevitable as that might be, now that she had this precious friendship, she was incredibly frightened of losing it.

Grumble must have been thinking something similar. "I'm forgetting what it was like to be human," he confessed. "I can't remember faces or names, my own included. I've forgotten what it was like to get out of bed in the morning. The feel of clothes on my skin. The taste of breakfast on my tongue. Food. I think I loved food, once."

Sunday's heart went out to him.

"But when I'm lost in your words, I see rooms and people and colors; I feel laughter and sorrow and curiosity. I forget that I am a frog. Instead I am simply a man, sitting here in the Wood beside his beautiful friend, listening to stories about her interesting life. You are magic to me, Sunday."

She bit her lip. Strange emotions welled in her again. It was the loveliest thing anyone had ever said to her.

"You have ruined me. I didn't realize how much I longed for the company of others until I had your words. When they are gone, the nights are darker. The silence is loud and bottomless, and I am empty. I miss them, my beloved Sunday, and I miss you."

It was no use fighting; the tears came. She was powerless

to break his curse, but she could give him what she had. She opened her book to the next blank page and started writing. When she was done, she leaned back and smiled at her friend. "'Sunday was nothing,'" she read aloud, "'until she met Grumble—a beautiful man, with the soul of a poet. He was her best friend in the whole wide world, and she loved him with all her heart.'" She closed the book gently in her lap. Her chest hurt. Her hands shook. "Oh, how I wish—"

"Sunday!" Her name was yelled loudly, from far away. "Sunday!"

Trix? What was he doing back so soon? She squinted into the high sun. He should have been gone another hour or two at least . . .

"Suuuuuun-daaaaaaaaay," Trix cried through the trees.

"Here!" she called out. "I'm here." And then to Grumble: "Well, like it or not, you're about to meet some of my family."

"It will be an honor," said the frog.

Trix crashed through the brush and stumbled into the clearing, quiver at his back, bow drawn with an unsteady arm. It was sweet that he thought she needed saving . . . and somewhat frightening that he was armed and dangerous.

Sunday held up a hand to stop him; the fantasy of dashing rescue fled his eyes, and he lowered the bow. "Ooooooooo," he said breathlessly. "A Fairy Well." Sunday grabbed his scrawny wrist before he could scamper off across the slippery rocks and break his neck. That was all she needed.

"Too right, young sir," said Grumble. "This is indeed a Fairy Well. I had almost forgotten." Trix froze and stared at the frog.

"Trix, meet my friend Grumble. Grumble, my brother Trix."

"Wow," said Trix.

"Enchanted," said Grumble.

"Did you see the fairy when she was here?" Trix asked him.

"I did," said the frog. "She took much delight in playing tricks on people who passed by."

The frog's answer puzzled Sunday. By the state of things, the well had been abandoned for a very long time. Grumble couldn't have been a frog for that long, or he would have forgotten his humanity entirely. Perhaps he was remembering some other story?

"Did she trick you?" asked Trix. "Is that why you're a frog?"

"No," said Grumble. "But I did ask if she could remove my curse."

"And what did she say?"

"Apparently, only the fairy who places the curse can remove it. All another fairy can do is . . . bend it a little. Shorten the sentence. She gave me one more year as a man before the curse took hold, and she provided an out clause."

"The kiss of true love?" asked Trix, wide-eyed.

"That very thing," said Grumble. He did not raise his head to look at Sunday, but Trix was too clever by half.

"Did you—?" Trix started to ask.

Sunday could not bear to revisit her failure. "The cow. You sold her so quickly?" Again, it was more of a hope than a question.

The wide grin he gave her was unsettling. "I am a shrewd

and lucky tradesman! I happened upon a man in the Wood who was on his way to market for just such a cow. Too bad you weren't there, Sunday, you might have learned a thing or two from your older brother."

The excitement that only minutes before had soared in Sunday's throat now soured in her stomach. *No. Please, gods, no.*

"I sold it to him for these." Trix slowly opened his palm, teasing Sunday with a glimpse of the contents.

"Beans." She was going to throw up.

"*Magic* beans," Trix said proudly. "That sly fox was going to give me only one measly bean. Clever me, I got him up to *five!* After all, what if one doesn't sprout? Smart thinking, eh?" Trix folded the orange-gold, sweat-stuck beans back into his pocket and patted them. "I will plant them under my tree house and then . . . Sunday? Are you all right?"

Sunday had stopped breathing. She was a dead woman. A stupid, stupid dead woman. What had she been thinking? Trix had been her responsibility, and she had let him go off alone and trade their best cow for . . . for . . .

"Sunday?" Trix was suddenly worried.

"Mama will kill me," she whispered. "We needed that money, Trixie. How will we eat?"

"You'll see." His voice was all childish wonder and infinite hope. "My magic beans will grow big, big as you've ever seen, and we will have food forever."

His innocence was as beautiful as it was frustrating. "Beans take time to grow," Sunday explained. "What will we eat to-morrow? And the next day?"

The severity of the situation seemed to sink in. "I'm sorry, Sunday," he said quietly. He put his thin arms around her shoulders and squeezed her tightly. "I don't want you to die."

"If I may be so bold."

In her misery, Sunday had completely forgotten about Grumble. The frog sat patiently beside a perfectly round, slime-covered rock. Trix left his sister to sit beside Grumble. "Whatcha got there?" He picked up the spherical stone.

"Something to save your sister's life," he said. "That life's become uncommonly important to me over the last few days."

Sunday shook her head. It was a sweet gesture. To Grumble, the ball must have looked like a precious gem or a fairy trinket or—

"Gold!" cried Trix.

"What?" Sunday snatched the ball out of her brother's hand; she was unprepared for its weight and almost dropped it. She scraped at the scum with her fingernail to reveal the smooth, hard surface beneath. "It is!" She laughed, jumped up and down, and hugged the bauble to her. And then she remembered that she wasn't a hoarding kobold. Sunday held the ball out to Grumble. "We can't take this."

"Sunday, I'm a frog. What use have I for such a pretty?"

"But its worth alone . . ."

"That and a hundred more like it wouldn't get me what I want most in the world," he reminded her. "But if it buys even a second of your family's happiness, then to me it is worth more than any moneylender could possibly exchange for it."

Her conscience still wouldn't let her take the bauble. Sunday's eyes moved from her brother to her friend, her mind weighing her needs against her morals. They both weighed about two pounds of solid gold.

"Please," said Grumble. "Consider it a gift."

A gift. He had not refused her gift, so she should not refuse his . . . though she had given him a bucket, and he had given her a family's happiness. Sunday wondered if Grumble had any idea how much power he had over her. She closed her eyes, nodded, and slipped the bauble into her pocket. She needed to leave before she changed her mind. But first, she crouched, scooped Grumble up in her hands, and kissed him heartily. "Thank you, my dear friend, more than you will ever know." He politely said nothing to her exuberance. "Trix and I must be going now, but church or not, I will find a way back tomorrow so that I can tell you everything! I promise!"

She did not hear him say goodbye. Excited, Sunday skipped beside Trix through the brush. They raced each other to the edge of the Wood until they spotted the towerhouse on the horizon. Their energy spent, they slowed to a walk. The weight of the golden ball knocked reassuringly between Sunday's book and her leg, reminding her how painful and how glorious life could be, all at the same time.

"He loves you."

The declaration startled her. Trix was like that. Full of snails and puppy dogs' tails one minute and unnaturally wise the next. What he said might have been true, but Grumble was a frog and Sunday was a girl, and between them lay a curse that might as well have been the ocean. Grumble might love her, but it did not change the painful and glorious way of the world.

"And you love him," Trix added.

Nor did that.

4

Godspat

WHEN YOU FIRST WAKE UP, you'll think you've just been boiled in oil and tossed on ice, in the midst of being flayed alive. You will vomit, though your stomach has long been empty, and it will feel like someone is shoving the world through a pinhole in the top of your skull. You'll wonder if every bone in your body was crushed beneath a giant's boot and then put back together in the wrong place. You won't remember how to talk. Gods, you almost won't remember how to think."

Rumbold would not cry. He would be six years old this summer. His father had told him he was not a boy; he was a man. Men did not cry. Princes definitely did not cry.

Jack plucked his thoughts right out of the air. "And you

will cry, long and hard, like a pathetic little baby. You will cry because in that moment your mind will be full of nothing but how amazing it is to be a man again. That's the most painful part of all." His voice got softer, and his head turned away. "Coming back is part of the price."

The young prince nodded silently. He had been bold enough to brave Jack's sickroom after the older boy's transformation back from a dog; Rumbold could not miss the opportunity to learn about the fate that would similarly befall him. Rumbold's fairy godmother had cursed Jack into a dog as penance for killing her godson's beloved pup. Jack's fairy godmother had shortened Jack's sentence to a year and cursed Rumbold to his own transformation on his eighteenth birthday. She had forbidden them all to speak of this countercurse. The king had actually agreed.

It wasn't fair. Rumbold hadn't cursed Jack, and certainly hadn't asked to have his birthday gift murdered. It had all been an accident. He'd seen his pup nip at Jack's heel for scraps. The swat Jack instinctively gave it with his foot wouldn't have harmed any of the other dogs in the guards' dining hall. Their godmothers had gone and overreacted for no reason. It just wasn't fair. But the deed was done: in twelve years' time, Rumbold would spend twelve months as a frog.

"To learn humility," Jack's brilliantly shining godmother had said. She'd said a lot of things that night, but Rumbold hadn't listened until she'd started talking about him. Losing his puppy had left a hollow place inside him that hadn't been full since his mother died. He hadn't even named it yet.

Jack scared Rumbold. Jack was a Great Hero. He went on Grand Adventures and did Amazing Things. Witches trembled at his feet. Demons quaked in their boots (if they wore boots). Jack was now the same age Rumbold would be when his own curse hit. The young prince hoped he would be half as strong. Half as stubborn. Half as brave. At the moment, he was just scared. He had a long way to go.

Jack bit off a small piece of dry toast. The nurse had said Jack could have solid food and would be "back on his feet in no time." The minute those feet hit the ground, they would walk right out the doors of the castle, and Rumbold would never see Jack again. This was his only chance.

"If you're smart," Jack said, "you'll keep this memory of us in a safe place. Think about it all the time: every morning when you wake up and every night before you go to bed and every time you take a bite to eat and every time you empty your bowels. If you can train yourself to do that, then in however many years' time, when you're waking up to the world again, this will be the first thing—the only thing—in your mind. Are you listening?"

Rumbold listened with his whole body. He heard the bedclothes rustle under Jack's legs. He heard the toast crush between his teeth. He heard the spoon stir the steamy broth on the tray. He heard the air Jack took in through his nose before he spoke. He even heard the gold medallion slide along the ribbon around Jack's neck as he straightened.

"There are two very important things. Number one: You must remember to breathe. Just like in swordfighting. Open mouth. Lungs. Air in, air out. Get your tongue out of the way. If you forget how to breathe, everything else won't matter. Got it?"

Rumbold nodded silently again.

"Number two: Stay still. Don't try to stand up." Jack flashed Rumbold a crooked grin. "Trust me, you don't want to be standing up when your mind comes back."

~~elle~~

He wanted to die, and it was the most wonderful feeling in the world.

Open mouth.

Lungs.

Air in, air out.

Nothing was happening.

Get your tongue out of the way.

Life burned into his lungs. On the exhale, he cried so loud and so long that the birds fled the trees above, leaving him naked and alone in the wild silence of spring.

He shook, his skin covered in cold, primordial slime. Skin. He retched again, and thought to move his head this time. Head. Stomach. Face. Skin. Pain washed in waves up and down his body. Body. He wiggled his fingers and toes, excruciating and wrong.

But not wrong.

Right.

So incredibly right.

He opened his mouth to laugh before he realized he'd forgotten how. It would come back, in time. He would heal. He would be himself again. He would stand on his own two feet, like the man he had been, like the man he was.

Stand.

He braced one hand against the ground and began to lift himself up.

Stay still.

The man's voice echoed sharply in his head. Was that *his* voice? He wondered what buried insistence could possibly want to stop him from jumping to his feet and running all the way home.

Home.

Memories surged and broke the dam the curse had built inside his mind. He didn't have time to scream before the blackness consumed him.

~ellee~

His own soft tears woke him. They made him smile.

Strong men did not cry. But even if doing so made him a weak man, he was still a man nonetheless.

Somewhere a woodpecker rapped. The air on his skin made him shiver. The sky was so bright he could see red through his thin eyelids. He opened them.

Too bright.

He closed them again.

One thing at a time.

He listened to the Wood for a while: the birds and insects, the wind in the leaves, the rustle of small animals in the brush. He breathed deep, smelling the moss, the dirt, and then himself as the warm sun made him sweat. He spread his fingers wide and felt the breeze dance between them. He ran his fingertips over the jagged, moss-covered stones beneath him. He eased a stick out from under his back, thrilled that he once again had a back to lie on.

He touched his belly, his throat, his face, ran his hands over his eyebrows, his ears, his hair, his smile. His eyes were damp in the corners and his lips had teeth under them. His tongue was attached to the back of his palate now, not the front. His hair was longer than he remembered it.

Remember.

He stopped before his mind lost him again in the full-scale regurgitation of his life. He took another slow breath and returned to the comfort of the Wood. He would start from here and work his way backwards. It would be easier. Safer. Less painful.

Instantly she filled his mind so completely, his heart forgot to beat. In his thoughts, the sun shone in her hammered-gold hair as she stretched out on the ground beside him. She took off her shoes and her skirts pooled around her fair-skinned feet. She was as fresh and wild and innocent and mysterious as the Wood itself. She knew so little of the world and yet saw everything through eyes of uncommon wisdom. She spoke, and the bright crystal tones of her voice soothed him. She laughed with her whole body, and when she smiled, she glowed. She was startlingly beautiful, like a newborn fawn, even more so in her blissful unawareness of the fact. She was at the same time self-ish and giving, ungrateful and kind. Her name was Sunday.

And she loved him.

Quickly he touched himself again to make sure that he had indeed come back as a man, whole and—despite the excruciating pain—unharmed. Thus reassured, he let his thoughts wander back to his girl. He would find her and bind her to him forever, as the gods willed it, and the world would be as it was meant to be.

He held a hand over his face and peeked at the color-saturated world through the spaces between his fingers. The air dried his eyes, and he tried to close an inner eyelid that no longer existed. The leaves in the canopy above were the brilliant green of new-birthed spring. A jay pecked about in the nearby grass, blue as a sliver of sky come down to visit.

A raspy sigh betrayed his thirst. Not yet ready for too-long legs, he crawled on hands and knees to the bucket beside the well. He raised the smooth, wooden edge to his lips with shaking arms and drank greedily from it, thrilling in the beads of water that ran down the sides of his face and onto his chest. He filled the bucket again and emptied it over his head, several times, washing the slime and sick from his body. He felt like a new man. He *was* a new man. The reflection wavering on the water examined him with its old and familiar face. The face of a prince. A prince *her* family would have nothing to do with.

In rage, he howled and smashed the bucket against the ruined well. He lifted some smallish rocks and hurled them a pitifully short distance into the Wood. It did little to appease him. Fate continued to be both mischievous and cruel, and life was still not fair.

He and Sunday were each victims of their history. She might have loved him truly, hopefully still loved him, but her love for her family was a bond he would never ask her to betray. Of all the women in the land, Fate had chosen Jack Woodcutter's little sister. It was a cruel, cruel joke.

He had to find her.

He tentatively stood up and stumbled forward, forcing his muscles to remember motions that for almost twenty years had been second nature to him. Thorns and branches scraped the language of the Wood in raw lines on his tender reborn skin. To his relief, a thin blanket of clouds politely moved over the scorching sun. He scanned the ground for the path his true love's feet had trod three days running.

He slammed straight into a memory: a vision of horses and hounds leapt before him. He'd done this before. He was a hunter. He had tracked the stag and wild boar and brought home the spoils for feasting and celebration. Food as far as the eye could see, song enough to fill the days and the nights unstopped, and women, such women . . . pretty shadows now in the memory of another life. He focused on a new memory, the one thing he had worth living for. She was a tiny thing with a gleam in her eye and a smile that made his blood sing.

The layer of clouds in the sky grew thick. The path disappeared. He raised his head, straining to see the edge of the Wood through the trees. An abyss of barkened trunks stared back at him. He bowed his head and shuffled on, eyes flitting from one bright stone to the next in the ever-increasing darkness. Finally, he found himself at the edge of the world. Only a few trees separated him from the grassy meadow beyond the Wood. The towerhouse stood bold against the sky, calling him back to the world of men. His legs burned. His chest ached. Rivulets of blood wept from scratches in his skin and cracks in his desiccated lips. Without the trees to buffer the plain, the wind swept freely across it, bending the high grass in waves and whipping his long hair about his head.

He came upon the high rock wall surrounding the towerhouse, followed it back to where a woman hurriedly unpinned sheets from the drying lines. They flipped and snapped to the beat of the oncoming storm. With deft hands, she kept a firm grip on the laundry without letting it fall, tossing garments one by one into the large basket she carried at her side. Her hair and eyes were the same intense gray as the threatening clouds.

"It's about time," she called over the lines to where he stood. "Don't just stand there. Come help your mother."

Clearly she had mistaken him for someone else, but he opened the gate and walked up to aid her.

"Are you going to . . ." She looked at him then, finally, her storm-mirrored eyes taking him in from head to toe. In all his pain, it had not occurred to him to be ashamed of his nakedness, and he thanked the gods that it did not occur to her to scream. There was a measure of surprise in her countenance; pity, perhaps; a dash of confusion; and then a stern control washed them all away.

"Gave the gods a stomachache and they spat you back out, did they?" She ripped more fresh clothes off the line and pushed them at him. "Put these on. My son's about your age. Not quite so tall and scrawny as you, but they'll do."

He stared at the bundle she'd shoved into his arms: rough, homespun material either brown faded with too many washings or white darkened by too many wearings. "Thank you," he meant to say, but his reattached tongue refused to get around the words, and he spouted only a single, wretched gasp.

"You look like a man, but you sound like a crow, what with all you've come begging on my doorstep. Go on, dress yourself, if you can manage it. I'll fetch some water."

The manner in which she barked her orders brooked no opposition. Awkwardly he tugged the shirt over his head and then pulled on the too-large trousers. The woman returned with a cup and a length of twine. She thrust the cup at him, and he lamented the few precious drops of liquid escaping down the sides. "Drink," she ordered. The cool water stung his lips and froze his throat, but he welcomed it. She knotted the twine around his waist while he drained the cup, and then she fetched more water. "Now sit while I finish up."

He shuffled to the bench she indicated while gently sipping the water. He watched as she worked, plucking the wild laundry out of the wind. Her gruff manners were curiously at odds with her kindness. There were animals in the Wood that acted this way when they were trying to protect themselves. Or their young. He wondered where her children were.

Something rustled on the bench. He looked down to see a familiar friend waving at him, its proud pages fluttering about. He picked it up, reveling at how small it now seemed, this little book that once had lain like a giant beside him. He wanted to hold it to his heart, smell it and see if her scent lingered there. He wanted to keep it, but that would have made her sad, and he could not bear to cause her pain. The wind turned the pages to the last words penned there. He allowed himself to remember her joy as she'd read the brief passage to him. When the words echoed in his mind, they did so in her voice:

Sunday was nothing until she met Grumble—a beautiful man, with the soul of a poet. He was her best friend in the whole wide world, and she loved him with all her heart.

She loved him. Reading those words refreshed him more than a million glasses of water ever could. She loved him, and the declaration of that love had saved him. She loved him, and it gave him the strength to do what he needed to do. She loved him. He only hoped she loved him enough to trust him, to still love him when all was said and done. He hoped she still loved him when she knew him for what he was.

The woman stood before him now, her laundry rescued from the wind. He held the book out to her, and she tossed it in the basket. "Absent-minded fool of a daughter. Come inside," she offered.

It took an inordinate amount of strength to shake his head. He took the woman's free hand and raised it to his ruined lips.

"You're a charming one," she said, her words soft and true and powerful. "You could have your pick of any girl in the land." And then that face of control returned. "When you're cleaned up, of course. You're not fit to be a troll's poppet in that state."

He smiled and pressed her fingers around the empty cup. "Thaaank y-you," he said carefully. This time it sounded more like what he meant to say.

"You're welcome."

He made a small bow and walked back through the gate in the stone wall. When he reached the bottom of the hill, he turned to look back at the towerhouse. His true love's mother stood at the gate, basket in hand and skirts swirling around her as she watched over him.

He had not yet reached the edge of the city before it started to rain. Big fat droplets kicked up the dust on the road and churned it into mud between his toes. Step by step, his pain returned and magnified. Mercifully, the gods sent a yellow-eyed man in a mildewing haycart to offer him a ride into town.

The castle was a dark beast on the horizon; its tallest tower plunged deep into the heart of the storm. It was dizzying to watch so many people bustle about the rain-drenched streets. He thanked the man once the cart came to a stop, urging him in as few words as possible to make himself known to the king. He had practiced his words on the soggy journey so that he would not stumble over them.

Walking was excruciating. The pads of his feet were blis-
ters. His muscles shook from strain. The hope that had energized him at the towerhouse waned under crippling exhaustion.
Not far now, he repeated to himself. *Not far now.*

At the guards' entrance, he was stopped with a spear.
"Now, where d' ya think you're going?"

"Aaawik."

"Come again?"

Concentrate. "Erik."

The guard turned his head and bellowed into the entranceway behind him. "Erik! Beggar out here to see you."

"A beggar? Good gods, I can't be bothered with . . ." A
stout man with a mop of red-gold hair appeared in the stone
archway. He wiped his mouth with the back of his hand, as
if he'd been summoned mid-meal. "Here, what's this all about?"

Erik had been a royal guard since Jack was in service. Of
all the king's men, Erik should have known him, the "him" he
used to be. The prince could only imagine his appearance now:
grim, gaunt, ghastly. Godspat. Not quite the glamorous return
of the prodigal son. His glimmer of hope waned further. He
straightened as much as he could and rested a hand on the
guard's shoulder.

"Erik. P-pleeease. Help me."

Erik's eyes moved through anger and confusion before finally arriving at recognition. "Rum—?"

He slammed his eyes shut, as if that might stop him from
hearing That Name. It had been ages since anyone had said it;

he needed to wait a while longer. The once-and-now-again prince put a trembling finger to his lips. "Please."

Erik threw a jolly arm around his shoulders and pulled him inside the castle. "It's been years, man," he said loudly. "You look like hell! Come in out of this tempest and tell me how your mother, my aunt, is doing? Still as beautiful a nag as ever?" Erik continued the charade through the Guards' Hall and kept up the monologue until they were well inside the castle walls. "Get Rollins out of his cups," he told an errant serving boy. "Tell him he's needed in his master's chambers."

Erik all but carried him up the back stairs and propped him up on the edge of his bed, where he shivered uncontrollably. "Cold in here," said Erik. "I'll make a fire."

He nodded, but the guard had already turned away. Every muscle in his body shook; his mind balanced on the edge of delirium. He hoped Rollins would not be long. His wish was granted.

"What is this blasphemy?" The short, well-dressed man hollered from the doorway; had Rollins's voice always been so loud and slurring? The prince summoned the last of his strength and began the speech he had practiced on the road. "There is a . . . man. Haycart in"—damn teeth needed to stop chattering—"rain. Will address the king. Com . . . compensate him."

Rollins snapped to attention. "Yes, Your Highness."

"Announce. Ball. Every young woman . . . in the land. Th-three . . ." He wasn't sure if his voice or his breath left him first.

"Three balls or three days hence, sire?"

His forehead broke out in a sweat from the effort of staying upright and keeping his words coherent. "Both. Also, send . . . missive. M-moneylenders." Rollins came forward, and the prince mumbled the details in as few syllables as could be managed. Rollins nodded, bowed, and backed toward the door. "As you wish, sire. Right away, sire."

"Rollins." His manservant stopped. The prince took a deep breath, concentrating on the importance of stringing the last of his scattered thoughts together. "Please tell Father . . . I've returned."

Rollins bowed once more, smiling. "It's good to have you back, sire."

Rumbold let the sentiment sink through his mind. Back. He was back. Spent, he collapsed onto the silk sheets, wavering in and out of consciousness. He heard Erik's deep baritone issue from where he crouched over the fireplace, coaxing a blaze out of the old logs.

"Well, well, well. This ought to be interesting."

5
Wicked

SUNDAY AWOKE to a poke in the side and opened her eyes to see her mother looming over her. The raging storm had sent them all to bed early. To Mama, that meant her family should wake all the sooner. Seven Wood-cutter had never been the soft, warm, cookie-baking type of mother. She had always been more of a "spoil the rod" sort. At least she wasn't using the rod on her children. Much. Anymore.

Sunday felt the familiar rustle of pages under her cheek; she had fallen asleep writing again. Her gaze flew to the candlestick on the bedside table and the small stub of candle there. Dear, good Friday must have snuffed it out. Sunday always received a severe tongue-lashing—sometimes more—whenever Mama discovered a candle burned down to the quick, for it was irrefutable proof that at least some of it had been wasted.

Beside the candlestick were the fairy stones and Grumble's shiny golden ball. When Sunday had presented it to her family, Mama's only comment was that Sunday had best not get too attached to the bauble. It would have to be spent immediately to cover the loss of the cow.

Despite Mama's penny-pinching, Sunday suspected that all the gold in the world would not make her happy. She wondered what might. She wondered if her mother had ever been happy. If so, she wished she had been alive to see it.

Another poke.

"There's been a Proclamation," Mama said by way of explanation.

Sunday groaned. Royal Proclamations usually meant more work, less food, and the loss of something they had previously taken for granted.

"Prince Rumbold is hosting three balls."

The prince whose evil fairy godmother had ruined her family forever. The suddenly reclusive prince who had been reported ill, missing, dead, or all three over the past several months, and who had evidently been restored to health, rescued, and/or resurrected. Whatever the true story, the spirit had apparently moved His Annoying Highness to throw a ball or three, so he was pretentious enough to announce them to the countryside like anyone cared a fig.

"Good for Prince Rumbold." Sunday rolled over. Her soft pillow smelled deliciously of sleep.

Poke. "All the eligible ladies in the land are invited. If you are very good and do all your chores, I will let you go."

Sunday couldn't think of anything she wanted to do less than attend some boring political event. She'd rather spend her time visiting Grumble at the well. "Have fun without me."

She felt the pages of her book slip from beneath her cheek. Sunday reached out to grab it, but Mama was too quick.

"You will go to market today and sell that golden bauble," Mama ordered. Sunday's eyes never left the book her mother held hostage. "Take Trix with you; he needs to make his amends as well. In addition to what we already require, purchase whatever Friday needs to fashion dresses for you girls. She's in the kitchen right now, making a list. Thank the gods for Thursday's foresight."

Or thank Fairy Godmother Joy for Thursday's magic spyglass. Or thank Grumble, whose golden bauble had saved them all. Or thank Sunday, who had made such a worthwhile and generous friend—but she was too distracted to argue.

"When you return, you will do your chores and Friday's for the next three days. At the end of those three days, you will attend the balls."

"All three?" Sunday whined.

"All three."

"What does Papa say?" With the horrid royal family involved, Sunday couldn't imagine her father letting the issue go without a fight.

"Your father has no say in this. Every girl in the country has been asked to attend; every eligible man of means will find an invitation. I don't care if it is that awful prince's doing. This may be my girls' only chance to snare a decent husband, and I will see at least one of you happily engaged before the week is out. Do I make myself clear?"

Sunday couldn't imagine anything "happy" coming out of this, but she nodded as Mama slipped the book into her pocket.

"Sunday." Mama's voice had changed. Startled, Sunday's eyes left the pocket that held her book prisoner. "You don't want to live here all your life, do you?" Mama's words had a singsong lilt to them.

"No."

"Please. Just do what I ask, and I will let you have your diary back before you go to bed every night. But I will take it away again every morning. Understand?"

"Yes, Mama." Sunday felt her mother's weight leave the bed. She could still smell the flour on her apron, or she might not have believed Mama had been there at all. For the first time in almost sixteen years, her mother had actually spoken *to* her, and not just *at* her.

Sunday dressed in a daze and picked up the golden ball from the table. She held the cold metal to her breast and thought fondly of her friend. Then she slipped the ball into her pocket and went down to collect her brother and sister.

The storm had not spared the Wood. Huge lengths of path were covered with branches, leaves, and mulchy detritus. Papa said that thunderstorms were caused by fairies upsetting the balance. Balance was imperative in magic; an imbalance could tear the very fabric of the world apart. So fairies never took a child without leaving a changeling in its place. They would reward one person and then punish someone else. When only one powerful fairy spell was cast or broken, it upset the balance. The storms were a way to get the gods' attention.

Wednesday had commented at dinner that it hadn't stormed this badly since Monday went away. Of course she used more flowery words than that; she didn't say it so much as imply it, and it *rhymed* . . . but Mama understood her perfectly. She had told Wednesday to leave the table and go up to her room, in exactly those words. Mama was not flowery.

Sunday followed Trix over a large boulder to avoid a splintered tree. She was too young to remember Monday's storm, but she would remember this one. Godseen or not, it had certainly caused a ruckus.

Friday twittered all the way to market, as if Sunday and Trix cared anything about threads or buttons or ribbons. Trix did cartwheels while Friday went on about hems and ruffles. Sunday imagined shapes in the clouds during Friday's lament over the lack of time for proper embroidery. Sunday watched Trix, making sure he didn't wander off. Friday wondered if they would have enough money left over for lace. "A luxury, to be sure, but just a bit of trim, you understand . . ."

Sunday halted when the pillarstone and the crooked tree came into view. They were her markers for the path to the Fairy Well, to Grumble. The temptation to leave her siblings was overwhelming, but Friday was far too sweet to take the upper hand with Trix. Who knew what mess they would make alone?

It would be hard enough handing the precious bauble to a moneylender.

"Sunday?"

Friday was calling her name. Sunday realized that she had frozen there, staring off into the Wood. Trix slipped his hand into hers and squeezed it. "Sorry," she said. "I'm fine. Let's carry on." Carefully, they continued together along the broken path.

The Woodcutter family had dealt with Johan Schmidt many times over the years; he loved hearing good stories as much as Sunday's father loved telling them. His hair had grown thin as his glasses had grown thicker, and he'd developed a stoop from poring over parchments and stacks of coins. He was scowling over a parchment even as they approached.

"Ridiculous," he muttered. "Simply preposterous. Why, it's just . . . Miss Woodcutter! So good to see you today."

"Good morning, Mister Schmidt," said Sunday. "How are you faring?"

"Fine, fine. How are your good parents?"

"They are both in excellent health, thank you." Sunday held the ball tightly in her pocket, hers for a few last precious moments. "I hope you can help us with something . . . of a slightly peculiar nature."

He raised an eyebrow. "'Peculiar' for a Woodcutter is peculiar indeed. I'll certainly do my best to be of assistance."

"I wonder how much you might exchange for this." The ball met the tabletop with a graceless thud. Her hand felt too light and empty, sorrow where there had once been substance.

Schmidt stared at the bauble. He looked at the parchment

in his hand, at Sunday, and then back at the bauble again. He lifted the ball in his fingers. "Well, I never." The moneylender cleared his throat. "Panser!"

A thin young man in a too-large suit stepped forward. Friday bowed her head without hiding her grin at the fellow's shaggy dark hair and ruddy cheeks. Panser grinned back shyly at Friday and nodded politely to Sunday. "Yes, Master Schmidt?"

Schmidt's eyes were still glued to the golden ball. "Fetch that purse on my desk. The purple velvet one. And be quick about it." Schmidt adjusted his thick glasses and peered over them at Sunday. She braced herself. He would now offer many times less than the little ball was worth, and she would argue about whatever he brought to the table. She had watched her father enough to know how the game was played. She could do this.

Schmidt cleared his throat again. "Miss Woodcutter, I need to confer with some colleagues as to the right amount to offer for such a rare and peculiar item."

"We can wait," said Sunday.

"I'll be quite some time—we old men enjoy quibbling over peculiarities." Panser returned with the velvet bag, and Schmidt offered it to Sunday without opening it. "I would not wish to keep you from your shopping. Use this bag of chits to make your purchases. They have my seal on them, and I will vouch for you at any stall."

After Trix's misfortune, Sunday was wary about trading her worldly goods for a handful of anything. She untied the bag the old moneylender had tossed to her. Inside was a quantity of metal tokens with a dragon stamped upon them, a derivation of the royal seal. If each chit was worth even a half-silver, it was more than she ever wanted to spend in one day. "But, sir—"

Schmidt held up a hand. "Trust me, young woman, you will not buy enough here today to waste this bauble's worth. Tell the stallkeepers to have your purchases sent here."

"Thank you, sir." She bobbed a small curtsey and let Friday drag her away before he changed his mind.

At Trix's insistence, Sunday pulled a few chits out of the velvet bag. She handed them to him with a stern warning. "Absolutely no buying more cows, or trading for more beans, or riding centaurs . . ."

"Don't worry," he said. "I'll be careful." With that, he disappeared into the crowd.

From stall to stall, Sunday watched her sister haggle over scraps and trimming. For all her good nature, Friday drove a hard bargain—perhaps Mama's traits hadn't completely passed her by after all. It didn't take long for the fascination to wear off, however, and Sunday let wares in other stalls catch her eye. Such distraction was in itself a luxury; the very poor couldn't afford to let browsing get the better of them.

Friday refused to carry the purse—a fact she used as a bargaining tool—so Sunday did her best not to wander far. She lingered by a goldsmith, missing both her golden bauble and her friend, while Friday cheerfully argued the finer points of lace. A woman heavy with child sat behind the stall, fanning herself despite the cool morning. "You're very pretty," she told Sunday.

"Thank you." Sunday wasn't used to compliments.

"Can I help you find something?" The woman placed a hand on her lower back and began lifting herself out of the chair.

"No, please." Sunday held up a hand. "Don't trouble yourself. I'm afraid your wares are a bit too extravagant for the likes of me."

The woman smiled in relief and settled back down. "I know what you mean," she said. "We can scarce afford to make them. But they are nice to look at, aren't they?"

"Yes," Sunday admitted. She was having a hard time looking away. The necklaces and bracelets were simple and elegant. The rings were intricately detailed and set with small precious stones. Judging by the woman's ragged gown and paper fan, she and her husband were forced to concentrate more on quality than quantity. It was a wise decision—the smaller pieces demanded a closer look and so stood apart from other stalls' bland accoutrements.

"Sometimes I imagine they're all mine," the woman's voice whispered softly in her ear. "As though I'm a princess." Sunday was so caught up in the designs, she hadn't noticed the woman stand and move across to her. Her wide-set violet eyes twinkled, and a lock of ebony hair escaped her kerchief to curl dramatically against her fair skin. She must have been a pretty young girl; since she was now burdened with child, being a princess would ever remain a dream. Sunday pitied the woman and wanted to buy something. Would that really be so terrible? Grumble had known she would have to sell the golden ball to save her family, but surely he would have wanted her to purchase something for herself, a token by which to remember his kind gesture.

Sunday's hand hovered over an exquisite comb. She did not recognize the small stones set in the bridge, a blue so pale it almost seemed white. The etching around the edges was particularly fine . . . Sunday bent closer. The tiny runes called to her. She could almost make out her name written among them. The woman picked up the piece, and Sunday wished she were holding the comb in her own hand. "Would you like to try it on?"

Sunday couldn't think of anything she wanted more. She had to touch the comb. She needed it. It was hers. It had been made for her. Could other people in the crowd not hear it singing her name? She stretched out her unworthy fingers to take the magnificent object.

"Oooh, what have you found?" Friday's chipper voice snapped Sunday out of her trance; the bump of her hip made Sunday miss the comb as she grabbed for it. "What a beautiful brooch. Sunday, did you see this?"

Sunday scowled.

"Any of my wares would be honored to decorate such lovely ladies."

"Thank you; you're very kind," said Friday, "but I'm afraid we have a long list of things to do today. Perhaps another time. Good day to you."

Sunday jabbed her sister lightly in the side as Friday escorted her away from the stall. "Friday, that was terribly rude."

"I'm sorry, but we don't have time for dawdling. There are too many things to consider! Undergarments, for example.

Have you even thought about what you're going to wear beneath your fancy silver dress?"

Sunday hadn't. She was forced to concede and thank her lucky stars that she had a sister who thought of every detail. Then she was dragged to the next stall and the next, until she hated shopping so much, she never wanted to visit another fair for as long as she lived.

"Friday," Sunday said finally, "I beg you. I have to eat something or I'm going to faint dead away right here in the dirt." Her head was pounding from the heat of the bright afternoon, the whirlwind of stalls, and the effort of quelling murderous thoughts about her sister. Her nose caught the scent of roasted meat and baking sweets in the air and her stomach churned noisily. "Please."

"Fine," sighed her tireless sister. "Give me a few chits, and I'll get some of the other things we need for the house. Find me when you're finished. And no dawdling!" Sunday handed over the tokens and watched Friday's patchwork skirts disappear determinedly around a corner. Oh yes. Friday definitely took after their mother.

Sunday's stomach growled again; she was overwhelmed by all the market had to offer. It was much easier when you were so poor you didn't have a choice as to how you filled your belly. Now she could have anything her heart desired! She wanted everything, and deciding between it all was making her ill.

She turned down another row, and the brilliant colors of a fruit seller's wares captured her attention. There were baskets of juicy oranges, ripe bananas, and various other strange shapes she didn't recognize, but they looked delicious all the same. The crown jewel, however, was the basket of perfect red apples. Sunday wondered at the bounty; it wasn't yet the season for fruit of any kind. The seller must trade with ships from the south, she decided, or with Faerie. Growing up so close to the Wood, Sunday was fairly used to seeing such unusual things.

She stood over the basket of apples, mouth watering. She could almost taste the crisp sweet flesh between her starved lips. "Excuse me," she called to the back of the stall.

A mass of tattered rags resolved into a haggard, hunch-backed, mostly toothless crone. "Coming, dearie," she cackled. "Old bones, you see."

Sunday waited impatiently as the old woman leaned on her crooked walking stick and slowly limped her way forward. The woman cocked her head and gazed up at Sunday with lavender eyes almost completely clouded over with age. "What can I get you, my pretty?" she asked, her gnarled hand already reaching for the topmost apple. She held it out to Sunday, its deep red surface so shiny that Sunday could see her face reflected in it. Hunger tied her stomach in knots so tightly, she could hardly speak. She pulled out a chit to pay for the apple.

There was a crash, and a cry of "I'll have your ears, boy!" filled the air.

Sunday exhaled.

Trix.

"For your trouble, grandmother." Sunday pushed the chit

into the old woman's hand and hurried off to rescue her stupid, rambunctious brother. She found him half buried in an upended piecart.

She grabbed Trix by an ear—the only part of his body not covered in juice and meat and pastry—and hauled him out of the wreckage. The pieman's face was so red, he could have baked a few more pies right there on his forehead. His jaw clenched and little veins popped out at his temples.

Any other day, Sunday would have been scared of this man and what he might do to her and her family. Today, she had a velvet purse at her waist and a boatload of confidence. "Please take this chit to Johan Schmidt the moneylender, sir. He can vouch for us and will reimburse you for your lost inventory."

The man stared at the small coin in his oversized hand. Sunday waited for him to open his mouth and cut her down to size. She clasped her hands together to hide their shaking . . . and watched as the pieman's color faded back to its normal ruddiness. He pulled the hat off his very bald head and clasped it to his aproned chest. "Thank ye, milady. Very kind of ye. I'll visit him straightaway."

Oddities she could handle aplenty, but this went beyond anything she knew. Were the very rich always treated with such courtesy? She and her brother deserved to be yelled at by this man, no matter how much money they had in their purse. Be that as it may, she was thrilled to have avoided confrontation. She silently thanked the gods, and then pulled Trix along to find Friday. She paused to scan the crowd for her sister's telltale skirts.

"It was an accident." The mischievous glint in Trix's eyes betrayed him, as did the syrup encrusted in his hair.

Sunday shook her head. "You look a mess."

He ran a finger along his cheek and sucked it. "A delicious mess." From a pocket, he offered her a slightly mashed pie. "For you, milady."

In the excitement, Sunday had forgotten the hunger that had threatened to tear her apart. She took the pie gratefully. "Find a way to clean up," she implored him. "Explaining you to Mama has only gotten me in trouble lately." He agreed, and begrudgingly she left him on his own again.

She found Friday gaping at an enormous array of ribbons. They hung from the stall in a million rainbows and swayed mesmerizingly in the wind, flashing and twinkling in the sunlight like fairydust. For the first time that day, Sunday was eager to help her sister.

The young, black-haired shopgirl happily folded their selections carefully into bags. Friday and Sunday bought more ribbons than they could possibly need. When Sunday made to pay for everything, the shopgirl beckoned her forward with smiling, deep violet eyes. Sunday had never noticed before how many people at the market had similar eyes; no doubt they were somehow all related.

"My family appreciates your custom, milady," the girl said as she accepted the chit. "More than you know." She pulled a bright blue ribbon down from the stall roof. "Please accept this as a gift with our thanks."

Sunday lifted her hair so that the girl could tie the ribbon around her neck. She was glad that she finally had something by which to remember this day, something she didn't have to feel guilty about buying, though she secretly hoped the girl included its price when she reported back to the moneylender. Sunday touched the silken strand at her throat reverently. "I will treasure it always."

"It matches your eyes." The shopgirl bowed her head. Sunday politely returned the nod, and then ran to catch up with her siblings.

Panser was at the moneylender's stall; upon seeing them, the apprentice went to fetch his master. Schmidt appeared at once, smiling and rubbing his belly like a cat just finishing his cream. Sunday held her breath, anticipating the bargaining they'd put off that morning. "I trust you've had enough time to confer with your colleagues," she said bravely.

"Indeed I have." Schmidt chuckled. "Indeed I have. You still have the purse?"

Sunday placed the velvet bag of chits on the counter. She and her brother and sister had hardly put a dent in their quantity, but Sunday now wondered how preciously the man would value each. She watched carefully as Schmidt counted out the number of chits, placing them in uneven stacks. He had not counted them out before giving her the bag, and she scolded herself for not having done so the minute she got them.

Schmidt snatched another bag from Panser, who was too busy exchanging smiles with Friday to pay attention. From it, Schmidt counted out one gold piece for every chit left on the table.

Sunday was confused. The gold on the counter could be melted down to make a ball easily three times the size of Sunday's bauble. Ah . . . he would finish and then subtract what they had spent, thought Sunday, but Schmidt did not. He slid the stacks of gold coins into the velvet bag and pulled the closing string taut.

"There you are, my dear. Panser has arranged a cart for you and your purchases."

She tried to say nothing, but this was too much. "Sir, I think—"

Schmidt peered sternly at her over his thick glasses. "You're not second-guessing me, are you, young woman?"

"No, sir."

"Then take the bag and hie you home. Give my best to your fine parents."

"Yes, sir," she whispered. The bag was almost too heavy to lift. "Thank you, sir."

Panser led them to the cart where the spoils of their day's labor waited. He helped Friday up onto the seat near the driver. Sunday and Trix climbed into the back with the bags and barrels.

The gold weighed so heavily in Sunday's pocket that it pulled on the front of her dress. She adjusted her pinafore so that the bag would sit more comfortably in her lap. Had they really been so frugal in their shopping? Sunday might have dissuaded her sister from her brutal bargaining, but Friday had loved every moment of it, and Sunday never would have stood in the way of her sister's enjoyment.

Stranger still was the ride back through the Wood, on the same road they had walked to get to the market. The path was clear now, as if there had never been a storm at all. Only one sizeable branch blocked their way home. The driver stopped the cart to remove it, dragging it into the brush past a pillar-stone and a crooked tree.

Oh, Grumble. It would be such an easy thing to hop off the cart. There was still a good bit of daylight left. No one would miss her, or the coins in her pocket, as they were hardly expected. But Trix would want to go with her, for sure, and then Friday would be offended if she was not invited to follow.

Sunday turned to look up at her sister perched prettily on the high seat. Dear, good, sweet Friday, with a heart of purer gold than any bauble that man or fairy could produce. Lovely Friday, with her mahogany hair and her eyes like gray smoke and the patchwork skirts that surrounded her like a halo of love. Sunday had seen how Panser fawned over Friday. They all fawned over her. For all Sunday knew, she herself was the only girl Grumble remembered. And for all that he might love her, Sunday did not know him well enough to trust that he would still love her after meeting her beautiful sister.

Sunday fingered the silk ribbon around her neck, the only tangible memory she would have of this day, and she felt a familiar vileness course through her. She knew what she was. Ungrateful. Selfish. Jealous. Wicked. Evil. There was no hope for it.

Trix followed her gaze to the pillar and then back to meet Sunday's eyes. He raised an eyebrow in question, and she shook her head. She did not want to share Grumble, even if it meant sacrificing another day in his company.

The driver finished with the limb and continued on the journey home. When he reined in at the front of the house, he offered to stay and unload the purchases. Friday batted her eyelashes. Sunday thanked him. Trix raced to the door, no doubt eager to tell their parents the fantastic story of an upset piecart and their newfound fortune.

"Mama! Papa! Wait until you . . ." Trix's words drifted into nothing.

They stared at the stranger by Mama's side. The woman was roughly a head taller than their mother but looked several years younger. Her very dark hair was pulled up into a loose bun, and the fire's reflection flickered in her equally dark eyes. She wore a tidy wool skirt and a crisp linen shirt with lace and a small brooch at the collar.

Had she been a few years younger still, she would have been the spitting image of Wednesday.

Sunday had no desire to speak. She let her sour expression introduce her.

"Well, well," said the woman. "It seems I have arrived just in time." She walked up to Sunday, pulled the silk ribbon from around her throat in one clean snap, and tossed it into the fireplace.

Sunday watched her beautiful gift smolder in the flames. As it burned, the fire around it turned green. Bilious smoke rose from it to hover above the logs. The smoke folded itself into the image of a snake that hissed and spat at them before evaporating up the chimney. What was left of the ribbon fell into ash.

Sunday turned on the woman. "Who are you?"

"Of course you don't recognize me, child. You were too young." She took Sunday by the arms and kissed her reluctant cheeks. "I'm your Aunt Joy."

6
Grim Harmony

IT TOOK RUMBOLD a while to realize that the fire had gone out. After months of greeting the dawn amidst the constant hum and bustle of Wood life, he felt a bit hollow and alone. Odd. He'd never imagined that he would miss anything from that enchanted otherlife. Here in the castle there was no buzz of insects, no hoot of owls about their nightly business, no rustling in the underbrush. No pale glow of moonlight fell from the heavens to light false paths in the darkness. The wind didn't whisper across the surface of the water as it lapped against the sides of the well.

But there was whispering.

A fear from his childhood seized his heart with renewed

vigor. The whispers had always lingered in and around his boyhood bedchamber in the witching hours, pestering him, filling his head with susurant syllables. If he stopped up his ears so he couldn't hear their disembodied chatter, they would hunt him down at the dining table or in the receiving chamber. They had faded with time, or perhaps his memories of them had simply faded with age.

While a frog, he had learned to survive within the constant conversation of the Wood. There it had guided him, reassured him. Here, the whispers shook him to his core.

Instinct screamed at him to hide, to pull the sheets over his head and plug his ears. He pretended the strange sounds were simply servants murmuring down the hallway. They were not in the room with him, not mouthless cries from beyond the veil, not long-ago memories soaked in stone and built into the cold, confining walls around him. He told himself stories, imagining the words being spoken in Sunday's sweet voice as the sun reflected off her golden hair and illuminated his soul. He concentrated on her sun-kissed skin, her lips like rose petals, her eyes like sapphires—

Alwaysss.

The drawn-out "s" caught his ear. Had he really heard the word? There had never been words in the whispers before, just an unintelligible mishmash of discordant sounds. Rumbold focused on extracting that one word from the noises in the ether. He was a man now, not a child. Instead of running from the whispers, he tried to listen for them. To them.

He honed in on a bass line: a low, syncopated thrumming like the beat of a heart. It could have been saying his name: *Rumbold. Rumbold.*

A note above that was the sibilant whisper, the words finally coming together for him in a hushed phrase: *I will always be with you.*

There was a sadness in the message, of lovers torn apart or family separated by time and grief. The lonely ache of it echoed inside him. As he embraced its discovery, he accidentally stumbled upon the next: *Kill me.*

Rumbold's shivers began again, and he regressed steadily into the fears of his youth. The whispers would no longer fade back into noise for him now. Each of the words was distinct in his mind, and together they haunted him with their grim harmony.

Rumbold. Rumbold. Rumbold.

I will always be with you.

Kill me.

Free me.

Over and over and over again . . . For all that he had initially strained to hear it, the dissonance was now deafening. He leapt out of bed—stumbling on foreign legs—and felt his way to the fireplace. If the whispers were tied to the darkness, perhaps chasing the darkness away would quiet them.

He scrabbled about on the floor; clean-swept stone finally yielded to ash and soot. He blindly searched for logs, kindling, flint, and steel. Of course, once he had them he had no idea what to do with them. He had managed to stay alive in the

Wood as a frog for months, but seeing to the needs of a human body was a very different thing.

Kill me.

Free me.

Try as he might, his meager sparks could not convince the wood to burn, so Rumbold pulled off one of his woolen bed-socks. On the third strike, the fibers caught and smoked. He laid the sock across the haphazard pile of logs, and finally they took up the blaze. The whispered words faded slightly, if only hidden under the crackling of the new fire. He peered back at his half-curtained mattress still shrouded in shadow.

There was a figure at the foot of his bed.

Rumbold could not make out the features of the human-sized shape, nor did he want to. He piled more kindling on top of the logs, urging the hungry flames higher and brighter, as if by sheer force of will they could become the sun and sweep the room clear of shadows. He pulled his knees to his chest and buried his head in his hands, unwilling to look upon his unholy visitor.

The prince rocked back and forth, the heat of the fire harsh at his side and on his back. He imagined the light of the flames surrounding him, protecting him. If desire was enough to make something true, he would be fine.

Rumbold awoke on frozen stone to the hollow chirping of a bird with no tongue and to the vague memory of a hero's sick-bed long ago.

Breathe.

He took a slow, deep, more-aching-than-painful breath and attempted to harvest his memories one at a time. The desperate cold beneath him was from the unforgiving flagstones of the hearth; the chirping resolved itself into the stirring of a silver spoon in a porcelain bowl. There was the subtle wheeze of a dying fire and the courteous shuffle of Rollins's shoes against the hard floor. The rest of the world was stone, soot, and blessed silence. There were no whispers in the daylight.

He dared not ask Rollins about the whispers in the darkness. There were surely enough questions as to the fragility of his mental state. He needed to appear sane, hale, and whole again.

He braved one open eyelid.

There was definitely some work to be done on behalf of his image of perfect health.

Much to Rollins's credit, upon discovering his charge sprawled uncomfortably before the fire, lamentably missing one sock, his skin and bedclothes streaked with ash, the manservant had greeted him with a simple "Good morning, sire" and continued bustling about the steaming breakfast tray. When Rumbold finally worked himself into a sitting position, Rollins extended a hand. He helped the prince off the floor and into a chair at the small table. The velvet cushion felt like a cloud beneath stiff muscles and aching bones.

"The fetes have been announced, as you requested, sire, and the local moneylenders are being informed of your wishes even now."

Reluctant to speak, Rumbold nodded his thanks. Before

him were a large pitcher of water, a bowl of brown broth that smelled like fresh stew, and a small glass of goat's milk. Post-enchantment day one: no solid foods. Cook had remembered. The sight made him starving and sick at the same time.

There was a slight pressure on his shoulder. "Take your time, sire," said Rollins. "I will prepare a bath."

Rumbold covered Rollins's hand with his own. "Meh . . ." Damnable words. "Ma faaathr."

He felt the muscles in Rollins's hand tense. "Your father bids you welcome on your most fortunate return. He will make time to receive you in his chambers tomorrow evening." It was an emotionless recitation, meaning the declaration had been emotionless as well.

And there it was. Enchanted into some vile beast, missing for months, unexpectedly reappearing long before his antici-pated return, and Rumbold was still not worthy enough for an unscheduled audience with his esteemed father. It was almost reassuring that so little had changed.

Rumbold waited until Rollins had slipped into the other room before lifting the heavy spoon with clumsy fingers. Sun-light winked at him from a jewel in the spoon's gilt handle, and the prince wondered at the uselessness of decorating a utensil. His focus shifted to the room, its walls draped in sumptuous linens and spotted with solemn-faced portraits in thick frames. Somehow, he had to find a way to reembrace this fanciful life of waste and excess. He must remember that he was a prince. A prince covered in cinders. A prince her family would have nothing to do with.

Love and rage burned inside his chest, crawled under his skin. They begged for his voice, his tears, his fury. He quickly gulped down the contents of the spoon. The liquid scalded the back of his raw throat. His stomach rebelled. Spices filled his nostrils and made his eyes water, but he refused to choke.

Boiled in oil and tossed on ice.

Swallow.

Breathe.

Open mouth. Air in. Air out.

Everything else doesn't matter.

. . . and she loved him with all her heart.

He would not cry. Strong men did not cry. He would exact what meager power he had and force his body to obey him. He would rule himself if nothing else. He remembered Jack: stalwart, brave, stubborn. Rumbold could do this. When the pain dissipated, he swallowed one more excruciating mouthful of soup.

Coming back was part of the price.

~eeleee~

Rumbold realized, as he lingered in the tepid bathwater, that many of his memories were missing. He could remember how to walk and talk, but he could not remember what he had done with the days of his Life Before. He could see himself as a child but not a man. The year immediately before his transformation was an empty page to him. The more he sought the memories, the more quickly they slipped away. He did not chase them.

He trusted that in time, they would all come back to him. He hated time.

Odd flashes hinted at a wealth of idle lassitude but nothing more, nothing that explained the monster rumbling within him. He should have been resting his weary body, taking this time to refresh and renew before he presented himself to the world, and to Sunday. But the crazed energy inside him would not accept that. It needed action. Now.

Since he could not remember his own life, Rumbold remembered Jack's instead. Young, healthy, and fit, even Jack had taken more than a few days to recover. Yes, Jack had endured his enchantment for much longer, but he had also been magicked into an animal of sound and speed and stamina. For a year he had been lead dog in the Royal Hunt; no fox had remained hidden long during Jack's reign of the pack.

Alternatively, for nine months Rumbold had lived the docile, minimalist life of a frog, never venturing beyond the small clearing surrounding the well. Now that he could walk (barely) and jump (possibly) and run (hardly) and talk (mostly) and sing (not that he had much before), he wanted to do all those things, at once, this instant, vigor be damned. He had the rest of his life to live, and he had no intention of wasting one precious moment.

That determination carried him all the way to the Royal Guards' training ground, Jack's home away from home. If Rumbold had no footsteps of his own to follow, he would tread in those he knew.

Rumbold found that he had an easier time walking if he

did not concentrate on it. When he tried to bring to mind the mechanics of the action, he faltered. So he left the task to his subconscious, trusting his body not to pitch him headlong to the ground.

And such ground he covered, so quickly on his long human legs with their impossibly large bones. He passed stones that the week before would have seemed boulders and patches of violets whose petals he might have worn for a hat. He pondered the existence of these trifles, wondering how long it might be before they fell beneath his notice once again. If ever.

He stumbled, and forced himself to stop thinking about his footsteps again.

Rollins had suggested he ride, but Rumbold knew from walking through town the night before that horses did not yet trust him. Horses could smell enchantments. Nor did he trust himself to remember how to ride, for all that he had grown up in a saddle. Basic walking was hard enough. He stumbled again.

A slight breeze ruffled the prince's newly shorn hair. After his bath, he had asked Rollins to hack off the ridiculous length. The result was anything but refined. Even wet it simply refused to yield to the royal comb and be properly tamed. Rumbold decided this adamant wildness was a leftover side effect of his enchantment. He was surprised to find it one he rather welcomed.

The trees lining his path were at the same time both massive and inadequate—they all towered above him but held none of the dignified majesty of the ancient sentinels of the Wood. All of the foliage here lacked personality and soul. The sky was overbright and bare of clouds, unframed by fat spring leaves. But the blue reminded him of Sunday's eyes, the sun of her smile shining warmly down upon him. He hoped beyond hope that when she finally met him as a man she did not find him as pitiful as he felt. As much as he craved memories, he did not think he could want anything more than he wanted to see his Sunday again.

The training ground was almost a mile behind the castle, on a hill that overlooked the forest. It doubled as an outpost. On a day like this he could see the river, a thin green line in the distance, and the silver-capped mountains beyond it to the north.

Jack had walked this path every day, but Rumbold had trained with the Royal Guard only in the summers as a boy. The prince could not remember the last time he had practiced with the guard before other amusements had drawn his attention elsewhere. But this was the first place to which Jack had returned after his recovery; it made sense that Rumbold should follow. Perhaps the blazing ball in the pit of his stomach would find solace here. Perhaps his strength would return. If he could not remember the man he was then, he could take pride in the man he was now.

Before him stood the small cottage that housed weapons and first-aid supplies. Off to the right, boys with long practice swords carried out synchronized formation drills. Behind them, a group of young men jogged the well-worn track around the field. To the left, a pair of men in their prime faced off with wooden staffs. One of the men was Erik.

As Rumbold approached, the cheering, jeering assembly of men came to a halt. A score of heads with broken noses bowed, and pates were patted where there were no forelocks to be tugged. Their loose-fitting garb was dusty from the sparring ground.

The prince clasped arms with Erik, who was coated in a healthy sheen of sweat that dampened his shirt and darkened his russet hair. There was more strength in the guard's arm than in Rumbold's entire body, but the unquenchable fire inside the prince maintained its stubborn defiance.

"Good morning, Your Highness." Erik did not seem surprised to see him. "You remember Cauchemar."

The prince's eyes met those of Erik's opponent. He did remember: Velius Morana, his own royal cousin and Duke of Cauchemar—though duke in name only. Seduced by immortality, Velius's ailing father still clung to life by desperate means in Faerie, at the queen's side. Unwilling to fill his father's shoes until they were legally his own, Velius had let his very capable mother run the estates while he trained with the Royal Guard. The arrangement suited them both, and had done for the past few decades. Like the view from the hilltop, Velius's lithe figure, raven ponytail, and even temper had been fixtures of the training ground since before Rumbold had practiced as a boy. Like Rollins and Erik, Velius had been there when Jack and Rumbold were cursed.

In all the time Rumbold had known him, Velius hadn't aged a day.

As he clasped wrists with his wry, dark cousin, Rumbold

realized that Velius . . . hummed. Not a sound but a feeling, and one Rumbold recognized. Reflected in those deep-set indigo eyes was the same fire currently banked in Rumbold's midsection. It was a raw lightning, vibrating at a frequency only slightly variant to the prince's own, as if in harmony.

Rumbold's mind flashed back to cold ashen flagstones in the dark of the night. *Kill me. Free me.*

Velius searched Rumbold's face. "He'd like to have a go," the duke announced, in a voice so calm a stone could be dropped in it and never form a ripple. He released Rumbold's hand in time for the prince to awkwardly catch the staff Erik tossed to him. He had not meant to spar today; he was still not sure why he'd showed up at all. But that burning inner beast possessed him, roaring with pleasure. He backed up a pace and nodded to Velius, suppressing a smile. He twirled the staff in his hand once, twice, testing its weight, balancing it, settling his grip.

What was he doing?

Don't think.

He must not think, or he would never be able to do whatever he was about to do. If he didn't think, then the demon inside him would take over. Maybe it would find some peace in the exercise and let him rest. He only hoped so. This was either very smart or very stupid.

Don't think.

They circled each other, step for step. Rumbold focused on Velius's eyes, their nightshade depths. They were the blue-black of a deep bruise, bright with life and vivid with—

Velius lunged forward, and Rumbold blocked his attack. Rumbold blocked again and then countered. Over and over their staffs met, faster and faster, the stained wood tapping out the staccato rhythm of an intricate dance. Sweat poured off the prince. His muscles screamed. The insubstantial beast raged on.

The prince's eyes never left the duke's. Velius's every movement was revealed in the brilliant darkness of his eyes. Rumbold saw further, deep into Velius's cold heart: unused, forgotten, forsaken, as clumsy with love as Rumbold's body would be when this fleeting fire left him. He could taste Velius's soul, the reluctant hopelessness bitter on his tongue. And there, there at the core of him was the flame, that burning, insatiable, unnameable need that mirrored his own.

One misstep let the duke rap his knuckles, another left Rumbold's side open for a smack, but still they kept on. There was no time for pain. The staffs became a blur between them, coming together again and again in such succession that the noise almost became one unbroken sound, a sound that completed a harmony between them, a harmony that fell magnificently to pieces at one word.

"Prince," whispered Velius.

And the spell was broken. The moment he remembered who and what he was, the magic left him. The demon fled, leaving Rumbold an unwieldy sack of bones to be swept off his feet. The prince landed hard in the dust, the duke's staff planted rigidly on his breastbone, pinning him there like an insect under glass. Not that he could have risen otherwise; his breath, sweat, energy, sinew, even his very essence seemed to have seeped out through his skin and into the dirt. Rumbold felt the pain of his beating tenfold. The bruise on his ribs pressed into his lungs. The split skin on his knuckles was wet with blood. He felt the confused stares of the men surrounding them, unsure about congratulating the winner of this duel.

The duke leaned over the prince with transcendental grace. Those violet eyes trapped Rumbold more readily than the staff upon his chest. "So, who is she?"

Shock. Surprise. Words sat ready to escape Rumbold's lips in reply, but nothing came. The months of inanition had finally left him paralyzed.

"No, wait, let me guess." Velius brushed a hank of black hair behind his ear. The duke was not perspiring at all, nor did he seem winded. "Skin of the finest porcelain. Hair of the softest silk. A voice like birdsong, a smile like sunshine, and a mouth . . . that could sate your brightest and darkest wishes."

Rumbold found his voice and troubled tongue. "You've . . . m-met her?"

A few guards in the crowd chuckled. The duke's brow creased in feigned seriousness. "Oh yes, my friend. We all know her. We've all pursued her. Some of us have even been lucky enough to have her." The duke raised his head to wink at the men, who jeered bawdily in affirmation.

"We've been drunk on her sin, become fools for her favor. She might have borne a different face each time, but her name was always the same." He eased off the staff and leaned closer. "Trouble."

Rumbold's pride gave in at the ribbing, and he mirrored the duke's wide grin. He overcame lethargy enough to raise his right arm to Velius in good faith, which the duke took and helped his cousin to stand. The guards let out their collectively held breath in congratulations and clapping. Erik moved behind the prince to dust off his back, planting a meaty hand firmly on one shoulder. Rumbold relaxed slightly. Between Velius's grip and Erik's, he would not disgrace himself by falling. He knew they knew it, too.

"Fetch a chair for His Highness," Velius called out, and three fellows jumped to do his bidding. "There are four things that make a man fight as you just did," the duke explained to Rumbold. "Love, despair, anger, or insanity."

Erik counted them off on his fingers. "Everything to lose, nothing to lose, someone's taken it, or you've lost it."

Velius's laugh echoed, deep and melodic, through the bones of Rumbold's arm. "Indeed. The fact that you're the crown prince rules out the middle two, and though you're still fresh from enchantment, you look fairly sane to me"—he gave Rumbold a once-over—"albeit a little worse for the wear."

Rumbold remembered the flame in the duke's eyes, the flame that still, deep down, had not been extinguished. Perhaps it had burned for so long now it never would be. "Aaa-and you?" the prince asked his cousin.

"I'm a little bit of each, Highness," Velius answered. "The most dangerous combination of all."

"Thank you," Rumbold said neatly, though he wasn't quite

sure if he meant for the fight, for the jovial welcome, for the sound thrashing and the pride stomping, for the understanding, or for his just being honest. He left his cousin to decide which.

"Not yet," said Velius. He held his free hand over the prince's bloody knuckles and closed his eyes. A wave of warmth washed over Rumbold, like an opened oven or a spill of bathwater. When Velius removed his hand, the prince's knuckles were covered in bright pink skin, unblemished by blood or bruises. "Can't leave you damaged for your parties, now, can we?"

Rumbold was glad he had already expressed his appreciation, for no words came at this. Velius and Erik led him to the small bench the three guards had brought to the edge of the sparring circle.

"We would be honored if Your Highness stayed for a while to watch our country's finest in action," said Erik.

"Of c-course," Rumbold replied. As if he could have walked three steps outside the training field without pitching face-first into the dirt. Velius remained at his side, a hand on his shoulder. The pressure was at the same time familiar and different. Rollins had placed his own hand there to reassure him. Erik had done so to give him strength. Even his wintry godmother had touched him there when she'd cast the spell that had started it all.

But Velius's fingers were warm, the heat emanating from them so strong that Rumbold was thankful for the presence of his shirt on the skin between them. Perhaps he would find a brand there later, in the shape of a thumb, palm, and four lean fingers. It would be worth it. His spent body savored the warmth.

Velius spoke once more, in a low tone for only the prince's ears. "I am glad you chose life, my cousin."

Rumbold didn't try to understand his meaning, but he took comfort in the loyalty the words conveyed. He sat in that chair at the sparring ground's edge, watching the men—his men—and let his tortured, fey cousin heal him. He vowed to return the favor someday.

7

All Relative

ATURDAY WOKE SUNDAY UP just by star-
ing at her. She sat cross-legged on the floor, her
ax in her lap. It had taken Sunday an eternity to fall asleep after
the previous evening's events; surely no one had had a good
night's rest. She wondered if Saturday had slept at all. Perhaps
her giant bright-eyed sister had finally come to put her out of
her misery just when things had gotten interesting.

They say that secrets live at the bottom of a wine bottle.
Mama had made it there the night before, slow glass by slow glass,
but she'd never spoken a word. Papa just pulled his chair up close
to the fire and smoked his pipe. The children perched on sofa
arms or huddled together on the floor and listened to their fey
Aunt Joy tell them all about the family they thought they knew.

It had never occurred to Sunday that "Fairy Godmother Joy" might be their mother's sister—after bestowing Sunday's nameday gift upon her, Joy had journeyed to Faerie and never returned. Joy's twin sister, Sorrow, was the prince's own equally powerful godmother. And Trix, their fey foundling brother, was in reality their cousin, son of wayward actress Aunt Tesera.

Nor had Sunday ever considered the prophetic consequences of being the seventh daughter of a seventh daughter. Her birth and subsequent optimistic normality had simply disproved Papa's fairy-tale notions. Aunt Joy had laughed heartily at that naïve insight and declared Sunday to be a delightfully silly girl.

Sunday's thoughts had played jump rope into the wee hours, searching back through her life for clues and pieces of a puzzle she had always been. "What time is it?" she asked.

"Not yet dawn," said Saturday. The candle was small; there was only enough light in the room to resolve her sister into a transubstantial shadow. "Life isn't fair," said the shadow.

Sunday considered her own circumstances: the sudden responsibility of unknown powers, her recent affection for a man trapped in the body of an amphibian. "I know," she said. She couldn't think of anything more helpful.

"It's no surprise that Wednesday's mostly fey, the way she speaks in riddles and all. I mean, look at her—she's the spitting image of the Fairy Queen, just like Aunt Joy. But the rest of us? Friday's an empath. Thursday's a seer. Peter's a sorcerer. Really? Peter?"

Saturday and Peter were as close as Sunday and Trix; Sunday understood how this revelation suddenly made a stranger out of a best friend. She did her best to ease her sister's mind. "Peter's a sculptor. You know how he is with wood. His name-day gift from Godmother Joy was a carving knife."

Saturday pointed to the door. "Which *Aunt* Joy is down in the kitchen right now teaching him how to etch runes with!" Sunday winced, and Saturday lowered her voice before continuing her tirade. "Trix isn't our brother, he's our *cousin* . . ."

"Saturday, he never really was our brother to begin with."

"But he was still family."

"He still is." It was pointless arguing with Saturday this early in the morning. Or ever.

"And you've got so many magical powers, Aunt Joy doesn't even know where to begin."

"I'm not sure that's a good thing," Sunday said. "How is Papa taking it?"

"He's positively giddy."

Sunday groaned.

"Papa always wanted to father some earthshaking wunderkind."

"He had Jack for that. I am hardly earthshaking."

"Well, he seems to think you will be. 'Destined for greatness' and all that," said Saturday. Her tone suggested that the stewpot was more deserving of the accolade.

"'Destined for greatness'? He actually said that?"

"Word for word."

Sunday wished she could fall asleep again and wake up

days ago, none the wiser, in a sun-filled glen beside a Fairy Well. "What about Mama?"

"Mama hates magic," said Saturday. "She won't have any part of it. She's been working in the kitchen like a madwoman since before daybreak."

"I thought it was before daybreak right now."

"Then since last night," Saturday clarified. "She's made enough bread for the week, started a stew, scoured the pots, and fed the chickens. Now she's rearranging the pantry." Sunday grinned at a chore list substantially shortened. "And she won't talk to anyone. Not even Aunt Joy."

Saturday said "Aunt" as if it somehow erased the fact that Joy was both a fairy and their godmother. "If Mama won't talk to anyone, then how do you know she's so upset about all of this?"

"She'll talk to *me,*" Saturday spat, "because I'm the *normal* child."

Ah.

Saturday held up her ax. "*This.* This was my nameday gift. Sturdy, reliable Saturday. My lot in life is to keep busy, working beside Papa in the Wood every day and watching my siblings master talents I will always covet. They will go off on grand adventures and have stories sung about them. They will be 'destined for greatness,' while I am destined for nothing but living and dying a poor woodcutter's daughter."

Sunday didn't believe any of that for a second, but there was no sense in trying to offer what had not been sought. Poor woodcutter's daughter indeed. "Poor" had more to do with Saturday's self-pity than the family's wealth. Saturday guttered the candle, but Sunday didn't need the light to know there were tears in her steadfast sister's bright eyes.

"Papa and Peter will be looking for me." There was a rustle of clothes as Saturday moved to stand. "Aunt Joy is expecting you soon," she said from the doorway. "Your lessons are to begin at breakfast."

Lessons, Sunday thought into the silence her sister left behind. Lessons to awaken something that had lain quietly ignored inside her for almost sixteen years. Lessons from a woman she had heard about all her life in stories spoken with love, a woman who in an evening had become a stranger Sunday wasn't sure she should trust. Lessons that would keep her from visiting the Wood for yet another day.

She dressed slowly and made her way down the stairs one by one. She lingered in the sitting room and finally moved to the kitchen. The smells of baking and frying and boiling and chopping filled the air. The floor outside the pantry was piled with broken jars, dried vegetables, and herbs gone to rot. She heard her mother rummaging around like a rat in the wall.

Fairy Godmother—*Aunt*—Joy sat patiently at the table, waiting for her.

Sunday took a generous slice of fresh bread and a hunk of cheese from where her mother had left them on the counter. She sat across from her aunt and slowly chewed her breakfast, wondering which question she wanted to ask first. One by one, Aunt Joy answered them all, many without the asking.

"The fey magic in your blood comes from your grandfather." She glanced at the pantry door. "*Our* father. He spent much time at the Court of the Fairy Queen. It altered his very nature."

"Do all humans change when they enter Faerie?" Sunday swallowed her bread and shoved a piece of cheese in after it. Table manners were currently the least of her worries.

Aunt Joy took no notice. "It depends on the length of the stay and their proximity to the Fairy Queen."

"Grandfather was very close to her?"

"He was her *lover*." Mama walked out of the pantry, angry eyes flashing. She bent and began to sift through the discarded piles, tossing the remotely edible bits into a slop bucket for the pigs.

"In the physical sense of the word only," Joy said to Sunday. "His heart still belonged to your grandmother and hers to him. Had they not been truly in love, there would have been no saving him."

Just as Sunday had not been able to save Grumble. Still, the words gave her hope, small and insignificant a shred as it was, and she clung to it.

"The Fairy Queen cannot give birth to her own children; instead, her powers are conveyed to those closest to her. Father was her favorite consort for a time, so his progeny were born fey-blessed." Joy patted her black hair. "Albeit some more than others."

"All except Mama," corrected Sunday.

Mama froze at her bucket. Joy arched a perfect eyebrow. "Your mother," said Joy, "is lazy."

"I never wanted any part of it," Mama said to the bucket.

"Only because you couldn't be bothered to think before you spoke!"

Sunday sat in silence while her mother and her aunt stared each other down, much in the way she and Saturday often did. Speaking. Words. Mama always reminded her that words had power. How did the rhyme go? *One for sorrow, two for joy, three for a girl, four for a boy, five for silver, six for gold, seven for a secret never to be told.*

As soon as she thought it, Sunday knew: things Mama said came true. This was why she rarely opened her mouth save to bark orders she knew would be obeyed. This was why she constantly scolded Sunday about what she wrote. Words had power. Mama wasn't being overbearing; she had been trying to keep her daughter from making huge mistakes.

Only, Sunday had made those mistakes anyway. Because Mama had eschewed her power, her daughter had no concept of the breadth and depth of her own. Thanks to Mama, Sunday had no choice but to learn everything she could from Aunt Joy. Sunday was furious. She wanted to write her own story, make her own choices, not exist as a result of someone else's silly decisions and past transgressions.

Saturday's early-morning tirade raced through her mind. If Sunday had the power to make things happen, then she would use it. She pulled the journal from her pocket and slammed it open on the table. In a heavy hand she wrote: *I AM NORMAL.*

A tear escaped down Sunday's cheek. No matter how many times she wrote those words, she knew they would never be true. She was the seventh daughter of a seventh daughter, and she was anything but normal. The ugly words mocked her. For the first time in her life, Sunday tore a page from her magic journal. She crumpled it into a ball on the table.

Joy opened the paper, read what Sunday had written there, and wadded it back up again. "Sunday."

Sunday bit the inside of her cheek. She might not have been able to stop the tears, but she refused to cry.

Joy blew softly on the paper ball and suddenly a white pigeon preened in her hand. It hopped onto the table in front of Sunday. Above the bird, her aunt smiled at her.

"Normal is all relative."

~~eelle~~

Sunday's first lesson was spinning wool into gold. They had brought the spinning wheel out into the garden so that Sunday could be close to her new pet; the bird cooed prettily in the tree beside her. Sunday wasn't sure what the lesson had to do with her writing coming true, and she told Joy as much.

"You know how to write, don't you?"

"Yes."

"Then why would I waste my time teaching you something you already know?"

Somewhat less than satisfied, Sunday frowned at the bag of wool. "Isn't it usually straw into gold? That's what all the stories say."

"Do you know where to get straw this time of year?"

"There might be some in the barn, but it's for—"

"And if I had straw, would you have the first clue as to how to spin it?"

"No, but—"

"Then quit dwelling on other people's stories and make up some of your own. I'll be back in an hour." With that, she turned and walked back into the kitchen to further antagonize Mama.

Next to planting beans, spinning was the most boring job in the world. Even Friday thought so. Sunday leaned over and pulled a handful of wool out of the bag; it was already carded. Thank the gods for small favors. She wound a leader of waste wool around the spindle and began.

Sunday turned the wheel with her right hand and let the wool pull through the fingers of her left. *Gold,* she thought. *Be gold.* She said it out loud. She closed her eyes and chanted it in her head. *Be gold.* She opened her eyes. No gold. Just old grayish yarn from old grayish sheep.

Some teacher Aunt Joy had turned out to be. Lessons were generally *taught.* How was Sunday supposed to learn with no guidance? And Joy had the gall to call Mama lazy!

Sunday sighed and kept spinning. Well, it was a chore Friday wouldn't have to do later. She was on her third handful of wool when Trix came along and sat down beside her. His bare hands and feet were covered in dirt and crusted under the nails with black. His trousers were muddy at the knees and his hair was mussed. Not unusual for Trix. Not much was unusual for Trix.

Sunday was desperate for conversation. "I'm spinning wool into gold," she said.

"You're not doing a very good job."

"I know." She tugged on the wool. "You look slightly grubbier than normal."

"Thank you! Papa left me his bag of seeds from Thursday. He told me to dig a trench and plant them all the way around the house."

"You can't be finished already."

"I asked the moles and worms to help me," he said, the same way Sunday would have said, "Well, of course the sun rose this morning."

"Moles and worms?"

"They were most obliging, but then, they always are. They'll talk your ear off if you lend them one. It wouldn't have taken half as long if I hadn't asked in passing about one's family. Moles have pretty extensive families. Is that sharp?"

Trix's finger edged closer to the wickedly tipped spindle. It was a silly question, but one she was much better equipped to discuss than moles and their numerous relations. She smiled a mischievous smile. "Don't touch it!" she yelled.

Trix jumped and snatched his finger back. "Why not?"

"It might be cursed," said Sunday.

Trix played along. "Do you think so?"

"One can't be too careful," warned Sunday. "There is a cursed spinning wheel somewhere in Arilland, but there's no way to know for sure if it's this one." She leaned in to Trix as if telling him a secret, much the same way Papa did. "No one can."

"What happened to make it cursed?"

Sunday looked into the sky dreamily as she spun, telling

the story as if she were reading it off the clouds. "Long ago there lived a young girl who hated spinning more than anything else in the whole wide world."

"Like you," Trix interjected.

"Very like me," Sunday agreed, "only more so, if you can believe it. She hated it so much that one day she declared she would rather sleep her life away than ever touch a spinning wheel again."

"Silly girl."

"Indeed. For in saying so she charmed the spinning wheel. And when she pricked her finger on the spindle, her blood sealed the charm forever."

"And she fell asleep?"

"She did! She slept for a hundred years. When she finally woke again, she was a frail, brittle old woman with no friends or family left in the world. Realizing her folly, she demanded that the spinning wheel be brought to her and destroyed."

"But it wasn't."

"No. When she fell asleep, they thought she was very, very sick or under a spell. They had no idea that the spinning wheel was the cause, so it was lost."

"What happened to it?"

Sunday absent-mindedly pulled more wool out of the bag as she spoke. "It fell into the hands of a vengeful fairy who had been wronged by a selfish king. On the king's granddaughter's nameday, the fairy gave the child the gift of humility, along with the spinning wheel. The parents could not refuse such a gift in front of their subjects."

"Clever fairy."

"Clever and mean and powerful. She altered the charm on the spinning wheel so that it would not only put the granddaughter to sleep for a hundred years, it would put the whole castle to sleep as well. The kingdom would be an easy thing to conquer; the fairy had only to trust the curiosity of little girls and pray she eventually pricked her finger on the spindle."

"Did she?"

"The night before her sixteenth birthday."

Trix gasped.

"The whole castle instantly fell asleep. The king and the queen, the cooks and the serving girls, the guards and the errand boys, the horses in the stables and the hens in the henhouse. When the spell was complete, the fairy surrounded the castle with a wall of thorns and set a basilisk to guard the gate so the castle would remain untouched, ready for her to inhabit in a hundred years' time."

"But someone got in."

"For some heroes, nothing is impossible. A young prince hacked through the wall of thorns and slew the basilisk. He made his way to the topmost tower of the castle, where the sleeping princess lay, and he woke her with a kiss of true love." If true love couldn't work the way it was supposed to in her own life, she could at least make it work for someone else. "The princess awoke and then the entire castle. The fairy was never seen again."

"What about the spinning wheel?"

"When the princess was well again, she ordered the spinning wheel brought before her to be destroyed."

"Just like the girl before her."

"And just as had happened to the girl before her, the spinning wheel was nowhere to be found. It remains intact, somewhere in Arilland, to this very day."

"Do you think it will ever be found again?"

"Oh, it gets found from time to time. You'll hear of a girl struck down with a sleeping sickness from which she will not wake. When her friends and family are questioned, they'll find she was spinning at the time she fell ill. They will look at the pad of her finger and see the mark of the spindle that stole her life. They will seek out the spinning wheel and try to destroy it, but it will be too late."

"Could this really be that spinning wheel?"

"There's only one way to find out." Before Trix could protest, Sunday reached out and pricked her finger on the spindle.

"No!" Trix cried, and immediately lanced his finger on the spindle as well.

Sunday watched the blood well up on Trix's fingertip. She'd meant to scare her brother with her story, but she'd never meant him harm. "Why did you do that?"

"If you fall asleep for a hundred years, then so will I. When we wake up, we can hunt down the spinning wheel together and make sure it's destroyed."

Trix was never one to question love or loyalty. If more people like him existed in the world, it would be a much nicer place. "Oh, Trixie. You're the best brother ever."

His face fell. The magic they'd woven between them blew away on the wind. "But I'm not your brother."

Sunday looked down at her fingertip with the bright red pearl of blood on it. She took Trix's hand in hers and pressed their two wounded fingers together. "You have always been family. In my heart, you have always been my brother. Now our blood is shared again. You have mine, and I have yours. You are my brother and I am your sister. Don't ever let anyone say otherwise."

"As it was, so it will be forever," he said solemnly.

Sunday's body tingled. She was working some small magic with her words, but she didn't care if she got in trouble. She wasn't changing anything major, just reinforcing a bond that had always been between them. If it made Trix feel better, it was worth it.

Trix pulled his finger away and wrapped it tightly in the hem of his dirty shirt. "So what are you going to do now that you've completed your task?"

Sunday looked down. The strands of gray wool she'd started with were now covered in a thick layer of fine golden yarn. She wasn't sure what exactly she'd learned, but she must have learned it all the same. Perhaps Aunt Joy wasn't as lazy as Sunday had originally thought.

She smiled at her brother-once-before and her brother-again-and-forever. "I expect I'll go find out what my next task is."

* * *

The afternoon sun burned high in the sky, Sunday's white pigeon cooed in the garden tree, and Aunt Joy made the beans grow. It was beyond strange to witness the beans they had planted only a few days earlier sprout and climb the sticks and strings that stretched down each row. The leaves uncurled and spread out in the sun; the vines wound around and around one another, flowered, and then sprouted fat velvety pods all over. Joy handed Sunday a basket. "Your next task."

"Picking beans?"

"Every last one," said Joy. "And while you are picking, think about how I just did that."

Sunday stood, dumbstruck, as her aunt turned to leave. Trix tugged on Sunday's sleeve, shaking her awake. "Can she have help?" he called to Joy.

Joy smiled benevolently and said, "Yes, she may," before disappearing back into the house.

Trix ran for another basket and joined his sister in snapping beans off the vines.

"You don't have to do this," she said.

Trix picked beans with both hands. "I want to."

"Thank you." The sun warmed Sunday's neck, and sweat trickled down her back. When her basket was mostly full, Trix emptied it into his and went to fetch another. He returned with a cup of water for her, and she gulped it down.

"Save some!" Trix said before she drained the cup.

Startled, she asked, "Why?"

"For your bird."

From the row of vines beside her, the little white pigeon

stared at her quizzically. Sunday stared back. A few hours earlier, it had been a piece of paper with a futile dream written inside it. Now it was flesh and blood and feathers and bone. Sunday hadn't the faintest clue what to do with it.

"I'm not even sure it is a bird," said Sunday. "Aunt Joy made it, but I never meant to keep it." She flapped her hand. "Shoo! Go away, bird. You don't belong to anyone, least of all me."

Trix laughed at her.

"What?"

"If the bird was made, it chose to be made. It's here because it chooses to be with you."

"I don't have any say in the matter?"

"You never did."

"Spectacular. I can't even take care of myself. What am I supposed to do with a bird?"

Trix put his palms together and cupped them. "Here. Pour what's left of the water into my hands." Sunday did. A few fat droplets escaped between his fingers. The bird hesitantly hopped forward and then fluttered to Trix's finger, where it perched itself to drink. Sunday studied its tiny eyes, its beak, its perfect, smooth feathers. They were impossibly white, like Sunday imagined an angel's might be.

"You should give her a purpose," said Trix.

"She's a *bird*," Sunday said. "Her purpose is to be a bird. I'm guessing she knows how to do that a heck of a lot better than I do."

"You should ask her for help."

"I am not talking to a bird."

"But you just did," said Trix. "When you told her to go away."

"I was being silly."

"You talk to Grumble."

And there it was. Sunday forgot all about the bird. Her eyes got misty, and her heart was suddenly too heavy for one person to hold. "I miss him, Trixie."

"Then go see him."

She had lessons to learn, a life's worth of magic to control, and an entire field of beans to pick. From here on out, her life would be one never-ending series of tasks after another. She was caught in a prison forged at her birth. "I *can't.*"

Trix pulled his hands slowly apart and the water rained to the ground. He moved the finger where the bird was perched carefully toward Sunday. Despite wanting nothing to do with the animal, Sunday raised her hand and held out her fingers. The plump little bird hopped into them. It weighed so little, she almost couldn't tell it was there at all. Its tiny feet tickled slightly.

"Ask her," said Trix.

Sunday exhaled. She could do this. Trix asked worms and moles for help, didn't he? Sunday finally spoke as if addressing a letter. "Dear bird, I would really appreciate it if you would help us pick all the beans out of this field." Had the bird bobbed its head? Sunday looked to Trix for guidance.

"Ask if its friends would like to help, too."

"And if you have any friends, we would be very grateful for their help, too." She whispered an aside to Trix. "Shouldn't we offer them something as payment?"

"Tell them they can have a basket of beans for themselves when they are done."

"Did you hear that?" Sunday asked. The bird bobbed its head again. "All right," she said, but the bird didn't leave. "Thank you very much." The bird flew away into the trees.

Sunday felt a fool. Talking to birds indeed. Enchanted men were one thing; wild animals were completely another. Trix was going to laugh himself silly. Sunday moved back to her row and started pulling more beans.

Trix put a hand on her arm. "Wait," he said softly. "Just wait."

So Sunday waited. The sun beat down on them as they stood in silence.

The small white pigeon flew back to them, alone. She landed on the row beside Sunday and Trix, snapped a fat pod off the vine, and dropped it into the basket on the ground.

"Thank you for helping us," Sunday said to the bird, "even if your friends didn't want to. More beans for you."

"Sunday, look." Trix pointed to a fluttering in the leaves three rows over. A starling poked its head out, flew straight for them, and dropped a bean in the basket on his way past. Everywhere Sunday looked, there were busy vines and shuffling wings. There were so many birds: martins and larks, turtledoves and jays, robins and snowbirds. They filled up Sunday's little basket in minutes. Trix fetched a few more.

"I don't believe it," Sunday said.

"If you want anything to work, Sunday, you're going to have to believe it."

Sunday laughed. He was right. Clever brother.

"Go," he said. "I'll watch the birds for you."

Sunday ran for the Wood without looking back. She was sweaty and dirty and her hair was full of feathers, her hands were chapped from spinning, and her dress was old and worn, and she had forgotten her book on the table in the kitchen, but none of that mattered. There was so much to tell Grumble. So much had happened in the short time—the eternity—they had been apart. She needed him to keep her sane, to make her laugh, to feel complete. She was so happy, it made her eyes water. She skipped through the lengthening shadows of the trees along the overgrown path and thought about what she would tell him: the family secrets, her strange powers, Aunt Joy's unorthodox methods of teaching . . .

What *had* Joy taught Sunday? She had spun gold, miraculously enough, but where had it come from? She'd felt magic when she'd named Trix her brother, but the gold had been spinning for some time before that. Both of them had been so wrapped up in her story, neither had noticed when it had begun.

That was it! That was where the magic was! The same magic that had pulled them into the story had changed the wool as she'd spun. For one spins a tale, doesn't one? Weaves it. And it hadn't been someone else's tale; she'd made up her own, as Aunt Joy had suggested. Sunday laughed at how obvious it was to her now. The lessons didn't have to do with writing because she had the ability to change things without writing them down.

Sunday pushed aside some branches and let them spring back behind her. So how had Aunt Joy created the harvest full of beans? The answer came as she thought the word: "created." That was her power, the crux of what Joy was teaching her. Sunday was a Creator.

Everything in the world was about creativity: belief and creation. Storytelling was the essence of both. Sunday had been teaching herself the rudiments of creative expression every time she scribbled in her journal. The beans had not changed on a basic level; Aunt Joy had merely let them be what they would inevitably be. Just like naming Trix her brother: Sunday had never believed for a moment of her life that he wasn't. Now, as it was, so it would be forever.

But the bird and the yarn had changed at their core. That was scarier. One day, Sunday would have the ability to turn men into animals. And one day, she would also know how to change them back. She wondered what Grumble would say to that.

"Grumble?"

Silence answered her. She called his name again, but suddenly she knew he would not answer. She could feel his absence like a tangible thing, knew it just as she knew her own name. She walked over to search the well, and when she saw the smashed remains of the tiny water bucket, despair clawed at her. She called his name a third time, in a desperate voice as broken as that bucket. There were no ripples in the water of the well, filled to the brim as it was from the storm two nights earlier.

The rocks had been disturbed, either by tempest or wild beast in rage. She hoped Grumble had run away and hidden somewhere, found an underground spring far beneath the well and swum to safety.

Silly girl, making up stories, her mind scolded. *He's dead and gone and you just don't want to admit it.*

I hope he went quickly, wept her heart.

She missed him with her whole body. And as that empty body turned to leave the well and the clearing and all their fond memories, she could almost hear him say, *Goodbye, my Sunday.*

The walk back to the towerhouse lasted an eternity. She felt neither sadness nor pain, only a thick numbness that wrapped itself in a cloak around her. She was not happy to see her garden gate again, nor was she surprised or excited to see that Trix and the birds had finished their task. Baskets and bags overflowing with beans lay in a heap by the edge of the field. She didn't care.

Sunday walked into the house through the kitchen, but she did not hear Trix's cheery greeting or her mother's mumbled complaints. She picked her journal up off the table and walked through the sitting room, past Papa with his pipe and Friday with her mending. Her melancholy march unaltered, she trudged slowly up the stairs. She did not stop until she had reached Wednesday's aerie, the topmost room in the tower, and there she sat at the window and looked out. Sunday did not see Wednesday curled up on her bed scratching down her latest lament on scraps of parchment; she saw only the clouds as they sailed by and turned gray and then pink and then gray again as the world succumbed to shadow and the gods sprinkled stars across the velvet sky.

She opened her journal and stared at the blank pages. She should force herself to write, she knew, to purge these feelings so that she might grieve and move on. But she wanted neither of those things. Right now the pain was a comfort. Right now he was still alive in her heart, closer than he would ever be again. Right now she needed her best friend, the one friend in the world she could no longer speak to. He was gone, and she had not kept her promise. She hadn't even said goodbye.

Perhaps she could say goodbye to him now.

Her pencil met the paper, but it would not write. Tears of frustration rolled down her face as she tried desperately to move the stubborn instrument. Her shoulders shook, her vision blurred. She closed her eyes to blink away the tears so that she might forget she had shed them at all. When she opened her eyes again she found that she had indeed written words on the page, but they were not the farewell she had been laboring toward. In a light, uneven, barely legible scrawl before her, the words she did not want to feel read: *I love you.*

Sunday tore the offending page out of her book and threw it out the window.

Sometime in the night she fell asleep on the hard window seat. Sometime before dawn Wednesday covered her with a blanket so that the dew wouldn't chill her as it beaded upon her skin and hair.

She awoke to the warm sun on her face and the soft cooing of a pair of white pigeons.

8

Portrait of Sorrow

LWAYS.

The fire had gone out again. He tried to hide inside the warm cocoon of blankets, but the cold seeped into his bones. When the whispers came, they scraped like steel down the length of him.

Rumbold. Rumbold.

His body shook. Before he'd gone to bed that night, he'd made the decision that if the whispers came again, he would not succumb to fear. With eyes closed so his imagination could not draw more monsters out of the shadows, he counted out the steps from the end of the bed to the wall and then along it, until his shin collided with the neat pile of wood Rollins had replenished. He fell to his knees in the ash and felt for the tinderbox. Beside it, Rollins had left two long, oil-soaked rags.

Free me.

The rags caught so quickly that Rumbold had to snatch his hands away. A circle of golden light surrounded him as the flames burned into the kindling. He tucked his skinny legs up and wrapped his thin arms around them, resting his chin in the ash on his knees. Boldly he peered into the whispering darkness, at the foot of his bed where the mysterious shape had formed the night before. He needed to know if what haunted him was old or new, mundane or otherworldly. It might have been pulled out of Hell during his transformation and given form by his fears. The stories of Soul Riders were gruesome tales ending in madness and death. Considering the power of his curse, it was entirely possible that a demon had followed him up the Fairy Well. If so, he bore the responsibility of seeing it returned.

A more frightening prospect, he thought as shadow began to resolve itself into shape, would be if it was neither ghost nor Rider but something else entirely.

He squeezed his legs until he felt bone against bone through skin and muscle. He tasted the cinders on his already dry lips. The form stretched and grew until it was roughly the size and shape of a man. The chill in the air deepened. Rumbold could see his breath before him; the translucence of it was only slightly more substantial than the presence at the foot of the bed. And then slightly less. In four frigid breaths, the shape had some semblance of a face; in five, a mass of brown hair formed on its head. What if it was him? What if the thing haunting him was his former self, wanting to be remembered? At the seventh breath, the hair grew long and spilled down the shoulders of the lithe figure in fat dark curls. Chestnut curls.

His mother wrapped her arms around herself and looked down upon him, her face a mask of love and fear.

There was no ninth breath.

She was more beautiful than he remembered. The firelight turned her skin and blue eyes golden. A shimmer of ghostlight upon her cheeks and temples made tiny white feathers across her brow; her sheer gown was also white beneath her sable cloak of hair. Great white wings spread out behind her and lit the room, far brighter than Rumbold's humble fire.

They stared at each other, not speaking, not touching, not daring to move and shift the impossible balance that had brought them together. Rumbold ached with shaking, silent sobs and shallow breaths. Tears soaked his nightshirt, but he let them fall, not wanting to turn his eyes from the sight before him. She cried, too, in her own way, her tears vanishing back into shadow before they hit the ground.

I will always be with you.

They stayed that way until the dawning sun's rays dissolved her image into daylight, until she faded so completely that Rumbold wondered if he had really seen her at all.

Rumbold woke on the flagstones again. His rumpled hair was matted with ashes, and cinder dust coated his tongue. This time it was Erik who roused him from the hearth. The guard stepped over Rumbold and unloaded an armload of fresh wood. He did not offer the prince his aid.

"May I?" Erik gestured to a chair at the small breakfast table. Rumbold nodded and the guard sat, stretching out his legs and lacing his fingers behind his head. He gave the room the same courtesy glance that he'd given Rumbold. He picked up the golden ball in the middle of the table and tossed it from hand to hand. "Rollins said you needed more firewood. He's fetching your breakfast." He snorted a half-laugh. "I've seen finer meals served to the damned."

Rumbold forced his sticky tongue to work. "I appreciate it."

"Then I suggest you reward Cook for her efforts." He said it without groveling or hesitation. It was a bold move. Rumbold nodded his agreement.

"Good. Just don't send flowers or jewels or something equally useless."

Rumbold shook his head this time, confused.

"What use has Cook for fancies? I hear she's been asking the steward to allot the kitchens a bit of land for an herb garden. There's an old walled-in garden on the south side of the castle that would do. Give her the key and an orphan to tend it. That would set her up forever."

"Yes," Rumbold managed. "I would like . . . to be useful."

The guard grunted. "Is that so." He put the bauble down, scratched his red beard, and folded his arms across his chest. "The soot suits you."

Rumbold's laughter quickly degraded into coughing. Erik handed him a small pitcher of water from the table. The prince gulped greedily, his lips barely moist enough afterward to spare a sincere "Thank you" as he handed it back.

Since Rumbold's return, Erik had always looked him in the eye, never averting his gaze or avoiding him as many servants and members of court did. Whether it was because the prince had scared them before or because his presence scared them now, Rumbold wasn't sure. He would never know if he couldn't find someone to talk to. So he chose to offer Erik two of the highest and most dangerous compliments that royalty can bestow: honesty and confidence.

"I do not remember who I was," Rumbold said carefully. He brushed the cinders off his knees; a cloud of ash rose before him, and he coughed again. "Velius said that he . . . he was glad I chose life. What did he mean?"

"Who knows half the riddles Cauchemar spouts." Erik uncrossed his legs, then recrossed them. He stared at the portrait on the wall in front of him, an elderly relation Rumbold didn't remember. Finally Erik's deep timbre filled the quiet room.

"Your mother died and Jack was cursed in the same season," the guard said. "You were too young to know all the games different hands played around you, too young to see their intentions, and far too young to carry such a burden of sadness and loneliness. You hid inside yourself and spent a quiet childhood.

"Your godmother cast her own counterspell to put off the inevitable, but for how long? You had walked on eggshells for so long, a boy on his best behavior, living in terror of what was to come. As time went on, you began to embrace the curse's deadline. You marked it as the time from which your life would start, when you would make your own choices and control your own destiny. You made every preparation there was to make as your eighteenth birthday came and went. The spell's postponement only prolonged your waiting, and you'd had enough."

Rumbold shifted uncomfortably on the flagstones. Erik tossed him a velvet cushion and the prince set it right in the ashes. "No harm could come to you until the curse had been fulfilled, but no one expected you to become . . . self-destructive."

"Was I mad?" Rumbold asked.

"In every sense of the word, and—to my mind—with every good reason."

"Did I hurt anyone else?"

"I don't think you gave a thought to anyone else. If anyone was hurt by your actions, you did not intend it."

"Did I . . . hurt myself?" Rumbold wondered, noting the guard's tense position and tenser pauses, if he had ever concentrated on the body language of another person so intently before. Another person besides Sunday.

"You're sitting there, so it couldn't have been too bad, eh?" But Erik's smile was gone; the lines on his forehead returned. "I will say, I would not trade places with you for the world. No man is meant to tempt Fate as you have. You were as much a victim of that fairy-feud as Jack was, and you deserved a happy ending for all they put you through. But your life from this moment will not be easy, my friend. You have only yourself to blame for that damnation."

So. This difficult path was the life he had chosen. Rumbold wished he could be as glad as his cousin about that. He looked at his hands still clasped around his knees, his fingers gray with ash, the soot caked in black lines along his knuckles and under his nails. His hands were bony, but they were also strong. These hands would forge his destiny, clear the brush from the difficult path, and catch whatever Fate threw at him. He could not change the man he had been, but these hands would make him the man he could be.

If he'd had friends in his previous life, they had not made themselves known upon his return. Now he found himself with three: Sunday, Velius, and Erik. He wiggled three fingers. Counting himself and Rollins, they all made a hand, solid, the first and best part of a body slowly rebuilding itself.

A strange framed ancestor sneered at the Cinder Prince on his dusty hearth. Rumbold squinted back at him, at an elegant woman in a black dress, at a pudgy boy with an equally pudgy dog at his knee. "Who *are* these people?" Rumbold asked Erik.

The guard burst into a belly laugh. "No idea. Stern bunch, aren't they?" Erik stood, extending a hand to the prince. "Come, Your Dirtyness. Let's get you clean and then take you down to the field to mess you up again. The boys will be looking for you."

Rumbold put his bony hand in Erik's meaty one and let his friend help him stand.

"Your father will see you now, sire."

Rumbold nodded to another steward—had he ever known their names?—and summoned the courage to walk through the massive doors. The expectation of disappointment roiled in the pit of his stomach. His feet sank in the deep red carpet; more unfamiliar relations looked down on him from their gilded frames. The painted ceilings felt miles away, their moldings hidden in the shadows of late afternoon.

Anyone walking this hall to the king's solarium was meant to feel small, to remember his place in the world, so very far below that of his wise and powerful monarch. To a man who'd spent half a year as a frog, size did not matter. Rumbold was nervous for some other reason buried in his mind along with his very quiet, very rebellious, and very cursed childhood.

The doors to the king's solarium were closed. Rumbold squared his shoulders and knocked, the sound almost completely absorbed by the polished wood. Perhaps his father would not hear; perhaps he was gone and Rumbold could call again another day. Perhaps . . .

A door cracked open to reveal his father, cheeks flushed, dark gold hair and clothes a rumpled mess. His amber eyes glimmered, and the lines on his face surrounded a broad, lopsided grin.

"Come, come! There's someone who'll want to see you." His father pulled him across the threshold and shut the door behind him. He dashed back across the room and knelt to continue his project on the floor. Rumbold smoothed out his sleeve, and the pressure of the king's hand there faded. *Someone,* the king had said. Someone who obviously wasn't him.

Thick tapestries covered the long, bright windows. Candlelight illuminated the king's collection of curiosities: a fairy crown, a horn carved from the bone of a hundred-year-old stag, the petrified heart of an Elder Wood tree, a silver apple, a golden goose egg. Each was a moment in his father's life; together they formed a timeline of the king's great quests and conquests. Each was encased in glass on its own pedestal. Had any of these items been moved, removed, or altered in any way, the king would have had a fit and someone's head, most likely in that order.

Rumbold wished himself under glass on one of those pedestals and knew it was not for the first time. But he was not a prize won or a gift treasured—to his father, Rumbold's existence was as constant, common, and unwanted as the sunlight squashed behind those oppressive curtains.

As Rumbold crossed the room, the dusky candlelight turned blue. The shadows in the room swam, all fuzzy at the edges. The golden egg turned the color of blood. The king had pushed his throne to the side of the great mirror, making the room seem twice as large and oppressive. He had thrown back the carpet to reveal a pattern of stars, circles, and symbols etched deep into the ancient wood floor, burned dark and painted over with clear lacquer so as to weather the years of shifting feet and furniture. There was a candle at each point of the largest star. Their flames were as blue as the clouds now filling the mirror with an unearthly glow.

The long shadows of the pillars strained toward the door, as if to escape. Rumbold found himself in his father's shadow and smirked at the irony. His heart roared in his ears and rasping whispers filled the air: *Rumbold. Rumbold. I will always be with you.* The king did not seem to hear them.

A woman came into the mirror, looking out at them as they looked in. "Dearest," she said to the king. Her faraway voice was like water rushing over smooth stones. "It has been so long. And yet . . ."

"Look who has returned!" Somewhere between the giddiness and the fairylight, the years on the king's face slipped away. At that moment, someone would have mistaken Rumbold's father for his brother. His younger brother.

"Has it been a year already?" The clouds parted, and the voice and image became clearer together, resolving a portrait of Sorrow inside the mirror's frame. Ebony hair, alabaster skin, and violet eyes. Her spectacular beauty only added to the inhuman unrealness of her.

Those bitter eyes lit upon him in the darkness. "No. Not a year," she said. "Your son should not be standing before you, my king."

"What? What are you saying?" His hands reached out to the mirror, the stones on his rings of office blazing with inner fire in the fairylight. "Is this not truly my son?"

A corner of her lip curved wryly. "It is your son, for all that he is missing a piece."

Rumbold thought back to his rebirth, took another mental inventory of all his vital parts, and did not come up short.

"What piece might that be?" The king's eyes were as violet as Sorrow's in the mirror's light.

"His heart, of course." She cocked her head and batted her eyelashes at Rumbold. "Tell me, Godson. What is her name?"

Rumbold said nothing. The ghostly whispers turned to screams in his ears, clawing their way through his mind, each vying to be heard above the others.

Rumbold! Rumbold!

Free me!

He couldn't breathe. The other two did not notice his distress, or they ignored it.

"He will not tell us," said one.

"Or he cannot," said the other.

Rumbold saw their lips moving but could not discern the speaker for the cacophony in his mind.

Free me!

Kill me!

Was this Fate's revenge? He clutched at his throat. Silly Fate. His life was going to last only a few more moments.

"I signed a Proclamation this morning," said the king, "at the behest of my son, ordering a series of balls to be thrown in honor of his return to the castle. All the eligible ladies in the land are invited. I thought it a bit extravagant, but I indulged him."

Open mouth.

Air in. Air out.

Gods, help me!

"They are all invited," said Sorrow, "because he does not know who she is!" Her laughter echoed from the mirror, her voice as large as the room. Fighting the pain, Rumbold slapped his hands to his ears, expecting his palms to come away covered in blood. The wavering fairylight shadows made him sick. He stumbled away from the star on the floor. He needed air. He needed light. He needed . . . reality. Stark, tangible reality.

Free me!

Kill me!

Rumbold!

The prince stumbled again, caught a thick tapestry, and pulled.

Daylight split the room into two sets of shadows: the fuzzy ethereal ones cast by the light of the mirror and the set that slammed sharply onto the wall opposite the setting sun. The pedestals and their treasures, the furniture, even the mirror's edge, all now cast two matching silhouettes.

His father did not.

On the floor before the mirror wavered the shadow of the king, but on the wall behind him stood an angel. She spread her wings and raised her hands in supplication. Then she reached down, lifted the shadow of the golden egg, and smashed it. The corporeal egg crumbled to dust beneath its unbroken glass dome.

The voices in Rumbold's head sang a chorus of jubilation.

The angel launched herself into the air and flew away.

The king collapsed.

As the angel vanished so did the cheers, fading first to

whispers and then to nothing. One last sentence was audible before becoming breeze. He had not heard this one among the others in the dark hours of the night.

I love you, my son.

The pressure around his throat released and Rumbold gasped, inhaling a precious lungful of air through his nose and mouth. He coughed, and breathed again. The air tasted purple, the way his mother had smelled, like lavender and lilacs.

Rumbold rushed to his father's side. The king's hair now ran with streaks of dull gray; spots and deep lines marred his once youthful features. No longer a brother now, the thin, frail man Rumbold held in his arms might have been his grandfather, or *his* father beyond that. The king's clothes were suddenly too big for his frame and his pale skin too large for the bones in his hands: it bunched along the knuckles and puckered on the fingertips. The purple air rattled morbidly in his lungs.

Lightning struck in the cloudless sky. The room was lit white for an instant through the open window; the subsequent thunderclap rumbled long and low through the thick stone walls and rattled the bones of the castle.

Sorrow stepped through the mirror.

His godmother had eyes only for the king. She sank gracefully to the floor beside him, calmly removing a pin of office from his breast and using it to prick her finger. Her blood was red; Rumbold had half expected it to be the deep violet of her eyes or the cold blue of fairy candle flame. Clouds still swirled in the mirror behind her, as if searching for their lost mistress or the errant bolt of magic lightning for which they'd been responsible.

Sorrow painted the king's lips with the blood on her fingertip. His color immediately rose with a healthy blush. His flesh filled out, and he was soon too heavy for Rumbold to hold. Sorrow ran her dark-tipped nails through the king's hair, golden once again. She patted the king's chest, and his breathing came, deep and easy.

"It is a good thing you have announced these balls." Sorrow's voice now seemed close and real and small in the spacious room. "It is time your father found a new wife." Her powerful violet eyes pinned him with their stare. "Welcome home, Godson."

9

The Greatest Story

THANKS TO FRIDAY, the whole family thought Sunday's depression was because she had a crush on Panser, the moneylender's apprentice.

Poor Panser.

Sunday might have laughed if she hadn't felt so old and tired, as if every muscle in her body realized that one small laugh from one small girl would never change the course of the universe and was therefore not worth the effort. The melancholy made her blood thick, her movements sluggish. Her heart was an invalid convinced that it would not survive many more sunsets.

Sunday had dark dreams of walking down long whisper-filled corridors. Party-dressed, flour-faced strangers scowled at her through gilded windows. The sheets of her bed felt like water, silken and cold. When she awoke, she was surprised to find her hands and fingernails free of cinders and soot. The nightmares left her sad and shaken.

The Panser issue might never have come to anyone's attention had Friday not had her own feelings for the banker's quiet young apprentice. Sunday neither confirmed nor denied an infatuation of any kind, so Friday moped in a productive flurry of lace, ribbon, and thread as she sewed her sisters' gowns for the ball. No one bothered to cheer her up or change her mind.

Saturday, still upset over the unfairness of her normalcy and the heartless notion of a balanced universe, was vociferously reluctant to attend the "ridiculous display of pomp and frippery" and took her anger out on several cords of wood. Papa was miserable at the thought of anyone attending at all, given the host and said host's well-known, unfortunate prior association with the Woodcutter family. Mama—who could always be counted on to display a certain measure of unhappiness—was even more out of sorts because no one else seemed excited about being invited to such a prestigious affair.

Sunday blamed herself for the drawn faces and sour moods, so she stayed away from the family rooms, thinking her distance might cleanse the air. Trix's idea of cleansing the air was to cart load after load of manure from the vacant cowshed and pile it atop the rose seeds he'd planted around the house. The resulting closed windows and doors sealed the Woodcutters' solemn tomb.

The cloak of numb quiet that Sunday wore became a

bridge from her subconscious to the inherent magic that had previously hovered so frustratingly out of reach. When nothing else mattered anymore, the world broke itself down and all that was left became . . . simple. Logic fell into place and introduced clarity. Everything that had once been such an obstacle for Sunday now jumped to do her bidding, soft and easy as the whisper of a kiss blown to the moon. As soon as her mind reverted to memories of love or pain, the power escaped her, but as long as she kept her heart in that tepid pool of nothingness, her mind detached and the magic was hers to control. Even Aunt Joy was stunned by her progress.

Sunday wished she cared enough to be proud of herself. She was too busy suffering over the inadequate love she felt for a man she'd never met and the frog who was her friend. Papa said some things were meant to be and some things were just meant to be good stories. If that was so, then Grumble was the greatest story of her life.

Dawns tripped into mornings, mornings stumbled into afternoons, and suddenly the eve of the first ball fell upon the Woodcutter household.

Sunday sat still in front of the mirror, a hollow statue clad in her silver samite gown edged with the magic gold she'd spun. Wednesday wove ribbons and Thursday's silver pins into her hair. Sunday could have easily done the task herself; she had already put a spring in her curls that was absent from her step and a blush on her cheeks that she did not feel. But she needed to bask in the calm sereneness of her shadow sister. Sunday concentrated on the relaxing play of Wednesday's fingers against her skin. She imagined them drawing the pain out of her heart, through the top of her head, and down the strands of her hair to fall like droplets of tar from the ends.

Wednesday was shrouded in her deceptively simple dress of fairy-kissed blue-gray silk and charcoal taffeta. Tiny clear glass beads twinkled along the trailing sleeves and down her skirts, making it seem as if Wednesday had just stepped out of the mist. Standing there behind Sunday, she might have only been her tall, thin image cast by the warm light of the setting sun as it bade its farewell outside the aerie's window. It was a melancholy day indeed when the sister of solitude was Sunday's silver lining.

Sunday's white pigeons perched together on the windowsill. The elder let the younger nestle in the base of its neck; the younger had a small crimson mark like a pinprick upon its breast. They looked to their mistress as if awaiting direction or sustenance, and yet she knew they would be just as content to sit there forever, as long as they were beside her. It made her life seem both lonelier and not as terrible all at the same time, though she felt guilty that the birds were forced to share in her sadness. They did not play or chirp or coo as birds should; she wished so hard for their happiness that at first she thought it was they who had started humming. And then Wednesday added words to her song.

> "When sad she brings the thunder
> And her tears, they bring the rain
> When ill she feeds a poison

To us all to feel her pain
Her smiles they bring the sunshine
And the laughter and the wind
And the birds they go on singing
And the world is whole again.

"Smile, sweet Sunday," Wednesday whispered in her ear. "The birds need your love so they can lift their wings." She planted a tiny kiss on the top of Sunday's head, now liberally sprinkled with white, red, and silver ribbons. Wednesday met her eyes in the mirror. "You look like . . ." she began dreamily, before wiping an imagined tear from Sunday's cheek. "You look beautiful." Wednesday said everything dreamily.

Sunday let her shadow sister lead her belowstairs, drawing her to the sitting room, where, like magic, all the sisters entered at once. Friday covered her gasp with hands that looked none the worse for the tireless work they had done the past three days. Mama stared at her daughters in wonder, eyes moving from one to the next and then back again. Aunt Joy's smile set her indigo eyes a-twinkle, making her look more like Wednesday than ever, only Wednesday never smiled like that.

The beauty that Sunday did not feel she found in her sisters. Friday had worked wonders with Thursday's bounty; the mix of textures and colors were a credit to Friday's eye and her skill with her magicked needle. Aunt Joy and Mama had assembled the basic kirtles, but Friday's artistry with the lace, ribbon, and small bits of glass and metal made the dresses surpass divine. There was enough detail on each gown strategically placed to catch the eye, but not so much as to burden the wearer or dazzle the admirer. Various sections were also replaceable, reversible, and interchangeable—Friday had kept in mind that they would need three unique dresses for three nights' worth of festivities. She had made her family look rich, a feat that at any other time might have been a felony.

Mama's gown was the most understated but not the least beautiful. The square-necked mauve brocade fell in straight lines to the floor. Small bits of gold and fur lined the hems and peeked through thin slashes in her sleeves. Her hair was swept back in a net; the iron gray bound in russet and gold weave shone like jewel-trapped ice.

Friday glowed in a scarlet taffeta. The flush of pleasure over her success colored her cheeks a similar shade. Ribbons and remnants of russet and gold edged her skirts and sleeves, setting the fabric aflame. In her dress Friday wore the passion of her heart for all the world to see so that all might share its warmth.

As hard as she tried to maintain her pout, Saturday stood regal in her damask gown. Sunday almost didn't recognize her tall sister, so stunned was she at the beauty that hid every day beneath a dusty cap and trousers. The deep blues and greens shifted in the light, overlapping within and without the decorative braid, spilling over one another to pool at her feet. With her square shoulders and those bright eyes, she might have been a goddess of the sea. "Normal" indeed. One day Saturday would have her adventure, in spades, just like Thursday.

Sunday wished she could see her father's face light up at

the sight of his beautiful girls. She wished she could feel his love and pride in her. She needed his strength tonight, but she knew she would not have it. Papa had made his disapproval clear.

There was a knock at the door.

Sunday moved toward it instinctively and then froze with her fingers on the handle. Right now there might be anyone on the other side of that door, closed as it was. It could be a Royal Courier announcing the cancellation of the festivities. It could be the prince himself come to apologize for hosting this farce and for all his past misdoings. It could be Papa, knocking on his own door to break the tension with his silliness. It was something Papa would do.

It could be Grumble, come forth as a man to rescue Sunday from the sadness of her life and the frightening events to come. He would fall to his knees and clasp her hands, her birds would fly down to light on his shoulders, and he would profess his love and beg her to come away with him. Sunday wanted that vision so much it stole her breath away and broke her heart all over again. If they had been destined for each other, her kiss in the Wood would have made a difference. It hadn't. That was just the way of the world.

The knock sounded again.

"Come along, Miss Molasses," said Saturday. "I want to get this over with."

Sunday whispered, "Trix."

Friday's pretty blush left her cheeks.

Since Trix had kept himself from being underfoot, no one had bothered about him. Only now did they remember that he had spent the day surrounding the house with fresh manure. They would dazzle everyone at the ball with their beauty and paralyze them with their stench.

Saturday closed her hand over Sunday's. "Let's give them something to talk about," she said, bright eyes twinkling, and they pulled the door open together. The room immediately filled with the smell of . . . roses, lush roses in the dead of summer, a scent sweet and thick as warm honey.

Aunt Joy turned her palms up and shook her head. "Gods bless the fey."

"Well, it's about bloomin' . . ." The liveried man's voice trailed off as he glanced up at Saturday . . . and up, and up. He blinked and then bowed low. "Forgive me, milady. As you might imagine, we're all in a bit of a rush this fine evening."

Saturday raised an eyebrow at Sunday, having suddenly realized the potential power of her own terrible beauty.

It was indeed a fine evening, warmer than usual for spring. Which was good, as no one would be expecting the Woodcutter women to be wearing cloaks they did not have. Sunday lifted her skirts, took the footman's hand, and climbed into the waiting carriage. Through the window she saw Aunt Joy silhouetted in the doorway, waving a smiling farewell.

Sunday caught a flash of movement elsewhere in the towerhouse: her father watched from his darkened bedroom, not so very absent after all. He twisted the small gold medallion—Jack's nameday gift, returned to their family upon his death—on its chain around his neck. Sunday sat back against the thinly cushioned seat and missed her father. She imagined he wished her well, but it was no secret how Papa felt about the royal family. She was betraying her father by even attending this ball. Worse, she was betraying Grumble.

Silly girl, said her brain. She could not betray a man she'd never met, no more than she could take the blame for obeying her mother's decision. Friday clasped Sunday's hand in hers throughout the carriage ride, and Sunday let her sister's excitement inspire her. She used her magic to keep her palms dry, her curls fresh, her dress wrinkle-free. Every little thing she had control over was another small plate fastened to the armor of her confidence. She was a warrior. She would be strong.

The carriage came to a halt long before it should have. Mama pulled the curtains aside as the footman opened the door. "I'm afraid this is as far as I can take you."

Between the open door and the far-off gates of the castle was a sea of people, animals, and contrivances of every sort. Carriages with teams of horses scraped past wagons pulled by oxen and haycarts tethered to donkeys. Girls poured out and off of every vehicle, squealing and chattering. Some arrived on foot with shoes in hand, sparing a moment to dip their dirty toes in fountains and horse troughs.

Sunday had never seen such a spectacle. Nor had the rest of the world; every member of the unwashed and uninvited had gathered to witness the event. Every living, breathing girl in the land seemed to have accepted the invitation, and—true to Mama's word—every eligible man of means had found a way onto the guest list. There would be songs sung about this night, and stories told around fires for generations to come. Sunday would have wished herself into them if she thought she had half a chance of being remembered.

Sunday and her sisters navigated the road—sidestepping ribbons and wraps and stray jewels scattered in the dirt and filth and livestock droppings—up the steps to where gaggles of other women waited to be announced at the Grand Entrance. The line wound through the lush hallways and out of doors, circling around itself on the cobblestones, colorful as a poisonous snake. The fashion ranged from gowns on par with Friday's subtle genius to outfits barely fit for the bean field. Brazen girls chose flash and frippery over decorum; innocents had come to chase a dream.

The rich decorations of the hall brought back Sunday's nightmares, memories of being cold, lost, and scared. She felt more the pretender with every step she took. Finally, the Woodcutter women passed over the threshold of the Grand Entrance and stood on the landing overlooking the ballroom floor. Below was a river of constant movement, a rainbow flowing in time to the beat of soft music. Above them twinkled a million lights reflected from a million faceted crystals that ringed the domed ceiling, like every star in the sky ever wished upon. Mama told Saturday to stop slouching.

Sunday and her sisters had attended spring fairs and fall harvest gatherings, so they were no strangers to celebration. They had joined in the revelry and often led it, singing along with the bawdiest of melodies and dancing until dawn. But this . . . this was another world beyond Sunday's wildest imaginings. She wondered if it surpassed even Wednesday's dreams.

"Missus Seven Woodcutter," the Grand Marshal announced, "and her daughters: Miss Wednesday, Miss Friday, Miss Saturday, and Miss Sunday."

Sunday closed her eyes, waiting for everyone to laugh at their ridiculous names. Thank the gods only the five of them had attended. When she opened them again, the Grand Marshal winked at her. It was such an odd, out-of-place gesture that she couldn't help but smile.

She steeled herself for the next challenge: to make it down those stairs and into that stifling sea of bodies. Her breath caught in her throat. Her face flushed. Her heart raced. She froze, unable to take another step forward. Friday's cool hand slipped inside her clammy one, giving her the courage to inch forward to the top of the red-carpeted stairs. Sunday immediately envisioned herself plummeting down them. Friday squeezed her fingers.

Concentrate. Curls in her hair. Ribbons in her curls. Smooth skirts. Every stitch reinforced in perfect place. Every light in the room shining for her, every color painting her memory. Another small plate in her armor was hammered into place with the beat of the music that echoed the mantra repeating in her head: *Why me . . . why me . . . why me . . .*

She was Sunday Woodcutter. She was a Creator, a tale-spinner, and she would be strong. She picked up her skirts in one hand and held fast to Friday with the other, leading her sister slowly down the steps.

The face that met them at the bottom was familiar to Sunday in the way she might have recognized herself in a wind-swept pond—if she'd been twice her age and ten times her beauty. Pale golden curls fell perfectly against a soft white velvet bodice and ended at a tiny cinched waist. Delicate hands were decorated with rings that matched the pearl-studded embroidery of her overskirt. Eyebrows arched like angels' wings framed almond-shaped eyes of deep dark blue, set in flawless skin as creamy as alabaster. A peach rose-petal mouth turned up ever so slightly at the corners. Upon her brow sat a thin circlet of more white gold, inlaid with more pearls.

Mama tilted her head and dropped into a perfect curtsey. "Your Highness."

The princess did not say a word, but her eyes were pleading.

Friday was less courteous; she strode over to the white princess and embraced her heartily. "Oh, Monday, how we've missed you."

Wednesday's gray shadow fell against Monday's voluminous skirts. She kissed her perfect cheek and held out a long, thin silk bag with a slip of paper tied to it. "From Thursday."

Monday's smile grew wider and her eyes sadder, the pearls on her brow like glistening tears outlining her ethereal beauty. "Thank you," she whispered, and pulled open the ribbon. From the bag slipped a stunning fan. Tiny jewels lined each ebony slat; fine black lace and downy dark feathers rimmed the edge. Small red symbols dotted the fabric between the folds of black and silver. Again, Thursday had chosen well. It was a beautiful thing worthy of such a woman.

Sunday's nose twitched. She thought of all the work her family did every day just to survive: mornings feeding livestock, afternoons in the fields, evenings shelling beans by the fire, rainy days spent spinning and dusting. So much for so little, and such nonsense over a stupid cow that wasn't worth half of the useless accessory her sister currently held so casually in her hand.

The sisters finally moved aside and left the youngest to the eldest's notice. The music beat inside Sunday's head: *why me . . . why me . . . why me . . .* Not knowing what else to do, she followed Mama's lead and dropped into a small curtsey. A perfectly manicured finger—one that never scrubbed floors or tossed pig slop or carded wool or had been pricked by a mending needle—slid under her chin and lifted it.

"She looks just like Tuesday," the princess said. Her voice was deep, sweet, and a little breathless, as Sunday imagined angels might sound. Or falling stars.

"She does, a little," Mama said after a pause.

It was the nicest thing her mother had ever said about her. It was the *only* nice thing her mother had ever said about her. "I'm not graceful," Sunday blurted, and then tried to make up for it by adding, "milady."

Monday's eyes brightened at the comment and instantly grew sad again. "Please," said the angel's voice, "don't . . ."

The music stopped. The room went quiet. Sunday was still too shocked at Monday's appearance, Mama's compliment, and her own rude outburst to notice anything. Monday was staring at a point just to the left of her. Behind her. Monday lowered her eyes and bent her head reverently.

"Miss Woodcutter," he said.

Sunday turned slowly and sank into a low curtsey. Biting her unruly tongue, she uttered the first words that sprang to mind that were not profane.

"Your Highness."

10
Monarchy and Magic Spells

THE INVISIBLE SOLDIER in the vacant suit of armor by the door filled out his breastplate better than Rumbold filled out his ceremonial garb. Even decked in layers of royal finery, the prince still managed to feel scrawny. Rollins straightened the maroon sash that ran from bony shoulder to bony hip and pinned a gold medal upon his breast. Rumbold's heart beat so fast he was surprised the medal didn't tremble. He would see her tonight. He would look upon his true love with the eyes of a man. One smile, one touch, and the world would make sense again. He would speak to her with the voice of a man who would say . . .

"How do I look?"

Erik and Velius, semi-engrossed in a game of chess,

shrugged at his appearance. Rumbold envied the ease with which Velius wore his clothes, the black silk draped over his strong shoulders as if it had always desired to be there and had finally achieved its dream. The prince was sure he had been that way once, so at home in his wardrobe that it never occurred to him to feel out of place. Right now, his skin was still only slightly less foreign than the shirt, sash, hose, and cloak that suffocated his new body. Would his true love's skin feel like that silk when he took her hand?

Velius leaned back in his chair. "What do you think?" he asked Erik. "Runny pudding?"

Erik studied the prince. "Weak beer."

"Hmm."

"No, wait. Boiled cabbages."

Velius nodded sagely. "That's the one."

"Maybe we shouldn't have let him play with the boys this morning."

"Is that a bruise under his left eye?"

"Leave it," said Erik. "Gives him a bit of color."

"We could always bruise the other side," said Velius.

"Wouldn't take much."

"And that hair." Velius sucked his teeth.

"There is no help for the hair," Rollins chimed in.

Rumbold let out a breath, making even more room between his breastbone and the sash that lay across it. "Am I really as bad as all that?"

Velius rose and placed his hands on his cousin's shoulders.

"Let's just say, rumors of your untimely demise were not that greatly exaggerated."

Rumbold understood what they were doing. Ribbing. Jest. Truth disguised with humor. Criticisms between friends. He smiled, a grin that split his face and shone from it all the gratitude, excitement, and affection he had no words for.

Velius raised an arm and covered his eyes. "Whoa! Be careful with that, Cousin. There are enough women ready and willing to say yes to you without *that* bringing them to their knees."

"He's the crown prince," Erik pointed out. "They can't say no."

Rumbold sobered. "He's right. What if—"

"None of that!" said Velius. "If she didn't already love you, you wouldn't be here."

"But she doesn't know who I am. *I* don't even know who I am. As for who I was . . ."

"Don't start that again," said Erik.

"Her family despises me and my father."

"They're not alone," quipped Velius.

"How do I fight that?"

"Look," said Velius. "The past is past. Not you nor I nor anyone else in this room can change that. There is only now. Who are you now?"

"I am a man who will hold tonight the most priceless treasure he has ever known. And I am scared to death of losing her."

"Then don't," said Erik.

Rollins draped the prince's short cape around his shoulders and secured the gold clasp. If Rumbold had any more material piled on top of him he would collapse. Two identical guardsmen opened the doors to the prince's salon in perfect synchronicity. They bowed low, and then snapped to attention on either side of the entranceway.

"After you, gentlemen," said Rollins.

"Come on, then," said Velius. "The sooner this circus starts, the sooner we can settle our boy down and fatten him up a bit."

Erik and the twin guards led the way. "I still say we should even out his coloring. He really shouldn't make his first appearance looking all lopsided like that."

"Fixing him would be cruel," said Velius. "The courtiers haven't had anything scandalous to talk about for months."

"I certainly don't want anyone to feel they have been neglected in my absence," said Rumbold.

"Ours is a compassionate monarchy with indefatigable attention to detail," said Velius.

"Without doubt," Erik agreed.

Rollins snorted at the banter, and the party of men came to a halt at the door to the king's chambers. The twin guards rapped upon the doors and then opened them, again in perfect unison.

Sorrow appeared, elegant as ever, in a wispy dress the shade of a bruise that floated lithely around her slender ankles. Long scarves wound around her neck and waist like serpents. The sight of his godmother had never set Rumbold at ease, but he could tell that there was something wrong: a hurry to her step, a ruffled air to her demeanor. Rumbold reached out and took her elbow before her quick footsteps let her escape.

"Godmother?" Her skin was pale, paler than its normal pearlescence. Her eyes were overbright, burning with a similar fire that had burned within both Velius and Rumbold that day on the training ground. "Are you well?"

"I am fine." Her words compelled him to believe their untruth. Rumbold felt her pulse like a bird's beneath his thumb. There was a raw, crescent-shaped mark on the soft flesh inside her elbow, and blood on his fingers.

"Shall I call a doctor?" He asked in a court-whisper so as not to alarm his companions, or the twin guards, who suddenly seemed very close by.

She politely wrenched her arm from his grasp and hid the offending mark with her palm. "I will feel better after an evening of rest in my rooms."

"We will be sorry to miss you," said Rumbold.

Sorrow placed a trembling hand upon his cheek. Had he always been so much taller than she? "Take care of him," she said.

His father, of course. It was never about Rumbold. "Be well," the prince said formally, "so that he might have the pleasure of your company tomorrow."

She smiled slightly before disappearing down the long corridor. Rumbold looked down at the hand that had touched her, his fingers spotted with drops of bright red blood. Instinctively, he raised his hand to his mouth.

Velius grabbed his arm. "Don't. Trust me." He thrust a handkerchief into the prince's fist.

"My son!"

The king exited his rooms with his arms raised in welcome and joy. His amber eyes also sparkled with an unearthly fire, but unlike Sorrow's, his cheeks were flushed with health. Light seemed to emanate from beneath his skin. Rumbold envied his father's broad chest and confident swagger and hoped he would not have to compete for Sunday's affections.

Once again he reminded himself that if her love were not true, he would still be wearing a frog's skin and looking up from the feet of the world. He had her heart. He only hoped she recognized it.

Rumbold decided to pretend that his father's affection was genuine—that the king was a confidant, an advisor, a mentor who put the best interests of his son above his own. It was like walking: if Rumbold didn't concentrate too hard on it, the illusion took care of itself.

The king clapped his son heartily on the back; it took all the prince's strength not to hurtle forward into Velius. "These fetes are one of your more bizarre requests," said the king, "but I'm betting they will benefit the reputation of this realm." His booming laugh echoed through the hall like thunder. "What are we here for if not to give those scrawny minstrels something to sing about for their suppers?"

"It will be many years before so fine a figure of a man will ever be seen again," said Velius. Rumbold thought him far too generous with his flattery, but it was exactly what the king wanted to hear.

"Indeed!" The king beamed. "Heed my words, gentlemen.

This is the Age of Glory. Our legacy will leave a mark on history that will last throughout time. Let us not delay!"

Velius and Erik stood aside so that Rumbold and his father could start the formal procession. They had made it but a few feet down the corridor when the king leaned in and whispered, "We are about to walk into a room full of beautiful women who worship you and who would do anything to curry your favor. Think about that. Anything." His father straightened his own scarlet sash and smoothed his hair. "There will be plenty of time to tie yourself down to one woman. Don't sell yourself too cheaply, my son. *Anything,* you understand. You just keep that in mind."

And with those words, the illusion shattered. Rumbold fell back a few paces and let his father lead the way onto the ballroom balcony. He heard music, light as air, more subtly repetitive than birdsong. Candles and torches and crystals lit the spacious room beyond like a dream under glass. The jewel-toned dancers on the floor seemed more painting than real.

He had known he wouldn't be prepared for the world after all those strange months in the Wood, but the sheer size and capacity of the ballroom took his breath away. A steady stream of guests trickled down the opposite stair. Even if he suddenly recalled all the grand balls he had attended in his misspent youth, he knew they would be insignificant in comparison.

He quickly scanned the crowd below, without attracting his father's notice, and was surprised that his true love's presence was not immediately known to him. Had he expected her face to shine like a beacon? That the sight of her would render him blind to all others? Doubt began to creep under his skin and settle in his stomach. Stripped of monarchy and magic spells, he was just a man in a mad world looking for the girl who shared his heart.

Rumbold felt a hand on his arm, and the unmistakable warmth of Velius's magic washed through him. "You have stood in this place a hundred hundred times before. This is no different." Rumbold turned to his cousin and raised his eyebrows. Velius smiled. "*Pretend* it is no different."

"Perception is everything," said Rumbold.

"She loves you, or you would not be here."

"And I love her and do not deserve her." He could not tear his eyes away from the room for long; what if he missed her? "Though I confess, at the moment, I am thinking only of myself and my shortcomings."

"That is your first mistake."

The song came to a close and the dancing company bowed as one. The heralds raised their long horns and trumpeted a short fanfare to announce the arrival of the king. Rumbold stood to the right and slightly behind his father; Velius took his place at the king's left, farther back.

"My friends. We come together these many evenings to celebrate the return of both the spring and my son to this cold land."

Rumbold bowed, courteously acknowledging the raucous applause and chorus of high-pitched squeals that followed his mention. The rest of the king's speech fell on many deaf ears, including those of his son. How many footsteps would he have to take until he saw her again? What if he didn't recognize her? He would have been just as happy if she came to the dance barefoot and pinafored. And her sisters! He couldn't wait to meet the legends themselves in the flesh. As his father droned on about duty and the good of Arilland, Rumbold tried to remember how many of Sunday's sisters had already married and left home. At least one—no, two—oh, and the one who had died . . .

The king ended the speech to polite applause. Rumbold was sure it had been full of appropriately eloquent and memorable words that he would ask Rollins to repeat later when he wasn't so scatterbrained. Later. Imagine! Mere hours from now the festivities would be over and the rest of his life would have begun.

Erik was suddenly very close to his face. "Let's go, lover boy."

"It is rather sweet," said Velius.

"Just as long as it's not contagious," mumbled Erik. "And of short duration."

"Come now. You can't say you don't indulge in a bite of cake now and then."

"I'll leave the ladies on pedestals to His *Highness*," Erik said. "I prefer mine a bit more . . . down-to-earth."

"You'll find no shortage of low women decorating the ballroom tonight," said Velius.

"Or earthy ones," the prince reckoned.

Erik smiled at that. "I'm counting on it."

"My cousin, I fear you have set in motion a madness of which you cannot *conceive*." Velius drew the word out. "I expect, thanks to these festivities, that there will be a marked increase in Arilland's population come midwinter."

And so the receiving line began.

"Ladies" apparently covered as broad a range of females as the word "eligible" did. Had anyone heard any part of the Royal Proclamation past the word "all"? Rumbold tried to suppress his awe at the volume and variety of material below tightly cinched waists and the notable lack of it above them. Nine months. Nine months covered in thick, slippery skin and now all this bare flesh on display. He was suddenly parched. His clothes scratched uncomfortably. His father's words came back to him, as did his cousin's. What monster had he unleashed? His eyes were drawn to the modest and not-so-modest couplings already taking place in the shadows. A night for the bards indeed.

Rumbold was overwhelmed with introductions, and Rollins did his best to keep them all at a respectable distance. He clasped hands: large and small, gloved and bare. His smile was received with giggles that offered much and coy smiles that implied knowledge of more. There were fear and frowns and frivolity and face after face; Rumbold saw his true love in all of them and none of them.

"Might we have some idea of what we're looking for this evening?" Velius asked discreetly.

"Sunrise over the Wood at week's end," he said, "and my heart." The woman he was not speaking to batted her eyelashes at his pretty words.

"So helpful," lied Velius. "The man in love ever finds himself the poet," he said to Erik.

"This man wishes he'd hurry up and lose himself again," replied the guard.

Rumbold had neither the time nor the inclination to reply as he nodded his head over another hand. Were there really this many women in the kingdom? Surely not. Several kingdoms and the outer reaches of Faerie, maybe. Somehow they had all managed to come from hither and yon with merely a few days' notice. Some smelled of spices, some had flowers in their hair, and some wore jewels that sparkled like his true love's eyes. Many brought him gifts: posies and portraits and little statues of gold and silver. None of them brought stories or a bucket of water.

He kept one ear trained on the Grand Marshal as he accepted compliments on his bold new hairstyle, hopes that he had safe travels, and best wishes for his future health and happiness. The prince thanked them all, confirming and denying each comment with steady inconsistency. The resulting speculation would make better tales than he had the energy to fabricate, and none of them would ever come close to the simple and beautiful truth about to walk down those stairs at any moment.

Rumbold bowed to the foppish marquis of a northern province he couldn't remember. Norland? Northshire? Neville? His head hurt and his neck was beginning to cramp. What if she didn't come? What if she was in the Wood, at the Fairy Well right now, waiting for him? No, she would not have stayed past sunset. She would not have missed this insanity. Would she?

"One wonders," Lord N-something said candidly, "if your mysterious return to the palace masks your father's announcement to take a new bride or if it's the other way around."

Rumbold puzzled for a moment over the proper response and then replied, "This is the Age of Glory. We are men of action." The marquis bowed again and shuffled off to his escorts, who instantly caught him up in whispered queries as to what had provoked more than a two-word reply.

Velius approached and bowed to the dark young woman in green whose trembling hand now clasped Rumbold's. "Forgive me. I need to borrow my cousin for a time."

"Yes, Your Grace." The girl curtseyed low and excused herself.

"For what?" asked Rumbold when they were clear of the receiving line. "How much time?"

"Oh, I'd say the better part of a *week*." Velius nodded toward the stair. "At least until *sun*rise." He breathed a short laugh and shook his head. "Fool." If his cousin said anything after that, Rumbold didn't hear.

She was a vision in a silver dress, though he missed her without the finery. He missed her quick wit and easy smile. He missed her laugh. He longed to coax one out of her, but he couldn't rush things. She would feel uncomfortable around him at first. As a man he was still a stranger to her; not just his title forced the distance between them. It was a distance he would not tolerate for long.

Enchanted, he moved closer, slowly, drawn to her. Minglers moved aside and voices hushed. She was just so . . .

pretty? He had thought so with his frog's eyes, but as a man he knew it. Yes, she was pretty, but so were many of the women who had paraded themselves before him that evening. Something beyond pretty radiated from inside Sunday. The folds of her dress called to him, the curve of her wrist beckoned, the silver pins scattered through her hair winked in invitation. She was beautiful. He wanted to tell her so every day for the rest of his life. Starting tonight.

"Miss Woodcutter." He had not meant to be so loud. Had the music stopped?

She looked up at him—*up* at him!—with those eyes as blue as the cloudless summer sky, and just as empty of recognition. *"It's me!"* he wanted to scream. He wanted to laugh, to cry, to scoop her up in his feeble arms and take her back to the Wood, back to their well, back to where they had fallen in love. Where she had healed him. Where she had given him the one thing he had never known he was missing and had made him whole. Where he had been born again. Where he had chosen life, for her. All for her. He wanted to fall to one knee and ask her the question that would bind her to him forever. He was the crown prince. She couldn't say no.

But binding only meant obligation, not willingness. He needed to take his time. Make her comfortable. Make peace with her family. Make her love him. And yet, how could he justify forcing her to fall in love with a man *he* still didn't really know? The boy he had been did not deserve her. And the man he was now . . . would start with a dance. One dance.

She curtseyed, a proper curtsey that a Woodcutter's daughter had little business knowing. As exquisite a picture as she made, he wished she hadn't.

Patience.

She loved him, he reminded himself. She already loved him, or he would not be here standing before her. Taller than her.

"Your Highness," she said coldly.

Breathe. Air in. Air out.

One dance.

11

Too Familiar

HE CROWN PRINCE of Arilland was asking her to dance. Sunday disguised her trembling hands in the folds of her gown and quickly swallowed the urge to vomit.

She had not prepared for this moment. She had hoped that this evening, and both subsequent ones, would be uneventful and quickly done. The sooner it was all over, the sooner they could all sit around nice bowls of stew, talk about the weather, and console Mama in her disappointment. Monday would go back to her palace, Wednesday to her tower, Friday to church, and Saturday to the Wood. Sunday would learn her magic lessons well enough and then Aunt Joy, too, would float away on the same stormy wind that had brought her to their door.

The prince was still there, hand held out to her, awaiting her reply. Turn and run, or stay and face the music?

She would have run, had there been anything left for her to run to.

Sunday took the prince's hand, and he led her to the center of the room. His fingers were thin and soft, like Monday's. She stared at the gold medal on his breast; fear more than decorum kept her from looking directly at him. He must have known of their connection; there were many Woodcutters in the land, but none with such ridiculously named daughters. Even if he had been too young to remember it, the prince could not have grown to adulthood without knowing his role in Jack's demise.

Was this a gesture of mending ways between their families? *In a perfect world, maybe.* Was he completely and utterly ignorant? *Certainly possible.* Was this his way of demonstrating to both her family and the world that he always got what he wanted? *Almost definitely.*

The orchestra started a waltz, and she mentally counted off the three-beat time. *Oh why me,* Sunday chanted silently with every movement. *Oh why me, oh why me, oh why me* . . . Over and over again as they turned eddies in the sea of beautiful people, over and over again—until she slipped and said it aloud. Her eyes widened in horror.

"I'm glad you asked," said the prince, casually, as if they'd been conversing all evening. "I need to know something, and you look like you have enough wit to answer my question honestly."

"As you wish, Your Highness." It was a natural reaction to curtsey at the title, and Sunday stumbled. The prince deftly spun her around to cover up the misstep.

"My fault," he said quickly. "Are you ready for my question?"

She nodded sternly.

"Do I look as stupid as I feel?" he asked.

Sunday bit her lips together and swallowed the laugh, which died as a snort in the back of her throat. One did not laugh at His Royal Highness. After a few more mental counts of three beneath the constellations of candles and crystals above, she felt calm enough to reply. "You could wear a sackcloth," she said, "or nothing at all. No one would ever think you looked stupid or be traitorous enough to say so."

"Exactly," said the prince, "which is why I'm asking you. I think myself a relatively good judge of character, and you seem the type of person who does not lie casually."

They'd only just met; how on earth would he know such a thing? Was it a challenge? "In that case," said Sunday, "you look fine. Very smart. Very handsome. As a prince should look. Although . . ."

"Tell me."

It *was* a challenge! All right, then. She had costumed herself for her mother's sake, attended this circus overflowing with strangers, and despite her inner turmoil had somehow attracted the notice of the crown prince himself. He had invited her to dance his first dance. He had taken her hand and not let go. He had asked for her honesty, and she didn't have the energy left to be anyone but herself.

"There is a rather large chunk of your hair sticking out on the left side." In truth, his hair stuck out a bit everywhere, but the left side was slightly more dramatic than the rest.

"I knew it!" the prince said through his teeth. "Damn nuisance. There's no help for it."

There's no help for either of us. Sunday hoped he couldn't feel her hand trembling in his. "I'm sure if you smoothed it down quickly, no one would notice."

"You said it yourself, Miss Woodcutter: everyone would notice. They will all say I am too vain for my own good."

She took in every syllable he uttered, but his eyes spoke to her in other words. He knew. He knew they were both pawns in a game long played by their elders, and he was as desperate as she to change the rules. "I would do it for you," she offered, "but then everyone would say I was too familiar."

The prince threw back his head and laughed loudly. Sunday tensed in his arms. Every eye in the room turned to them, and every other mouth whispered her name. She was instantly reminded of her place in the world. Perhaps it was a good thing. She had been feeling entirely too comfortable with this man who was supposed to be her enemy. She felt her cheeks turn instantly red, which no doubt sent more tongues wagging.

"I love that you blush."

"Why did you do that?" Sunday whispered.

"Because everyone was looking," he said, "and now everyone assumes that you are too familiar, so you must dance every other dance with me after this. In order to save yourself the humiliation of dancing with a lunatic all night, you have no choice but to tame my wild locks."

"Scoundrel." His playfulness drew her in. She reached out a hand and gently coaxed his chestnut hair back behind his ear. It was thick and silky, and her grooming was over with far too quickly. His eyes never left her face; they continued to tell her things she wasn't sure she was ready to hear.

Half the room gasped. Sunday didn't care. She saw no harm in letting a handsome, powerful man adore her for a while. She looked the prince straight in the eye and returned his smile, and they danced on. In that moment, she was the most beautiful woman in the room.

Too soon, the dance came to an end. The prince stepped back, released her, and bowed. A chill swept over her. She was surprised to find that she wished she were still in his arms, still talking, still smiling, her body still engaged in an activity that distracted her from the sadness and complications of her life. He had shocked and confused and embarrassed and scared her, but she had *felt* those things. She'd been nothing but numb for so long; it was blissful beyond belief to feel anything at all . . . and even better to feel so admired.

Without his support, her hands were free to tremble once again. She grabbed a handful of skirts and curtseyed, noticing how clean and unworn his shoes were. He probably had a new pair for each day of the year.

Even as he bowed, those intense eyes never left her; she could feel the heat of them. It would take her a few seconds to rise, and then those bright and shining shoes would be on their way to some other corner of the room, dancing on some other part of the floor, brushing against some other skirts, setting some other woman's blood boiling for entirely different reasons. He had promised her other dances, yes, but Sunday could guess the weight of a wayward prince's promise. There was no sense getting her hopes up only to have them dashed again. The only intentions she trusted were her own. At the moment, even those were suspect.

He did not leave. They both just stood there in the middle of the floor, memorizing each other. The musicians awkwardly tuned their instruments. Sunday stared back into those dark eyes, braver now, looking for answers to questions she had no right to ask. She could not quit the dance floor until he escorted her off, but he made no move to do so. A new song began, and a few brave dancers took up the rhythm. The prince remained exactly as he was. Had he taken ill? Again?

"Do you want to know why I danced with you?" he asked into the music.

"Why?"

He leaned into her, and her heart raced. He did not touch her again, but she could feel his breath stirring the soft hairs beside her ear. He smelled of fire and ash, wood smoke and secrets. Sunday remained still, her hands clenched in her skirts. The room blurred. There was no crowd, no music, no castle, no ceiling of candlelit stars, no time. There was only his voice. "I want to be one of your stories."

Sunday lost her grip on the perfect magical control she'd

been maintaining for the last two days. A seam beneath her arm gave a little, and the curls went limp in her hair. A silver ribbon slipped from Wednesday's ministrations and fluttered to the floor between them.

Her eyes were not the only ones that followed the prince as he knelt to retrieve the ribbon. Instead of returning it to her he let it lie, a limp river of sparkling moonlight across his palm. "Stepping away from here will be like going into battle."

Sunday stayed focused on the ribbon. He hadn't really danced with her. He wasn't really saying these things. He would return her ribbon, and she would vanish back to her worn linens and quiet tower and slightly less-than-normal reality.

"It is customary for a soldier to accept a lady's favor before going into battle. Would you do me the honor?"

He was joking. He had to be joking. This was some mischievous scheme to make a mockery of her and her family, but for the life of her, Sunday couldn't figure it out. She should refuse. She should turn away and leave. But he had been nothing but kind to her. He had made her welcome and made her smile. He had made her forget, for one unforgettable dance, about the pain and the numbness that awaited her outside these walls. She liked him. The only person she could hate for that was herself.

"That's an awfully long pause," he whispered. "Please say something."

"Yes."

It was more of a breath than an answer, but it was all she could manage of either. She lifted the ribbon from his hand without touching his skin and tied it around his left arm, near the shoulder. Her fingers were too clumsy to fashion a bow, so she tied a simple knot and pulled it tight, letting the ends of the ribbon trail down past his elbow. Sunday knew what it meant. Every woman who held this arm tonight would remember that she'd been there first.

This time she did step away. She stared at the hem of her silver gown, which matched the favor he now brandished. She did not want to look into the crowd and discover how many enemies she had just made. Sunday experienced a dreadful moment of inadequacy.

A slender man appeared at Rumbold's side, with blood-violet eyes and hair as black as night. "May I present my cousin Velius Morana, Duke of Cauchemar. He will escort you back to your family." Sunday curtseyed again; she wasn't sure her legs would hold her much longer. "Look after her," the prince said to Velius.

"My pleasure, Your Highness." Velius took her arm and led her off the dance floor, back to her stern mother, her princess sister, and the throng of strangers hovering around them who suddenly wanted to know everything about her. She hesitated. The duke placed his body between her and the rainbow of onlookers.

"Perhaps you would prefer another dance?" He bowed. "Please allow me to oblige."

The words came out in a rush of relief. "Thank you, Your Grace."

Velius spun her away from the crowd and swept her up in

a flawless minuet. It was similar enough to a harvest festival dance that she learned the steps quickly. The unfamiliar melody mirrored her sadness and loneliness. She wanted so badly to be loved by someone worthy, someone who cherished her, someone like the frog she'd met in the woods one sunny afternoon. With or without him, she belonged in that glade by the well, not all tarted up and sharing whispers with a boy dressed as the man who was supposed to be her enemy.

Sunday was suddenly too aware of the heat of the duke's hand beneath her own, the pressure at the waist of her elegant gown—but it was not her gown, never hers, and the skin beneath its layers was not her skin as she fled her body. She closed down before she lost control, blocked out her surroundings and remembered her magic. She concentrated on the steps of the dance, the ribbons left in her hair, her breathing, the ersatz night sky. Sunday focused on a flame in a far-off candleholder. No one would notice one candle's absence. If she could just think hard enough, center herself . . . The flame disappeared.

Counter to the dance, the duke lifted her in his arms and spun her around. "Stop it," he said.

"What?" Caught off-guard, Sunday gave no thought to titles or propriety.

"The magic," he said. "You don't want to attract attention to yourself."

Oh, really? "Thanks to the prince, I've already attracted more attention than I ever wanted. I just needed to—"

"You need to relax and enjoy the dance."

Enjoy the dance. Dressed like this? In a sea of elegant strangers? In a castle that defied description? Surrounded by all those eyes and whispers and . . . ? Fool. What did he know of her mind? *Easier said than done.*

He laughed as if she'd spoken the words aloud. "Just because the most powerful fairy at this fete is currently indisposed does not mean she welcomes any and all strange new powers that traipse through her doors."

"My powers are no competition for anyone."

"Not yet," said Velius, "and there are indeed enough haefairies present in this crowd to mask your tiny indiscretions. But, Miss Woodcutter, you are a seventh daughter, are you not?"

"Seventh of seventh," muttered Sunday.

The duke rolled his eyes. "Gods' mercy. The first thing they should have taught you, little star, is not to go marking a stronger fairy's territory unless you mean business. There is no fairy stronger than our dear Sorrow. So unless you plan to serve her every ounce of your magic for breakfast . . ."

"Sorrow is here?" Sunday whispered.

"Not presently, no. But she is in this castle and still powerful enough to notice when a star winks out of the decorations."

"All these people make me nervous."

"You are more like him than you know." Before Sunday could ask whom, for he could never mean the prince, Velius motioned to the candle she had extinguished. It guttered and then burst into flame once again. "If she should ask, I'll tell her I was showing off to impress some sweet young thing."

It might have been true—he certainly seemed to have the hair and eyes and power to match. "And there are other . . . what did you call them?"

"Haefairies," said Velius. "A common term for those of us with some significant amount of fey blood in our veins. Come now, you didn't think you were special, did you?"

"I . . ." Sunday hadn't expected this evening to come with another lesson.

"Close your eyes," said Velius. Sunday did as she was told. The warmth radiating from Velius's hands was like sunshine on her cold bones, working its way through her muscles and setting her at ease. Had she thought the music sad? It thrummed joyously inside her now; her feet skipped gaily across the ground as if she were floating on air.

"You are young and beautiful," Velius whispered in her ear. "You have a smile as bright as the sun, a heart as big as the moon, and a destiny so great that you may never understand its importance. There is a storm coming, one like this world has never seen before, and you and Rumbold scamper before it as it nips your heels. But you are not alone."

The words sounded like a spell, and Sunday's eyes snapped back open. The crowd was gone. Her brow furrowed. Had he somehow sped up time? Had he put her in some sort of trance? Had her sisters left without her? She quickly scanned the room. It would be just like her mother to abandon her, so caught up in her own . . .

No, her sisters were all there, as was her mother, still at

the far edge of the room where Sunday had left them, chatting as if nothing had happened. In fact, as Sunday looked closer, none of the people in the room acted differently. Which was odd, as some held detailed conversations with thin air, and a few on the floor danced alone. A small, dark woman in a green dress held her arms up before her and stared longingly into the eyes of no one. But that couldn't be.

Now that over half the room had vanished, Sunday had a clear view to the archway where Rumbold stood, bowing dutifully to a gaunt man in a gray uniform. Behind the general, a shorter man in a bright turban waited his turn to greet the prince. A shame, thought Sunday, that of all the people Velius had spirited away, he had not managed to eliminate the ones who currently added the most complications to her life. The few people who . . . who Sunday knew had fey blood. Rumbold's mother had been fey.

"Catching on now?"

"All of us?" Sunday said in awe. "All of us are haefairies?"

"We are all made of stars," said Velius. "Not just you, little one."

"Won't someone notice?"

"Worry not; it will fade in a moment. No, sorry," he corrected himself. "I should say it will reappear in a moment."

"The prince is looking at us," said Sunday. Her cheeks grew warm again. "I think he knows."

"The prince is looking at *you*, little star," said Velius. "You've caught his fancy, and I've captured his prize."

"You have a silver tongue, Your Grace." She would not look

at the prince; there was more there than her heart was prepared to handle. But she was a silly girl and too full of curiosity
to resist the temptation. Their eyes locked again across the
room, and Sunday felt a click in the back of her mind.

The dance came to an end, and the duke bowed. Sunday
rose from her curtsey and found herself once again surrounded
by her mother and sisters. The bustling ballroom had set itself
to rights, all attendees visible and accounted for.

"Thank you, Your Grace. It's been . . ."

But Velius was not looking at her.

Wednesday held Monday's elbow, and they whispered like
small girls sharing secrets. Sunday was unsure which sister held
Velius so transfixed. Wednesday noticed his stare and stopped
her conversation.

"This can't be," said the duke.

Wednesday placed herself between the duke and her family and bowed her head. "Wednesday Woodcutter," she introduced herself.

"Velius Cauchemar." The duke bowed automatically but
never let Wednesday out of his sight. He seemed on the verge
of saying something else, and Wednesday waited politely. Was
he smitten? Would he attempt to out-poet the mistress of verse?
Sunday imagined all the various ways this scene might succeed,
or crumble into a flaming disaster. What she did not imagine
were the words he finally did say.

"You are not safe here."

Wednesday had the briefest moment to furrow her brow
before Velius was brushed aside by none other than the king

himself. He was a vision of broad-shouldered handsomeness, oozing with charm.

Something other than humility made Sunday back away from him. She supposed his features were similar to Rumbold's if she looked long enough, but she didn't want to. There was something *wrong* about him, something unnatural, something inside him that didn't belong.

The crowd around them dropped into low curtseys and bows—some patrons even prostrated themselves on the floor—but Wednesday stood tall. Velius kept his head bowed, his mouth drawn in a tight line.

"Your beauty enchanted me from across the room," said the king, "and I found myself helpless against it. I am under your spell, fair maiden." He took Wednesday's hand in his own, kissed it gently, and led her away for his first dance of the evening.

Wednesday said nothing.

12
Beautiful Stranger

OOK!"

Gasp.

"Over there."

"Oh, my goodness!"

"Who is she?"

"Have you ever seen anything so beautiful?"

Sigh.

It was the first time that night the full attention of the assembly was not upon him, and so Rumbold saw what everyone else saw. He noticed when the next woman in line did not extend her hand in greeting. The prince looked past her powdered yellow curls, plump shoulder, and equally plump bosom, following her gaze to the opposite side of the ballroom, just to the right of the main stair, in the direction that Velius and Sunday had gone after the last dance. The chatter lowered to whispers, and a sea of eyes turned to ogle the events.

Only two people in the castle would have commanded such attention, and to the best of his knowledge, his godmother still rested in her chambers.

The dancers scattered like autumn leaves on the polished floor, and the king swaggered through them, his boots rapping a confident *Me, Me, Me, Me* as he crossed the room. Everything about him gleamed: his hair, his boots, his hose, the stitching on his coat. His perfect form caught eyes, but his face held them. For the first time in as long as anyone could remember, the king was not brooding or scowling or looking ready to eat someone alive. No, he seemed . . . giddy. Enchanted. Energized. The company stared, many open-mouthed. Rumbold forced his own mouth to stay closed. He wished, too, that his father had ever glanced in his direction without disdain or duty.

"About time, if you ask me."

"He deserves some happiness, lonely man."

"Isn't she a picture."

"Why, she doesn't even look surprised."

"Probably in shock, the poor dear."

It was the fantasy of every woman in that room that few dared dream for fear it might never happen: To be so singled out. To be so special. To be so unabashedly *wanted* by such a man. To be held in such arms and whisked away with such strength. That promise was what had brought most of these bodies to the assembly tonight. As the king strode across the room, each woman he passed wished with all her heart that someday someone would look at her with that much desire. All of them would be disappointed.

He could not have known her; the king made a point of being intimate with none of his subjects so that they might all speak with one voice. His indifference meant their equality. It also meant that the object of his current affection was nothing more to him than a beautiful stranger.

"I can't believe it."

"Could it be?"

"Oh, I wish . . ."

Sigh.

Rumbold experienced a moment of panic. He had a sixth sense when it came to Sunday; he now knew where she was in the room even without looking. Didn't everyone else notice her? Every time he closed his eyes, he dreamt of her. Each blink brought him the sound of her voice, the shape of her lips, the curve of her neck, the smell of forests and firelight and candles, and his heartbeat as they danced.

That same heartbeat refused to continue until the far side of the room bowed low and his father stepped aside to reveal exactly whose hand he was taking. Yes, that was Velius next to the king and—relief flooded Rumbold—Sunday's hand still rested lightly inside his cousin's elbow. The woman they surrounded did not bend, however. She was a thin streak of darkness in the bright room, like a cloudless night peeping through the gap in a brocade curtain. Her silver-gray dress and wispy black hair added to the aura of magic about her.

"So enchanting."

"Very ethereal."

"She's fey, of course."

"She looks like . . ."

Gasp.

Rumbold was not close enough to see the color of her eyes, but he could guess they were some shade of violet. A score of years or so earlier, in softer light, this woman might have been Sorrow. No wonder she had drawn his father like a lodestone. His godmother would not be pleased.

The king took the woman's hand and led her out on the dance floor. The plump woman in yellow sighed and held over her heart the hand Rumbold was to have taken. The king and his stranger were beautiful and romantic; their dance was a confection for lonely souls. The sheer power of it eclipsed Rumbold's dance with Sunday as if it had never happened.

He was light and she was darkness, sun and shadow, fire and ash. They danced without words, spinning around and around so gracefully, it seemed as if their feet never touched the ground. They stole the breath of everyone they swept past. Every woman grew weak at the knees, and every man, overcome with sudden courage, turned to the closest woman and asked her to dance. Soon the whole company was caught up in the feeling. When there was no more room on the floor, people danced on balconies and steps and tables and chairs. They would all remember this night and tell the story again and again for as long as they lived. Bards crouched in the nooks and crannies, already composing tributes to this magical evening. The charming king of Arilland had fallen in love at first sight. There was no question that he would soon take this beautiful stranger as his bride. Fate had brought them together. Destiny. It was intoxicating.

No, Sorrow would not be pleased at all.

For the first time that night, Rumbold's head was not filled with thoughts of his beloved or himself. Instead, he feared for this woman's life.

~elle~

When claustrophobia got the better of him, Rumbold removed himself to his velvet-cushioned chair on the balcony. From this vantage point, it was easier for Erik and him to keep watch over Sunday and her sisters, suddenly the most sought-after women at the ball. Despite all the energy from the monster inside Rumbold, physical weakness was getting the better of him. He would be devastated to collapse at the dainty feet of his beloved. Would she care? Once proven, was true love forever or just a fancy? He'd witnessed one too many affairs to be ignorant of the fact that the heart was a fickle beast. "Affairs." The word tickled the edges of memory. He probably knew a great many women at this assembly far more intimately than their spouses ever suspected. There was so much unhappiness in the world; once upon a time he had drowned himself in it. He pitied people who'd never lost their hearts and souls to someone else. And minds. Yes, Rumbold was definitely losing his mind as well.

Velius all but leapt over Erik onto the balcony beside him. He had been absent now for the better part of two songs and was slightly worse for the wear after elbowing through the mad dancing throng. His jacket was crumpled, his boots were scuffed, strands of his perfect hair had escaped their queue, and his eyes were wild. Then again, his eyes were always wild.

"I am a fool," he said.

Rumbold was glad he wasn't the only one. "Erik," said the prince, "your memory is currently a great deal more reliable than mine, but I would guess that my dear cousin has apologized for nothing since the beginning of time. Am I right?"

"Correct, Your Forgetfulness."

Velius fell into the lavish chair opposite Rumbold and poured himself a healthy glass of red wine. "Stop being an idiot," he said. The goblet was still as he held it, but the liquid trembled inside. He drank it like the traitor it was.

"I'm merely attempting to assess exactly what kind of trouble we're in," said Rumbold. "What happened out there?"

"I was a fool," Velius repeated.

"We've established that. Then what happened? More important, is Sunday safe?"

"Yes, Cousin, your beloved still has all her limbs, though I imagine they are a bit worn out from dancing." His gaze fell to the empty glass in his hands. "It's her sister I'm worried about."

"Her sister?" Erik asked. "Weekday or weekend?"

Velius grinned a little at that. "Wednesday."

"'Our Lady of Perpetual Shadow,'" Rumbold quoted.

"An apt description," said Velius. "And your father's current dance partner."

Erik turned from his post near the entranceway. *"What?"*

The dancing couple was easy to spot. Despite the crush on the floor, there was a buffer of space around them. They spun like the sun chasing the moon. No words passed between them, only that unwavering stare. The romantics in the crowd whispered that it was love; to Rumbold, it looked more like each was sizing the other up.

"But how . . . ?" He meant to ask after the strange resemblance. Velius answered a different question entirely.

"I'll wager your girl is just as tormented as you are, Cousin. She also holds quite a bit of magic for one so fair. She's a seventh-seventh, you know."

"I thought that was a myth," said Erik.

"It is and it isn't," said Velius. "Like most myths."

"She told me once that the things she wrote down came true."

"It's a bit more than that, my fine cousin, but hopefully not more than her teacher can handle. I was only concerned that she not alert your godmother."

Something niggled at the far reaches of Rumbold's mind, and the prince recalled a vagueness about fairies and their power struggles. It was eclipsed by the small jealousy that his cousin knew things about Sunday that he did not.

"I disguised her magic with a glamour of my own so that if Sorrow commented, I could truthfully admit I was showing off to impress a lady."

"What sort of glamour?" asked Rumbold.

"One that would make her feel slightly less alone in the world," said Velius. "I showed her how many of the partygoers had fey in their blood."

"I didn't notice anything strange," said the prince.

"You have only what little fey you inherited from your mother," said Velius. "You wouldn't have noticed. Few at this assembly are powerful enough. Sunday is one." He took another sip. "Your father is another."

"My father doesn't have a drop of fey blood in him," said Rumbold.

"He did tonight." Erik huffed. "A snootful of the most potent stuff in the castle."

Rumbold started to ask the guard what he meant, but he had seen it himself. Sorrow had bent over the king and painted his lips with her blood, reversing some terrible aging spell. Tonight, the king had displayed boundless energy that Rumbold wished his own frail body possessed. There had been bite marks on Sorrow's arm, angry and red for the world to see. The prince put a fingertip to his temple and massaged the searing pain there. "Is this something I've always known?" he asked his cousin.

At least Velius was honest. "I believe it's something you've always suspected. But Sorrow has not been in residence for some time, so there must be some other key to his eternal youth."

"How old *is* my father?"

"No one knows," answered Erik.

"The kingdom forgot long ago," Velius added. "Right around the same time we forgot his name."

Rumbold felt the searing pain again, more like his rebirth in the woods than ever before, and he was thankful to be sitting down. He concentrated on the cool velvet beneath his clammy palms, soft like Sunday's skin. He rubbed the silken silver ribbon between his fingers. He took several long, deep breaths, emptying his thoughts of all but her smile and the woods on a spring morning.

"Don't try to recall it," Velius warned him. "You can't."

"It shares that trait with the rest of my life." Rumbold peeked through his eyelids when he felt his body was once again under control. "So many memories are still hidden, it never occurred to me to think it odd that I didn't know my father's own name." *Deep breath. Velvet like skin, comforting and familiar.*

"What I would like to know," said Velius, "is why Wednesday Woodcutter is the spitting image of your fairy godmother."

Steady now, Rumbold drew upon his last reserves of energy and stood. He disguised his imbalance by smoothing invisible wrinkles out of his doublet and straightening his sash. "Let's go find out."

~eeQee~

It was amusing how few people cared when Rumbold crossed the ballroom a second time. Whatever eyes were not on the king and his bewitching lady were fixed on their own partners, tapping into the sea of sensual energy that surged from the royal couple. The prince: he and his exploits were already old news. Nothing was so sensational as the couple in the middle of the dance floor. Ridding Sunday of her current dance partner was easy; Rumbold thrust him into the arms of the closest un-accompanied female.

"Hello again," he said.

"Hello." She was glad to see him. He could die a happy man. "I didn't think you'd come back."

"It is my honor to surprise you."

"And pleasantly so." Exhaustion caused her to throw for-mality out the window, and he was glad of it. The space taken up by the number of people in the room—and the dizzying amount of material from the skirts on half those people—forced him to hold Sunday close. The hem of her dress brushed against his legs, threatening to trip him. He didn't mind. The pace at which they danced was slowed considerably as well, and obligatorily free from fancy spins and flourishes. They moved together in warm, comfortable silence, the kind a friend might find in the sanctuary of another friend's embrace. The volume of the music had risen to cover the din of the crowd, and the voices had risen further as a result. Rumbold did not feel re-quired to add to the already deafening level of noise. When there was a lull, they both spoke at once.

"If I may—"

"Why is it—"

Their voices wrapped around each other, dancing with the

same rhythm. He liked the sound of them. Sunday bowed her head and blushed again, completely disarming him. "Please," he said. "I suspect our questions have the same subject."

He felt her take a breath. "Why is your father dancing with my sister?"

"Ah." He spun them to a slightly less crowded space. "Why does your sister look so much like my godmother?"

"Ah," she repeated. "I found out myself only recently. Your godmother is my aunt: my mother's eldest sister." She took another deep breath; he swore he could feel the tension in the muscles of her back beneath his hand. "Which makes *us* . . ."

". . . blessedly unrelated," Rumbold finished. "Have you ever met Sorrow?"

"I have not had that pleasure," she said, too formally.

"She has been my father's closest advisor since"—Rumbold made the mistake of trying to think in earnest and was greeted with a world of pain for his efforts—"since anyone can remember." Since before the king had relinquished his name, apparently. "Wednesday's resemblance to her is strikingly uncanny."

"How did you know my sister's name?"

Had he given himself away so soon? No. "By now there are few in Arilland who do not know her name."

She laughed a little at that. Triumph. "Of course. Forgive me; I'm a tad out of sorts."

"Never! I was just this very moment envying your calm grace." Even in the stifling heat she smelled divine. "It's turned into a bit of a madhouse, hasn't it?"

"Indeed," she said. Sunday tossed a fat lock of golden hair over her shoulder and tucked it behind her ear. A tiny bead of sweat rolled down her exquisite neck and vanished into the lace at her shoulder. He wished he could steal her away to somewhere cool and private, under the open sky where the stars were real and he could be himself, instead of a trickster playing with an innocent girl's heart. What was he doing?

The dance ended, and they each bowed as deeply as the crush of people would allow. He clasped her hand, desperately and reluctantly, not wanting to let go. Only this time, when he began to pull away, her grip tightened.

"Please." He was sure the look in her eyes mirrored his own, and he was anxious to know the reason. Her explanation came out in a breathless rush. "I recently lost a very close friend of mine, on top of the strange truths I've just discovered about my own family. My sister who speaks in angels' riddles has enchanted a king. I'm not sure how much longer I'll be able to manage this 'calm grace,' as you so politely called it, and I'm very worried about what might happen if I can't control my . . . self. I know this is out of line, and rude, and completely . . . well, rude . . . but I'm so very tired, and for some reason you of all people are amazingly comfortable to be around, and I—" She took a breath. "Please," she said more calmly. "Please stay here with me."

"Yes," he wanted to cry. *"Yes and yes and yes. Happily, now and forever, until the end of time and after."* Would that he had already confessed his soul to her at the beginning of the evening, but then she might not have felt as comfortable with him as she did

now. No matter. What was done was done and she was here now, speaking to him the same words he had been too afraid to say himself.

"That's an awfully long pause," she said. "Please say something."

He resisted the urge to crush her in his arms and kiss the breath from her; his bursting lungs ached to shout his joy. He shrugged his arm to indicate the silver ribbon that still hung limply in its place of honor, and then bent to lightly kiss her hand. "I am my lady's servant," he said.

He wished he could bottle up the smile she gave him and save it for a rainy day. Of course, if all went as it should, he'd have those smiles every day, bottle or no, rain or shine, now and forever, until the end of time and after.

13

Swallow the Sun

THE NEXT DAY started so much like the one before it that it took Sunday a while to realize the ball hadn't been a dream. Blessedly, those dreams she did have had been quietly free from winding, portrait-lined hallways. She awoke to the feel of pages slipping beneath her cheek as her mother pulled her journal out from under her head.

"Candle burned down again." Mama clicked her tongue. "Wasteful child." She pried the remains from the holder, pulled another from the drawer, and lit it. The air beside Sunday filled with the scent of tallow and flame. She lay helpless as her journal disappeared inside the pocket of her mother's apron. The pages would be gone for another day, but the emotions of last night still bubbled up inside her.

"Don't yawn at me, young lady. You lost sleep on your own time." Sunday mumbled an apology to the march of her mother's hips as she vanished back down the dark stairwell. Like magic on her heels, Trix slid out from under the bed.

"Having breakfast with the nightmares?" Sunday asked him.

"Even the nightmares tremble in Mama's presence." Trix brushed dust fluffs off his shirt and sneezed. The candle at the bedside flickered and set their shadows dancing. Dancing. Oh, to be dancing again.

Sunday laughed. What were princes and dances next to charmed brothers and sorceress mothers? Suddenly, her new life didn't seem like such a fantasy. "How long have you been down there?"

"Long enough to tunnel a way from my dreams to yours," he said. "Dull stuff there. Not enough flowers and sunshine. Now come on, get dressed." He pulled open the wardrobe and tossed her a shirt. "I have to show you something very important."

Snails' trails and rainbows were of great importance to Trix. Sunday sniffed the shirt to make sure it hadn't already seen a day's worth of chores and noticed her silver dress tossed over the chair in the corner. She wanted to hug that dress, clasp it to her breast, and dance around the room, recalling and reliving every single detail of the night before in the exact order it had happened. Every word, every touch, every step.

"Mama will have my hide if I don't get all my chores done—and Friday's—before we leave for the ball again." Possibly Wednesday's as well, since Mama had already decided she'd given birth to the future queen of Arilland. Not that there was anything out of the ordinary with Wednesday leaving her chores undone and unremembered.

"The chores will get done. Mama said so."

"That she did." Sunday sighed, never forgetting for a moment the burdens of a seventh daughter. The world would do as Mama bade, whether it liked to or not.

"Don't worry, she'll be distracted by other things soon enough." Trix did a little jig. "The day won't be longer, but the chores might be smaller. Trust me."

History proved that more dangerous words had never been spoken. Trix skipped down the stairs; Sunday had no choice but to follow. She tossed off her nightgown, pulled the shirt over her head, tugged a skirt on, and blew out the candle. Before she reached the stairs, she ran back to the chair and pulled the silver dress to her in a fond embrace, breathing in the memories, indulgently spinning around once before taking it down to the sitting room. Friday would need to alter it for this new night's festivities. If it were up to Sunday, she wouldn't change a thing.

Nor would she change a thing about her brother. Trix didn't have to do anything to attract chaos—it ferreted him out eventually, and with alarming regularity. Over the years the mayhem had become more expected than feared, but there was still an element of surprise left in discovering the new adventure. The surprise this time was that the catastrophe was not Trix's doing; it was Aunt Joy's.

When Joy had sped up the growing beans for Sunday's second lesson, that power had infused itself into the soil. Thursday's rose seeds were already sprouting. The spell had further spread to the ancient tree whose sturdy branches held Trix's beloved tree house, and around whose trunk Sunday's fey brother had tossed that cursed handful of magic beans.

If it hadn't been for that ill-fated purchase, Sunday's life might be very different. And Trix's tree would not currently be swallowed in mutant beanstalks.

The green vines twisted and twined, up and over each other, around and through, weaving a net that covered the bark and limbs and leaves so completely that the tree became one giant beanstalk itself. The air smelled green and new and elec-trified, like it had before the storm. There was a soft hissing as the stalks slid along the bark; the giant trunk creaked beneath as it adjusted to the new weight. Most of Trix's tree house was already covered in vines: only half a shuttered window and a small section of roof still peeked through. The beanstalks melded together as one, and the monster grew.

Magic and monsters, all before breakfast. Sunday wouldn't have it any other way. She bravely cupped a hand around a bud-ding leaf; its new velvet skin tickled her palm as it unfurled and continued to stretch its way heavenward. The monster stalk's leaves yawned above the tree's top into the breaking light of dawn. The vines plaited themselves into a mass as thick as the trunk of the tree at its base. Sunday's feet itched, remembering her own waltz as she watched the vines dance.

There had been moments when the prince reminded her of Grumble: something the frog might have done or said, and how she might have reacted. These thoughts were unfair to the prince; he was a unique individual comparable to no one. But she couldn't just erase those memories, nor could she change what had come to pass.

"Let this be another lesson for you, child." Joy looked oddly at home in one of Mama's homespun frocks, her immortal elegance encouraging the overworn threads of the cloth to become young and vibrant again. "All actions have consequences. Ones that affect you"—Joy waved her hand at the furiously rising monolith before them—"and ones that affect those around you."

"And never sell your cow to a strange man for a handful of magic beans," added Sunday.

"Everything still happens for a reason," said Joy.

"That's what Mama says," chirped Trix, skipping merrily past them.

"Even the harmful and awkward and stupid things?" asked Sunday. "There are reasons for those?"

"Especially those," said Joy.

Sunday lifted her head at the sound of birdsong. Her pigeons played in the upward-crawling beanstalk, white as spry ghosts against the green monster, darting in and out of the serpentine mass and chirping as cheerfully as Trix. Sunday hoped they did not tire soon, or that if they decided to alight somewhere, it would not be for long.

"Is it ever going to stop?" Friday asked Aunt Joy. She and Mama had finally appeared from within the house, with Wednesday floating softly behind them. Sunday's dark sister seemed both younger and older than the day before.

"It will grow as high as it needs to," said Joy. "Like most plants. And children."

For a woman who had just become a favorite for the throne, Wednesday didn't seem very happy. "Maybe it will swallow the sun," she said. In one of the stories they had heard at Papa's knee, an old god had done just that. A young boy tricked him into sleep and cut open his belly to set the sun free so that the world might live on. Sunday shaded her eyes against the dawn; the sun was in no danger of being swallowed for half a day yet.

"Those beans worth eating?" asked Mama.

Sunday could almost see the piles of gold adding up in Mama's mind as each tiny white blossom burst to life, withered, and bore fruit. Sunday would never let a bean from this beanstalk past her lips; she couldn't imagine selling them to anyone else. Joy gave her youngest sister a look. Mama grumbled a little and said nothing more.

Trix continued to hop around the trunk of the beanstalk tree, laughing and waving and cheering it onward and upward. And why shouldn't such an insane and spectacular thing be celebrated? Sunday leapt forward and clasped hands with Trix, spinning with him. She threw her head back and laughed heartily at what had once been the tree's top.

Her birds fluttered and danced with them, a blur of snowy feathers. They flew at her, catching up locks of her hair. Sunday threw her hands up over her face so as not to catch an errant beak or talon in the eye. Their chirps were frenetic, cacophonous cries that sounded like . . . words. *Blood in the shoe. There's blood in the shoe.*

Friday's scream cut through their merriment. She tore down the hill, patchwork skirts a blur, mahogany curls streaming behind her. Papa and a shirtless Peter walked slowly toward the house, each bearing Saturday's weight between them as she limped on one leg. The other leg was covered in bloody rags from the knee down. Both Peter and Papa looked concerned, but the agony in Saturday's bright eyes was disproportionate to the amount of blood on her leg. Sunday suspected foul play.

"Speaking of stupid things," Aunt Joy said to no one but Sunday.

~eelee~

Aunt Joy healed the terrible gash on Saturday's leg, where her beloved ax had slipped on damp wood and bit deep into her calf. No one else's nameday gift had ever harmed them—Sunday was amazed Saturday's ax even *could* draw blood. Mama pointedly asked Papa about the wisdom of Saturday traipsing about in the woods every day. Papa argued on Saturday's behalf, praising their daughter's previous work ethic and reliability and other useful words that did not improve Saturday's demeanor. Friday mopped up the blood that led into the kitchen and pooled under the chairs where Aunt Joy administered to the wound; years of tending to the poor and sick gave Friday the ability to stay both busy and out of the way. Wednesday disappeared to her aerie. Trix crawled under the table and held Saturday's hand, resting his head against her good leg in support. Peter sat on the other side of the table, staring at Saturday as if waiting for the answer to a question he'd long since asked. Saturday would not meet his eyes.

Sunday watched Joy as she deftly fused the muscle and broken skin with the pinch of her fingers. She applied a poultice and wrapped Saturday's leg tightly in bandages that Mama had boiled and dried.

"You need to keep this elevated," Joy told Saturday, gently placing the wounded leg in the chair beside her. "Stay off it for the better part of a week if possible."

"But—"

"You heard me, Seven," Aunt Joy snapped before Mama could doom her daughter to action. "My abilities can return the appearance of things to normal, but there is no replacement for time when it comes to true healing. Your daughter needs to stay out of the woods for the next few weeks for her own safety." *"And the ball,"* she didn't say, but everyone heard. *"Saturday will not be attending the royal ball tonight or any other night."* Saturday let her long hair fall into her face, but Sunday could tell she was smiling at her lap.

"Fine," Mama said to her youngest-but-one, "but I'll not have you sit there useless. Your hands still work just fine. You'll help your sister with her sewing." Saturday bit her cheek, bobbed her bowed head, and silently accepted the task. Sunday wondered if Saturday's graceless fingers could even accomplish anything so delicate, but since Mama had ordered it, Saturday would have to try her best. Papa poked idly at the logs in the fireplace. He would not be losing all his daughters to the royal family tonight.

Friday returned to the re-cleaned kitchen with the dresses, her new sewing box, and the bag of lace and trimmings. She tossed the shimmering rainbow onto the table in front of Saturday, who gave the requisite grimace and stuck out her tongue. Mama shooed Papa and Peter back to work and the rest of her children off to do their chores. Joy stayed in her chair beside Saturday; she took up the blue-green dress and pulled a line of lace trim from the hem. Good, thought Sunday, Aunt Joy would keep the peace between Mama and Saturday. And with Mama so preoccupied, she'd stay out of her youngest daughter's hair.

Sunday scooped up the feed basket and walked out to the yard. She tossed great handfuls of dried corn at the chickens, at her pigeons as they swooped down to join her, and at Trix, when the pigeons perched cheerfully on his head and shoulder. He laughed as the cracked corn bounced off his chest and bare feet. When they were a safe distance from the kitchen window, he asked, "What happened last night?"

"My, my," Sunday clucked with the chickens. "There's something you don't know? I find that hard to believe."

"I'm as shocked as you," Trix said. "This ball was all Mama could talk about for days. Now everyone's mouths are clamped shut like you're all hiding some big secret. Mama was all whispers with Aunt Joy over the stewpot this morning, and I'm sure Saturday told Peter and Papa during their walk to the Wood before . . ." His voice drifted away. "Sunday, why would she do such a thing?"

Sunday halted mid-toss, closed her eyes, and put herself in each of her sister's dancing shoes. "It scared me, too, at first: all those people and all that noise. Saturday was as miserable as she was gorgeous. She's not one for dressing up for a room full of ninnies pretending to be who they're not."

"Ugh," groaned Trix. Having to put on shoes was horrible for Trix. "I bet she wished she had her ax the whole time."

"Mama told her to stand up straight, so she looked down her nose at all those pompous ladies, as if she could trust them about as far as she could throw them."

"Saturday could throw them farther," said Trix.

Sunday chuckled. "I bet you're right. Oh, and Monday was there."

"Of course!" Trix danced gleefully; the pigeons scolded their unstable perch. "How is she?"

She thought back on their princess sister, perfect as a painting with her jewel-studded fan. Sunday had spoken more to the prince than to her own estranged sibling. "Beautiful," she said finally.

"Oh." It didn't seem to be the answer Trix was looking for. "And what's the matter with Wednesday?"

Funny he should say that; of all of them, it was Wednesday who was acting most like herself: aloof, despondent, and largely uncommunicative. "The king seems to have taken a shine to our Wednesday. The two of them dancing together was something out of a bard's tale."

"Aiming to outdo our dearly departed brother, is she? I thought these balls were being held for the prince."

"They were. Are." Sunday turned her face into the cool wind, hoping the blush would fade before he noticed.

He noticed. "Oh no," said Trix.

"Oh yes," said Sunday.

"Do you like him?"

"Rather a lot, unfortunately."

"Do you love him?"

"I hardly know him."

"Hmm," said Trix.

Sunday threw back her head and let out a laugh that came straight from her toes, filling her whole body with joy. How long had it been since she had felt so real? "'Hmm'? I pour my heart out to you, O He of the Unusually Wise Comments, and all you have for me is 'hmm'?"

Trix's smile could have outshone the sun, had it dared peek from behind the morning clouds where it hid from the hungry beanstalk monster. "Sometimes 'hmm' is the wisest thing to say."

"Indeed." Sunday tossed the rest of the handful of seed onto the ground. The grains fell hard and fast, more like stones than corn. Trix bent and rescued a few pieces before the closest chicken had a chance to snap them up. He examined them and then held his palm out to Sunday. She sighed at the contents.

Her laughter had turned the seed to gold.

* * *

The hired carriage was a little less cramped that night. Saturday might not have been there in body, but pieces of her were still with them: Friday had retrimmed each of their dresses with bits from Saturday's. Friday's bodice and sleeves were now edged in blue, and Mama's in green. Saturday's decorative braid now lined Sunday's own hems, and her damask overskirt transformed Wednesday's soft gray clouds into a storm-tossed sea. Friday had sewn the last scrap of material into a slender tube, stuffed it with strands of each of the sisters' hair, and given it to Saturday as a bracelet. Sunday saw the blue-green flash of it on her sister's wrist when Saturday raised her arm at the door to wave goodbye. She leaned her weight on Peter, and he helped her hop back into the house. The coachman snapped the reins and drove the rest of the Woodcutter girls to their second night of adventure.

Wednesday had found an old pair of gloves with which to cover her ink-stained fingers. No one but Sunday noticed that Wednesday's penknife—Joy's nameday gift to her poet god-daughter—had crept back to its usual place in the knot of her hair. A small comfort, Sunday knew.

The lane to the castle's inner courtyard was once again crowded, but the driver managed to get them closer to the entrance than before. They only had to wend their way through a small maze of muck and horseflesh before their slippered feet hit stone. So many people were enjoying the crisp night air that it was difficult to tell who was in line for receiving and who was simply milling about. Sunday was swept up in the sea of skirts and smoke from gentlemen's pipes. The crush was all around her:

shoulder to shoulder, back to front, and within ever-quickening heartbeats, she could not see her mother and sisters. Sunday called out, but she could hear no one answer above the din.

Sunday pardoned and excused herself, but instead of letting her pass, the crowd squeezed closer. A few times, the press of bodies lifted her off her feet. She tried to remain calm. The only faces she could make out were all strange to her. No one seemed to notice her predicament. If they did, no one bothered to help her. And then the two girls next to her turned . . . and snarled. A third girl landed the first punch into Sunday's stomach.

Sunday doubled over and struggled to regain her breath. Hands tore at her ribbons and ripped her dress to shreds; she heard shrieks like wild animals above the rending of fabric. Her cheek was scratched. Soot was rubbed into her hair and face. One particularly strong blow sent her to her hands and knees, and someone's—or several someones'—pointed slipper connected with her ribs. If she did not stand, she would surely be killed. Pain blinded her briefly, and when her vision swam back to her, she saw blood on her fingers.

The blows came too quickly. She brought her free arm up in a futile effort to protect her head. Sunday focused on the angry feet surrounding her, the gray cobblestones, the blood on her finger, just as when she had pricked it for Trix on the spinning wheel. She should perform some magic . . . but what could be created from such madness? There was only one thing she wished for. She drew a small circle on the cobblestones in blood and breathlessly mouthed, "Quiet."

The pain in her head died almost instantly. The blows stopped, and she fought to stand. She stumbled drunkenly through the mob, pushing against strangers, propelling herself closer to the castle wall. She forced her eyelids to stay open as she felt along the wall, step by step, brick by brick, until she came to a doorway and fell inside. The smell of bread and oven fires surrounded her. A scullery maid bolted the door behind her, while another gingerly lifted Sunday's head and cradled it in an apron that reeked of cinnamon and onions.

"Please don't tell him," Sunday begged her bright-eyed, stringy-haired savior.

"Who, milady?"

"The prince," she said, and suddenly wished she hadn't.

14

Pain and Punishment

WHERE IS SHE?"

"The main kitchens, sire."

"Take me there?" It was more of a request than an order; Rumbold couldn't have found the main kitchens if his life depended on it. How many kitchens were in the castle? Had he ever visited them? He bowed to the Count and Countess of Wherever, frozen in mid-salutation. "Forgive me," he said, and spun about to chase after Rollins.

The castle never seemed so large as it did when one desperately needed to be at the other end of it. When he and Rollins emerged into the blasting furnace heat and bread-and-beast stench of the kitchens, it was all he could do not to collapse at the foot of the crowd gathered by the back door. Rollins parted the onlookers, and Rumbold hit the stone floor beside Sunday, his beloved Sunday, torn and tattered and tossed to the ground. Her hair was a mess, her dress was in rags, her shoes were gone, and there were holes in her stockings. What skin wasn't covered in filth was red from scratches and slaps. A skinny, mousy-haired girl knelt on the opposite side of Sunday and gently tried to wash away the mask of blood and soot she wore.

"What happened?" he whispered to anyone.

"She fell in through the back door," said a waif with flour on her cheek.

"There was a riot in the courtyard," said a freckled scrap of a boy.

"Who started it?" asked Rumbold. "Have the guards apprehended anyone?"

But for the bubbling of tureens, the spitting of roasting flesh, and the crackle of fire in the ovens, the kitchen was silent.

"They are all asleep, sire." The black, bald, and barrel-chested butcher towered above them all. His voice came from deep within that chest, like the bottom of a steel drum. The words stepped crisply off his tongue, as if common speech was not his first language. He punctuated the statement with a definitive chop from his enormous cleaver. "Every last one. Fast asleep."

Rumbold stood slowly, so as not to lose his balance, and still had to look up at the man. "You are familiar to me," he said, relieved to be on the verge of an actual memory. "What is your name, sir?"

The butcher wiped the blood from his hands onto his already massacred apron. "Jolicoeur, Highness."

"I need you to carry her, Mister Jolicoeur, for I have not the strength to do it myself. Would you do that for me?"

"Yes, sire." The giant knelt and easily lifted Sunday in his arms. Her face was so pale against the butcher's dark skin. Rollins led the way to the closest guest chambers. The mousy-haired girl followed behind Jolicoeur, swallowed in his shadow. Cook, with her meaty hands and determined strides, caught up with their strange parade as soon as she had restored order to her demesne. A giant, a waif, a cook, and a scrawny prince: Sunday would have enjoyed this motley crew.

Rollins threw back a dusty velvet coverlet and patted the silk sheets beneath. "Set her down here, please."

"Awfully clean sheets for one awfully dirty girl," said Jolicoeur.

"They can be washed," said Rollins. "I'll fetch a few more ladies with fresh water. And bandages, just in case." As he breezed past, Rumbold heard him mutter, "And a dress. She'll need a dress."

Rumbold stood with Cook at the foot of the bed while Jolicoeur gently settled his battered angel on her ivory cloud. The mousy-haired girl slipped silently under the butcher's massive arms and continued tending to Sunday's face with her now-dirty rag and no-longer-clear water.

"As terrible as circumstances are," Cook said to the prince, "I'm glad I've the opportunity to thank you in person, sire."

"Thank me?"

Cook indicated the mousy-haired girl. "She is my new herb girl, per your command, Highness."

Rumbold understood now. "You saved my life, what wretched little there was left worth saving."

"I merely have a good memory, Highness. And a long one."

"Would that more had your memory and put it to such good use." He took her strong, pie-and-vinegar hand and kissed it.

Cook blushed. "I like you better than the reckless sod who used to live in your clothes."

"As do I." Rumbold turned back to the mouse. "What is your name, child?" His question was met with silence.

"Forgive her, sire," said Cook. "She is mute. Quick of mind, though, and enthusiastic. I'll take those qualities over a nightingale any day."

"Did the orphanage have her name?"

"There was no record, sire. I took her out to the garden and told her to pick me a flower to be her name."

"Let me guess," he addressed the mouse. "Iris? Lily? Are snowdrops still in bloom? Oh dear, you're not Skunk Cabbage, I hope." The mouse rewarded him with a smile.

"Nothing so dramatic." Cook laughed. "Rampion. It will do."

"Thank you, Rampion. Welcome to our band of misfits." Rumbold studied the soul beneath the rags and the skin and bones of her. She was older than he'd first imagined, closer to Sunday's age.

"If you don't mind, sire, Mister Jolicoeur, Rampion, and I are needed elsewhere."

"Yes, of course," said Rumbold. "Thank you." He bowed to the mouse-girl, then took the giant man's hand and grasped it firmly. "Thank you all so very much."

"She will heal," said the butcher. "All of us heal in time. The strongest are born again." He placed a hand on Rumbold's upper left arm. "We only keep the scars we choose to keep."

Visions surged through Rumbold: a knife at Rumbold's throat, a whip at his back, the sting of salt in his eyes, and beneath Jolicoeur's palm, the burn of a blade as it tore through the flesh of Rumbold's arm. A fight? A sea voyage? His frustratingly elusive past lay just there beyond the veil.

Rollins returned with two women: not sequined ladies' maids but women whose statures spoke of years of hauling about everything from firewood to reluctant youngsters. With startling efficiency, they hefted a steaming basin of water to Sunday's bedside, followed by one armload of towels and another of shimmering gold he could only assume was a dress. They closed the bed curtains around them to work. Rumbold paced.

When the curtains finally slid back, the light that shone from the figure on the bed dimmed all other lamps in the room. The simple golden gown suited her coloring; it would have matched her hair were that not darker from being slightly damp. Somehow, her face showed neither cut nor bruise. He was relieved to see her unblemished.

"She needed no bandages, sire," said the woman on the left. The black- and blood-streaked rags she bundled in her hands indicated otherwise. She tossed the ruined scraps into the tub of dingy water between them.

"With your permission, sire," said the woman on the right.

"Yes, of course, you may go. Thank you both." Why wasn't Sunday awake yet? He dared to touch her hand, warm and pliant, not cold and stiff as the mask she wore. It was sleep, then, and not death. But an enchanted sleep? Who had done this to her? What exactly had happened in that courtyard?

Rumbold forced the impatience back down his throat. He would have all of his answers when she woke. And perhaps—he fingered a stray lock of her hair and ached to touch the lips that might one day say his name—when she awoke, he would tell her the truth. She deserved that. They both did. She would be happy that her friend the frog was still alive, happy that she had saved him, happy that . . . that Fate had bound her forever to a man her family despised.

No. He clenched his fists. If Sunday was to walk that path, she should do it because she chose to, not because the gods had bound and gagged and marched her down it. Sunday deserved the truth, but she also deserved a life. She deserved the freedom he'd never had.

"Is it this one?" Rumbold heard Erik before the door was flung open. The guard paused only long enough to let Rollins through with his contraption: a wheeled chair for invalids.

"Rollins, you are a genius," said Rumbold.

"I thought some fresh air might do her good," said Rollins. "And neither you nor I are Mister Jolicoeur."

"Bah," said Erik. "I could have carried her. Is she all right?"

"She sleeps," the prince said. "Other than that, I believe she's fine."

"They're all asleep," reported Erik. "The entire courtyard. Anyone whose feet were touching those cobblestones when the ruckus started simply fell in their tracks."

"Was it my godmother?"

"If it was, then she orchestrated it all blind. She is resting up in her rooms, same as last night."

Which meant that she had once again passed her blood, her energy on to the king. "I take it my father is attempting to regain control over the situation?"

"With the same vigor he applies to everything," Rollins said judiciously.

"And a sledgehammer," added Erik.

"Right," said Rumbold. "Best we stick to the gardens, then."

Warm in his arms, Sunday slept on. Beyond the thick hedge, Rumbold could hear the muffled commotion from the courtyard, and his father's voice, bellowing above them all. Rumbold pretended the king's bark was wolves howling through the Wood and that the chatter of guests was the chirp of sparrows and chickadees as they discussed the evening. He laughed at himself, for he couldn't remember the last time he had done anything so ridiculous and innocent. He kissed the top of Sunday's head in gratitude for her influence.

"What is this place?" she said into his shoulder. His heart soared at the sound of her voice. When she turned to smile up at him, the garden, the palace, and the whole world smiled, too.

"Welcome to my sanctuary," he said. "I find myself despising crowds of late."

"They will hate me for making you miss your own ball."

"The hellions should be grateful I did not call off the evening altogether," he said. "Witnesses said they had never seen such savagery."

"The female of the species . . ." Sunday chuckled, and then coughed. As Rumbold suspected, only her external wounds had miraculously healed.

"It is my fault for singling you out."

"It is my fault for wanting to be singled out," said Sunday. "The curse of an interesting life: there are either very good times or very bad times." She winced as she shifted in his arms. "Tonight was the price I paid for yesterday."

"Do not attempt to justify their actions." He smoothed her hair with his hand, and she did not tell him to stop. "This will not happen again tomorrow."

Sunday lifted her head from his shoulder. He saw a trace of pain in her eyes, but not enough to worry him. "There can be no tomorrow," she said. "Surely you realize that."

"There will be a tomorrow, just as there will always be a tomorrow that follows today. I will send a carriage at sundown, and my guardsmen will accompany you and your family to the entrance. You have my word; no harm will come to you."

"But . . ."

"Please," he said. "It's the least I can do."

"What of my mother? And my sisters?"

"They are welcome, too."

"No, what of them now? Where are they? Are they all right? Were they—?"

Rumbold moved her body so that she could sit beside him on the bench and converse properly. He took her hand so that he could keep touching her for the short time they had left together. Here in the garden under the stars was the perfect place to tell her the truth of his enchantment. But when he opened his mouth, he said only, "They are fine, I think."

"You *think?*"

"They're all asleep."

"Asleep."

"As you were. By all accounts, everyone in the courtyard just fell asleep."

Sunday covered her mouth with her free hand. "This is all my fault."

"I am as much to blame as you," said the prince.

She pulled her other hand away; he refused to let her see how much it wounded him. "You don't understand," she said. "*I* did that. *I* put everyone to sleep. Me. I am—"

"Good," said Rumbold.

Sunday halted mid-rant. "Good?"

"It stopped the riot. It stopped anyone else from getting hurt." He touched her hair again. "It stopped them from killing you." *And me from having to kill them.*

"It was all I could think of. I didn't even know what would happen, or if anything would happen at all. I was only thinking of myself. I could have hurt someone."

"I've hurt a lot of people," he admitted, "and never for

anything so noble as saving my own life. So tell me"—he lifted her chin—"which of us is more selfish?"

The bellowing and murmuring beyond the hedge grew louder. Erik coughed and then appeared through the gate. "They are waking up, sire."

"Please," said Sunday. "I can't face them."

"As you wish," said the prince. "But you have nothing to fear."

"I fear myself," she whispered.

"I do not fear you," he whispered back.

She smiled. "Perhaps you should."

"Erik, please secure a carriage for my honored guest. The evening has taken its toll upon her and she must rest"—he winked at her—"so that she may return tomorrow."

"Of course, sire," Erik said grandiosely.

"Discreetly, friend," said Rumbold.

"Like a thief in the night," said Erik.

"Thank you," said Sunday.

"I will convey your whereabouts to your mother and sisters and offer them a carriage as soon as they wish to leave," said Rumbold.

"Thank you again."

"And if they wish to stay, I will woo your mother and dance with your sisters until every other woman in the room is green with envy. Now, would you grant me the honor of pushing your humble contrivance to the gate?" He gestured to the wheeled chair.

"I'm sure I can walk."

"If I were stronger, I would ignore your protests and carry you to your carriage," he said. "I am the prince, after all."

She swatted his arm. "You are a beast."

"I have been called such before, but unfortunately I don't have the energy to live up to that either. So I will only offer you my arm and hope you will take it."

She did. He led her to the carriage Erik had called to the north gate, away from the courtyard, and helped her in. Before he shut the door after her, he kissed her hand. "Good night, my Sunday."

"Good night, my prince," she answered, and the carriage bore her away into the night. *My prince.* One day soon, he would not have to watch her leave him again.

"Come on, lover boy." Erik clapped him on the shoulder. "We're needed to save an innocent barrel of wine from a lecherous duke's son."

~~eelee~~

Considering the volume of alcohol needed to make a haefairy like Velius as well and truly drunk as he was, it was a wonder there was any wine left in the castle.

"He's been like this since they discovered the sleepers," said Erik. Rumbold helped him pour Velius onto a bench at the edge of the courtyard. Slumped over like that, his angelic face pressing into the stained wood, his cousin looked about fourteen. Velius obviously still felt responsible for whatever he'd done to bring Wednesday to the king's attention. "It got even worse after they woke up."

"I would know who started this rabble." Rumbold scanned the sea of victims and servants until he found his father addressing the Woodcutter household.

A woman wearing a silver-pink dress and a circlet on her brow held Seven Woodcutter's hand. *Princess* Monday, Rumbold recalled. With her long golden hair and bright eyes, she was a vision of what Sunday might look like sitting beside him on a throne one day. Her skirts were pristine; of course she and her husband would have rooms at the castle. She wouldn't have been in the courtyard when the riot had happened. Monday said something soft and beautiful enough to deflate the king without annoying him. The king actually stepped back, accepting Seven's reticence and ignoring the trembling Friday, who hugged herself tightly and kept her head bowed.

But there was one Woodcutter sister who was not afraid of the king. Wednesday met the king's eyes as blatantly as she had the night before, and then completely ignored him while she twisted her hair into a knot and fixed it into place with . . . some sort of knife? Rumbold felt sure he had seen a wicked gleam flash from it. Wednesday's dress tonight was a shroud of tears and trouble, a symbol of the emotions that hung, invisible but palpable, above the courtyard. When she raised her arm to silently indicate the instigators, it was as if they had been marked by Death himself.

There were seven of them, reluctant, regretful, and resigned, and they were brought before the king. Each of them wore at least one bandage. Most of them limped. A line of blood still trickled down one girl's cheek. The Woodcutter sisters had all fought back. Proudly, Rumbold squinted at Wednesday's hair again. Perhaps that *was* a knife.

"What would you have me do to them?" the king asked Wednesday. His voice carried on the cool night air down to the water, the Wood, and the next kingdom. "What should be their punishment? Lashes? The stocks? Or perhaps"—his eyes gleamed—"they should be placed naked in barrels staked with nails and dragged through the streets by two of my best chargers."

What had gotten into his father? But Wednesday was not ruffled. "They know their crime," she said. "They know their shame."

"It is not enough for me," said the king. "It is not enough for what they would have done to you, what they have already done to . . . the woman I love." On the humble cobblestones he knelt before her, and the crowd gasped. "Now that I've found you, I don't know what I would do without you. Dear Miss Woodcutter." He took her pale hand. "Wednesday. I have this kingdom and riches aplenty at my disposal, but my life is as empty as my heart. I can't remember the last time I was as happy as you made me last night."

Can you not, Father? Rumbold wondered if his father had said similar words to his mother, or the woman before her.

"I would be honored," the king continued, "if you deigned to stay and further your efforts toward my happiness."

"For how long?" she asked. Every breath held, though each soul already knew the answer.

"For as long as we both shall live."

"Yes," Wednesday said without hesitation, though Rumbold suspected her haste was more due to expectation than emotion. "Yes, I will marry you."

A cheer rose from the assembled crowd, the population of which had more than trebled since the mishap. Hands clapped and feet stomped and wine poured, and three violinists struck up an impromptu jig.

There were some who did not cheer: Rumbold, Erik, the still-not-drunk-enough Velius, and the seven women whose punishment had been postponed long enough for their small insurrection to become attempted murder of the future queen.

After kissing the hand of his wife-to-be, the king addressed the accused. "These women will remember the harm they have caused for the rest of their lives," he said. "I would have the rest of the world know their dishonor as well. Call for the pigkeep." A servant scurried to obey. "Each of their forearms will be branded with the royal seal as a reminder of the debt they owe to the crown."

Slowly, each of them curtseyed, accepting the pain and punishment they had brought upon themselves. Slowly, Wednesday closed her eyes, in patience or prayer or something else. Slowly, the crowd parted along the walk to the Grand Hall.

Sorrow had risen to join them in the courtyard.

"Forgive my tardiness, Highness. I have not been myself as of late." Rumbold had never seen his godmother so small and pale as she was now, swaddled inside her robes, old beside Wednesday's ethereal youth. For all that they seemed mirror images of each other, when they were set side by side, the mirror cracked.

The aura of power around Sorrow, however, was rivaled by no one.

"I understand congratulations are in order." She turned to Wednesday. "Hello, Niece."

15

The Third Time's the Charm

HE HOUSE WAS DARK when Sunday arrived home. She gently climbed the stairs to her tower room, tiptoeing past the rooms where Saturday and Trix and Peter lay sleeping. She bit back pain as she eased the new dress over her bruised body, slid her weak arms into the sleeves of a nightgown, and tossed back the thin covers of her bed. Her journal sat on her pillow, small and lonely and wanting to know her troubles, but after only a few tearstained paragraphs, she simply didn't have the strength. Nor did her mind have the serenity required for sleep. She dreaded another torrid night of wandering long strange hallways in someone else's shoes. What Sunday needed was calm and comfort.

Without Mama, the kitchen was just a memory of yeast

and herbs and a dying fire. Aunt Joy was waiting for her there. "A little birdie told me what happened. Can I offer you some tea?"

"Yes," Sunday said automatically. And then, "No. Wait."

"What, dear?"

"Please," said Sunday. "No magic tea. I can't take any more magic today. I don't care if it will solve all my problems and make everyone's dreams come true. I just want to be me, with no help from the birds or the gods or the universe"—she glared across the table accusingly—"or you."

Joy laughed, an expression Sunday was still not used to seeing on the face Wednesday wore most days. It suited her aunt, drew lines in her cheeks and around her eyes that made her seem more . . . human. Another word she rarely associated with Wednesday.

"Cheers, little one." Joy took a cup and saucer from the cupboard, delicate pieces from a set of china Thursday had sent Mama long ago, after her infamous naval elopement. "It's just tea, I promise. It comes with nothing but conversation. And a biscuit. And sugar, if you like."

"Some of both, please." Sunday plopped down in her chair in front of the fire. "It's been such a very long day. My life has been one string of very long days lately. Ever since . . ." She decided to burn her tongue on the tea rather than finish her sentence.

"Since I arrived?" asked Aunt Joy.

"Very near then." She blew the stray floating leaves to the edge of the cup, let the warmth of the porcelain seep into her palms. "Once, not so very long ago, I was just a girl made of nothing but silly wishes and fairydust, who wrote stories and pretended she was a gypsy or a pirate or the queen of the world."

"And now . . . ?"

"And now," Sunday said, as if that would suffice.

"Now you are a young woman in love with a prince."

"Am I?" asked Sunday. "Am I really in love with him? I thought I loved someone once, but I didn't. Or, rather, it wasn't enough."

"I loved someone once," said Joy. "A street magician, a conjurer of cheap tricks, a shyster, my father said. But, oh, he was so much more than that. He caught my eye and bewitched my heart, and I was a fool for him."

"How did he die?"

"Sorry?"

"You're not together," said Sunday. "I just assumed."

"No, child. He is very much alive."

Someone as powerful as her aunt had let the man she loved slip through her fingers? "What happened to him?"

"I don't know what became of him, in the end."

Sunday realized she'd asked the wrong question. "What happened to *you*?"

"I had a sister," she said. "Women began speaking in snakes, children disappeared into the Wood, the king of Arilland lost his name, and I had a dark sister."

"Can no one else keep Sorrow in check?"

"No one like me," said Joy. "No one is as close to her, who

can tidy as quickly and neatly the messes she makes. I was not there for the first royal wedding, nor was I there when Queen Madelyn—your dear prince's mother—died. This is my last chance to undo what she has done."

"The last?"

"It must end here, because this time it involves my god-daughter."

"But I'm not going to marry the king," said Sunday. "I'm in love with the prince." The word slipped out so easily. "Love." The echo of it hovered in the air.

"I know." Joy smiled again. "But, like me, you have a sister."

A chill settled over Sunday, one that she could not shake and that the small fire could not dispel. "Wednesday."

"The king has asked for her hand in marriage tonight, and she has accepted."

"But you were supposed to stop it," said Sunday. "Why aren't you there stopping it right now?"

"I cannot stop the unstoppable."

"Then why are you here?" Sunday cried.

"I am here to right a wrong," said Joy, "and to teach you." She took Sunday's empty teacup. "You should try and get some rest before your sisters get home."

~eelee~

When Mama poked her awake the next morning, Sunday screamed. Her mind was still fresh from dreams that tasted of storms and sea and blood and hunger. Her ribs were still bruised from the beating in the courtyard, but she didn't want to alarm her mother. "I'm sorry," she said quickly. "You startled me."

"You started quite the scandal, disappearing with the prince last night."

"I was badly hurt. They carried me inside and took care of me."

"No one saw you leave the courtyard, and everyone else involved in the ruckus woke up exactly where they had fallen." Mama rubbed a bruise on her right cheek. "Including me. And then some brawny, fire-haired guard told me you'd been escorted home in the royal carriage."

"They knocked me to the ground, and I managed to crawl to the kitchen door. That's all I remember, Mama, I promise. I was very ill."

"So ill that you lost your dress?" Mama scoffed. "Don't lie to me, Sunday. It isn't you." Sunday opened her mouth, but Mama held up a hand. "Don't tell me the truth either, because I can't lie to your father. Just tell me this: are you in love with the prince?"

"Yes." All her torment filled up that one word and spilled over the sides.

"That's what I was afraid of," Mama sighed. And then the strangest thing happened: Mama softened. "Come with me, child."

Sunday dressed as quickly as she could and followed her mother down the tower steps to her parents' room in the main house. Mama led her to the trunk at the end of her bed, a fixture for so long, Sunday had forgotten it was there. Mama pulled off the quilts and pillows—more of Friday's handiwork—stacked on top of it. The lid creaked as she pried open the long-neglected hinges. Among the sundries inside the trunk was a box. Inside the box was a dress of silver and gold, the most beautiful dress Sunday had ever seen.

"This was Tuesday's gift from Joy," Mama said. "I think she would want you to have it."

"What happened last night, Mama?"

"The king asked your sister to marry him."

Sunday didn't need to ask which sister. "And she accepted?"

"As if she could have done otherwise."

But Wednesday *could* have refused to marry the king . . . and then he could have ignored her refusal and ordered her to marry him anyway. Aunt Joy had said the event was unstoppable. "When will the wedding take place?"

"Tonight," said Mama, to Sunday's astonishment. "Friday will have her hands full today making a brand-new dress for Saturday. The gods know how we're going to move her around the castle with that leg."

Sunday remembered a wheeled chair resting near a bed of small white flowers in the garden. "We'll find a way. What about Wednesday's wedding dress?"

"Wednesday stayed at the castle," said Mama. "Monday is taking care of her there."

"Monday."

"I've made my peace with her, fool girl," said Mama,

though Sunday wasn't sure if the "fool girl" Mama referred to was Monday or herself. "I have a daughter about to become queen. Holding the rank and title of princess against my other daughter seems trivial." Mama took Sunday's hands in hers. "Or *daughters,*" she added.

"You mean me," said Sunday.

"I saw the way you and the prince looked at each other that first dance," said Mama, "as did everyone else in that room, before his father's ridiculously dramatic display erased their memories. I've seen that look before. It was a look your father and I shared, once upon a time."

"Do you still?" Sunday asked desperately. "Do you still look at each other like you once did, back at the beginning of the story, when everything was a question you were too afraid to find the answer to?"

"If you can pull yourself away from your own ridiculous drama, you'll find out." She motioned to the dress in the trunk. "Go on."

Sunday lifted the dress by the shoulders. It smelled magically of honeysuckle and sunshine, not thirteen years of storage. Aunt Joy's gift had not saved her sister; Tuesday's death must have been one of those unstoppable events. As with Jack, so much in the world had hinged upon Tuesday's life, and the ending of it.

"Are you sure?" Sunday asked her mother.

"What do you mean am I sure? I said so, didn't I? You know I mean what I say, whether I like it or not," she scoffed. "The dress is yours, Sunday."

It was always meant to be hers. Sunday saw that now. Clever Aunt Joy. It wasn't just Monday with whom Mama meant to make peace. She had to make peace with her own powers.

Seven for a secret never to be told. Seven Woodcutter had stopped having children after seven daughters, just as she'd said. She had called Trix family. She had announced that one of her daughters would be engaged by the end of the week. She had cursed those elfin red shoes of Tuesday's to never wear out and doomed her own daughter to death.

Not knowing Grumble's fate was hard enough. Sunday couldn't imagine having to live with the guilt of killing your own daughter. "Monday said I looked like her," said Sunday. "If my putting this dress on causes you pain, I won't do it."

"Everything happens for a reason," Mama said. "I was the reason your sister died, plain and simple. I have regretted those words every day since." She sat down on the edge of her bed, as if every syllable she spoke held a weight she was long tired of carrying. "I miss her," she admitted. "I miss them both. I didn't realize how much until I saw Monday again." Mama stroked Sunday's cheek. "Your resemblance to Tuesday is the gods' way of giving me back, in some small part, a piece of the daughter I never got to know. I have to accept that and appreciate it." She dropped her hand. "I can't do that if I push you away, too."

Sunday hugged her mother tightly. "I love you so much, Mama," she said. "No matter how hard you push."

Seven Woodcutter put her arms awkwardly around her

youngest daughter. "I love you, too, Sunday. No matter what happens."

For once, Mama didn't have to say it for Sunday to know it was true.

~elle~

Sunday found Papa in the back garden. He was whittling a birch branch to nothing and watching the sun spin the clouds into pink candy. She sat down beside him without a word. Her white pigeons cooed softly in the holly tree beside them. The wind barely ruffled the grass below; the sky barely moved above. Mama would be calling for her any minute, but she needed something. Finally, her father gave it to her.

"There was once a beautiful young girl," he said. The breeze and the birds and the sound of his blade on the branch blended into a song.

"Was she the most beautiful girl in the whole wide world?" asked Sunday.

"Yes," said Papa, "but that's another story. So this beautiful young girl—"

"Was her name Simone?"

"Her name was Candelaria," said Papa, "but that's another story. Candelaria had a cat—"

"Was it a smart cat?"

"Cats are neither smart nor dumb. They are just cats. And being cats, they have an extraordinarily good sense of balance."

"That they do."

"Which is why Candelaria was caught by surprise the day she saw her cat fall and, quite ungracefully, not land on its feet."

"Was it hurt?"

"Only its pride. Cats possess even more pride than balance. 'If you promise to never share what you have seen here today,' said the cat—"

"Cats can talk?"

"When they choose to," said Papa, "but that's another story. 'If you promise to never share what you have seen,' the cat said to Candelaria, 'then I will grant you one wish.'"

"Did she wish for a unicorn?"

Papa held up a finger. "Being given this wish was a miracle," he said, "for Candelaria's father was deathly ill."

"Did he have a cough?" asked Sunday. "And the chills?

"A cough and the chills and bumps and a rash and a fever and black toes and a gremlin sitting on his chest."

"That's not good," said Sunday.

"They had not the slightest hope. But Candelaria now had a wish."

"Did Candelaria wish for her papa to be saved?"

"No," said Papa. "She wished for a unicorn."

"Ah." Sunday curled her toes into the cool wood of the bench and rested her chin upon her knees. Not quite the ending she had hoped for, but for that brief time during the telling, they had been just Sunday and her papa, and nobody else. Just like the story, their time was now over, their ending bittersweet. Unless . . . "What color was her unicorn?" asked Sunday.

"Oh, she didn't get a unicorn," said Papa.

"She didn't?"

Papa turned to her, and that smile Sunday had missed so much of late suddenly appeared on his face. She almost cried aloud with relief and happiness. "Of course not," he said. "She got another cat."

"Another cat?"

"Yes indeed," said Papa. "For the only things in this life more selfish than beautiful little girls are cats."

Sunday wrung her hands. "I'm so sorry, Papa," she said, her voice choked with invisible tears. "I am so very sorry that we never had a cat."

Papa's bark of laughter startled the birds, who scolded him properly, and he pulled Sunday to him in a hug so wonderful that she didn't mind her scrapes and bruises. "I don't want this nonsense to come between me and my little girl."

"Neither do I, Papa."

He tossed the useless branch away and sheathed his knife. "I still don't like him, though."

"The prince?"

Papa scowled. "Or his father. Just because you are the king and you can get everything you command doesn't mean you should."

"He did *ask* Wednesday for her hand," said Sunday, "or so I'm told."

"Yes," said Papa. "But he didn't ask me."

No, he hadn't. But he was the king. He didn't have to. And that was the point. Sunday worried then that the sins of the father would be visited upon his son as well. "And what about the prince?" she asked casually.

"He hasn't asked me anything yet," said Papa. "But I suspect he hasn't asked you anything yet either."

"No," said Sunday. "He hasn't."

"You have nothing to worry about," said Papa. "If you are . . . don't." Sunday put her chin back on her knees. Parents always told their children not to worry about things. "If you'd like, I'll do my best to reserve judgment until I've met your prince."

Her prince. The words felt like a warm breeze. *Her prince.* "I think that's wise," she said. And then, "Yes, I would like that."

Papa leaned back on the bench with his arm around Sunday; she snuggled into the shoulder that had been molded over the years to exactly fit a daughter's head. "So tell me about this fellow I haven't met yet."

"He makes me laugh," said Sunday.

"*I* make you laugh," said Papa.

"As much as I hate the crowds and the costumes," she said, "I feel strangely comfortable around him."

Papa harrumphed. "That's my job, too."

"He seems to go out of his way to seek me out," she said. "He worries about my mood and my well-being. He seems to genuinely care about me. Why would he do that, Papa? He doesn't even know me."

Her father sighed. "My dearest Sunday," he said, "I wasn't scared of losing you until that last part."

"You'll never lose me, Papa."

Mama yelled for her from deep inside the house.

"See?" he said. "Your mother's trying to spirit you away already."

"We probably should get ready. The royal carriages will be coming for us." She tried to stand up, but her father squeezed her tighter.

"The royal carriages will wait," said Papa. "We could sit here until tomorrow and the royal carriages would wait."

"But Mama will not." Sunday heard her mother call once more, this time for them both, and louder.

"I know that, little dove." He closed his eyes and took a deep breath of twilight. "I also know that there's a reason they say the third time's the charm."

And so they remained there, in guiltless peace, until Mama called again.

16

Shadow Angel

HE WHIP SLICED into his back. The barbed end of the leather came away with bits of his flesh, his blood, and his pride. Was this a dream? Was it a memory? Either way, it hurt like hell.

"Again," Rumbold said. His wrists were raw from pulling at the rope that bound him to the ship's mast. The captain had ordered ten lashes; he'd counted only seven. "Again!" he yelled to the black giant who stood behind him like a late-afternoon shadow, but no more came.

The captain slid into Rumbold's blurry field of vision. "You *want* him to hit you?"

"I know the punishment for disobedience. I disobeyed you. I should be punished the same as any man."

"Any man wouldn't have disobeyed my order in the first place."

"I am not any man." Sweat stung his eyes, and the salt from the spray stung his back. He basked in the pain. "But I mean to be reprimanded as such."

The captain knew who he was, but Rumbold was not sure how far down the ranks this knowledge had spread. "Nor do you *act* like any man." She brandished her knife and sawed through his bonds. "You ask too much expecting me to treat you as one. Besides," she whispered, "this will be a greater punishment to you than any physical torture I could ask Mister Jolicoeur to exact."

She was right. It burned Rumbold more to think that he was still being singled out and treated differently because of who he was. Well, if the captain would not willingly finish carrying out the prescribed punishment, he would force her to. Heedless of the raw, broken skin at his wrists, he captured her waist and kissed her full on the mouth. She tasted of fresh air and apples. The men hooted and hollered. She kicked him in the groin and sent him crashing to his knees on the deck before her.

Rumbold heard the first mate snap the whip in his giant hands. Now, he thought. Now she would punish him properly.

Instead, she laughed at him. Her brown eyes and red-gold hair sparkled with sunlight, freckles sprinkled like spice across her nose. "So," said the captain, "what do you suggest we do with this one?"

"Make him walk the plank," one man suggested.

"Keelhaul him," said another.

"Make him swab the deck," offered the man currently swabbing.

"I think we should promote him," said the Pirate King.

"So do I," said the captain. "He's a complete pain in my neck, but he's got spirit."

"If anyone should be fond of that particular asset, it's you, my beloved," said the Pirate King.

"Plus, he's not a terrible kisser," said the captain.

"Keelhaul him!" cried the Pirate King.

"Stand him up," said the captain. The giant Jolicoeur helped Rumbold to his feet without touching the fresh wounds on his back. The captain slid her knife beneath his jaw. "You are lucky, boy," she said. "I should split you open, cut out that silver tongue of yours, melt it down, and buy myself some pretties. Unfortunately, I am bound to keep you in one piece. So, as you are nothing but trouble, then 'Trouble' it is." She sliced a "T" deep into the meat of his left upper arm.

The actual cut did not hurt as much when it happened as it did when the first mate took up the swabbie's pail and doused him in salt water. Rumbold screamed, shook, and defiantly refused to fall to his knees before her again. The captain noticed. "Oh, I do like you," she said. "Far more than I should."

"Just remember that you're mine," said the Pirate King.

"That I am, beloved," said the captain. "Forever and a day, until the seas dry up and there are no more ships to plunder." She kissed her husband lightly, and then turned to Rumbold. "T for Trouble," she said. "And T for Thursday. You are not just any man now, Prince. You are family."

Rumbold smiled. "Yes, Captain."

eeQee

Rumbold's chamber door opened, and Erik entered with a flourish. "May I announce His Grace Velius Morana, Duke of Ouch-More."

"There's nothing wrong with me, you twit." Velius slapped the back of Erik's ginger head.

"*Au contraire,*" said Erik. "There are many things wrong with you. A hangover just isn't one of them." He sat in one of the velvet-covered chairs and poured himself a glass of water. "Your fey cousin here has the miraculous ability to hold his liquor—and mine, and yours, and the king's, and half the country's, I expect."

Velius waved a hand. He really did look no worse for the wear, despite his pitiful episode in the courtyard the previous evening. Rumbold hated him a little for that. The prince was proud merely to be eating solid food.

His dreams had become more vivid, though, and more draining. He pulled down the left collar of his nightshirt and ran his hand over the skin of his unblemished arm. It was hard to tell anymore which were dreams and which were memories and which were both. At least he hadn't woken up covered in soot on the floor again.

"Inferior spirits," said Velius, "both wine and wit. You humans have such weak constitutions."

"You asses are far more sturdy," said Erik.

Rumbold was too distracted to play along. "Velius, did my mother know she was going to die?"

"Gods, now I do need a drink," said Erik.

"Leave it to you, Cousin, to sprinkle salt on our confection," said Velius. "The truth is I don't know. Madelyn had many friends but few confidants. She spent all her time with you."

A woman who had known her life was going to be cut short might have spent all her time with her only son and not have made close friends. "Perhaps she thought the death of the first queen was just a tragedy."

"First time's a fluke; second time's a coincidence," said Velius.

"Third time's tradition," finished Erik.

"There will be no third time," said Velius.

"So Wednesday has cause to be alarmed?" asked the prince.

Erik answered. "I wouldn't want to take her place."

"Then why are we all in here?" said Rumbold. "We need to go to her and find some way to prevent whatever's going to happen from happening."

Velius cocked his head. "I think I liked you better when you were a raging idiot."

"No, you didn't," said Erik.

"Carrots is right," said Velius. "I didn't. But I still should have thought of that first. Let's go."

After dressing his charge, Rollins directed them to the guest wing of the castle, where Wednesday had been installed in Monday's rooms. Erik knocked on the door and a young maid answered, slightly flustered and mildly surprised. "Oh! I thought you were the man with the dress."

"He could put one on for you," said Velius. "He's got the legs for it."

Erik winked at the maid, and she blushed mightily.

"We have come to call on the future queen," said Velius, closing in on the maid with a predator's skill. "Please take your time in summoning her."

"I'd thank you not to render Marta completely insensible, Velius. Wednesday will be out in a moment." Monday walked to the maid and whispered, "You'll want to assist her ladyship while your innocence is still intact." Marta curtseyed with a giggle and scurried out of the room.

Erik quickly dropped to a knee. Velius spun like a dancer, bent at the waist, and took the princess's hand. Monday wore a dress of the lightest blue, a fabric one might have taken for ivory but for the deep azure of her eyes that brought out the shade. A pale golden circlet crossed her brow and disappeared at her temples into similarly golden hair. Each alone, her features were too large, too broad, and too sharp; together, they created a face so fair that no man could easily tear his eyes away.

"Dearest Monday." Velius's voice was as smooth and dry as the kiss he placed on the back of her hand. "You look ravishing, Your Majesty."

"Thank you, Your Grace," she said. "I'll be sure to summon you as soon as the desire to be ravished comes upon me."

"I won't hold my breath," said Velius.

"I would be very sad if you did," said Monday. "I would hate losing one of the few friends I have at this court. No, yours is not the heart I wish to carve out and serve this afternoon." Monday extracted her fingers from Velius's grasp as smoothly as he had captured them. Her eyes moved to Rumbold. "I have larger prey to snare."

"Please," said Velius. "It wasn't his fault. It was I who made your sister's presence known to the king."

She put a hand to Velius's cheek and smiled with those rose-petal lips, a gesture so much like Sunday's, it stole Rumbold's breath. "Do you really think the king wouldn't have found Wednesday on his own? My poetic sister, the perfect image of the woman he will always love but never possess? It was inevitable, my darling. All you did was hasten the meeting." She moved to stand before Rumbold, though she still clearly addressed his cousin. "I thank you as well for turning the attention away from my youngest sister and her scandalous escort."

"It was my honor, Your Majesty."

"Tell me, Velius, what do you suppose your cousin's intentions are toward my sister?"

"He loves her," said Velius.

Monday raised one curious eyebrow at Rumbold, a talent that the prince himself did not possess. Her face was not only beautiful but expressive. "Love? After only one night of dancing and one night of—well, no one really knows where they disappeared to last night, do they?"

Rumbold could no longer hold his tongue. He knew Monday's legend. "Many years ago, was a dark and stormy night not enough to breed its own love?"

It was a jest intended for a future sibling. The prince did not expect the cold reserve that washed over Monday's face. "It was not," she said. "Nor was the decade following."

Rumbold bowed low to Monday, wishing he were a frog again. "Forgive me, Your Majesty."

"A man born four times has nothing left to speak but truth," said a voice to his left. The prince straightened. "Wouldn't you agree?" Wednesday's thin frame haunted the chamber doorway. Rumbold wasn't quite sure how to address her, this woman only several years his senior but oceans wiser, and who would become his stepmother before the night was over.

"Four times?" he asked.

"Boy, menace, beast, man," she counted. "You will take more roles in the future, but you have made your last transformation."

He was relieved to hear that there would be no more shape-changing in his future, and slightly annoyed to be labeled a menace for those years the spell had been postponed.

Wednesday read his mind. "You were no more a menace than any other rebellious teenager born with more privilege than sense. I would tell you to take heart, but it seems you already have my sister's."

"I gave my own in return."

"What is a heart bundled in lies?" she asked.

"What is a heart without love?" he fought back. Neither Monday nor Wednesday had a response. "I did not lie to her."

"No," Wednesday agreed. "You have tortured her with silence. You let her grieve for a soul she did not lose, mourn a heart that should not have broken, and berate herself for betraying the man she loves . . . with the man she loves." She was tall enough in her stocking feet to look him straight in the eye. "It can't be 'true' love without truth, Rumbold."

Wednesday's wisdom astounded him. He was perhaps a fool to think he could find a way to save his future stepmother better than she could herself.

"We are all fools," she said before he could respond, "blessed with the knowledge that certain events will come to pass no matter what path we take to get there." She said "blessed" in a tone that meant just the opposite. "The wise ones follow their angels while they may." She looked to Monday, whose fey-kissed features certainly seemed divinity incarnate.

A sharp rap on the door brought Marta scurrying out of Wednesday's chambers to answer it, and a footman navigated his way into the salon. He carried an enormous white dress as if it had once been a woman who'd fainted and then shamefully faded to invisible in his arms. Some sort of form held the bodice of the dress in place—a form that would have been modeled after the last body to wear the queen's bridal gown.

Rumbold's mother.

A woman entered the rooms directly after the dress. The

inky waves of her hair framed her cherub face and set off her skin's magenta hue. She was from the north, then, of the mountain folk, which explained her hearty build and shrewd eye. The footman held the dress out before the woman while she closely examined the fabric. Satisfied, she nodded to the man, and he gently laid the dress out on the nearest sofa. There was a slight breeze as the skirts settled, and Rumbold smelled lavender.

I will always be with you.

"Yarlitza Mitella." Velius bowed to the magenta woman and crushed her palm to his lips like a lover. "It has been too long."

"Yet you are still a picture, damn you." Yarlitza Mitella made a show of pulling her hand away and gently slapping his face. "I am the same woman in not the same body, alas."

"I see before me the woman who once haunted my dreams," said Velius, "and still does." Was there any woman who didn't succumb to Velius's charm? Rumbold rolled his eyes . . . right over to where Wednesday stood. Perhaps there was one after all. But just the one.

Yarlitza Mitella swatted the duke's arm again. "Enough. Introduce me now to this woman who shall be queen."

Velius took her elbow. "Miss Woodcutter, this is Mistress Yarlitza Mitella, the esteemed seamstress."

With a fist, Yarlitza swept her skirts up to the small of her back, displaying layers of intricate black ruffles and shiny leather heels. She leaned forward in a gesture that was half bow, half curtsey, and wholly of the mountains. She drew her thick black eyebrows together and scrutinized Wednesday's face as intensely as the wedding dress. "We have met before, yes?" Yarlitza asked of Wednesday.

"Once or twice," said Wednesday. "In the future."

This seemed to make sense to Yarlitza, though it made none to Rumbold. "You are She Who Will Be." Yarlitza deepened her bow. "I am honored, my lady." Her sentiment was followed by a sentence in the mountain tongue that sounded like a prayer, or a message of sympathy. "Now if you gentlemen will excuse us, I need to squeeze every moment out of the precious few hours I have left. *Avas!*"

Rumbold spared one last look at the queen's gown as Yerlitza herded him and his companions to the door Marta held open. He should have felt upset about Wednesday wearing his mother's gown, but even his mother had not been the first woman to don it and bind her soul to king and country. And as he hadn't been born yet, he held no sentimental memory of seeing her in it.

Or did he?

Rumbold halted in front of the empty dress on the couch and the invisible woman who listed drunkenly inside it. He *had* seen this dress before. His mother had been wearing it when she had come to him in his dreams, the waking nightmares drenched in soot and ash. He reached out to touch a sleeve and then hesitated, not wanting to sully the pristine fabric with his cinder-covered hands. He looked down at his fingers; they were clean.

Rumbold. Rumbold.

"What?" he said to no one.

"Stop up your ears," Wednesday answered. "Listen with your heart."

Rumbold's brain was too filled with sisters and riddles. The smell of purple rising from the dress gave him a terrible headache. He was tired and needed a nap before the long evening to come. A very long evening. He needed to tell Sunday the truth, and the anticipation weighed upon him. It tasted like fear. He wasn't sure he could go through with it, and yet he knew it must be done. It must be done.

Kill me.

"Until this evening," said Velius. "We bid you gentle ladies farewell." Yarlitza couldn't move them fast enough; had there been a broom handy, she would have surely swept them out with it.

"Listen with your heart," Wednesday repeated softly as Marta closed the door.

Free me, said the voice in Rumbold's head.

In full court dress, Rumbold wandered the halls and fought with the monsters in his mind. How was he supposed to tell Sunday the truth about himself now? She liked him well enough, he hoped, as a man. She had that way of looking at him that made him feel like he'd built the world for her and given it to her as a gift just that morning. The second he opened his mouth to tell her the truth, that smile would vanish. She would walk away and never look back. He was an idiot.

Wednesday had told him to listen to his heart. Sunday was his heart; did she have something to say that he needed to hear? No . . . Wednesday had told him to listen *with* his heart. He put his knuckles in his ears, closed his eyes, and listened. Anyone who walked by would see him and say, *"Look at the crown prince of Arilland; the insanity of kings runs thick in his blood."* Thankfully, he didn't particularly care what "anyone" thought.

Listen with his heart. Listen. Listen.

Listen.

Nothing.

He braced himself for Sunday's scorn and hatred. That would never happen, but he would expect it nonetheless, to lessen the blow from whatever disappointment lay ahead. That matter settled, he opened his eyes and watched the wall sconces lining the empty hallway before him gutter and extinguish.

Perhaps he really was insane.

He stepped back; the lamps behind him were still lit. He continued backward slow step by slow step. He refused to run from this darkness, but he wasn't fearless enough to walk blindly into it. Rumbold backed up far enough to reach a junction. The corridor to the right was pitch-black. To his left, the torches between each sculpture and mirror and portrait still flickered, happily ablaze. The darkness wasn't just whispering; now it was *leading* him.

In the corner of his eye, a shadow fled on enormous dark wings. Rumbold caught a whiff of lavender. He walked down the hall. The cold darkness closed in behind him. *The wise follow their angels while they may,* Wednesday's voice said in his head.

The shadow angel led him down several more hallways and up several flights of stairs. Up and up. The lack of garish furnishings suggested that few others took this path. The purple smell became muffled under the odor of dank and dust. Rumbold ran his hand up the bare stone wall. He must be in the tower beyond the clouds.

"It should be you," his father's voice sounded from far above him. "You are meant to be by my side."

Rumbold froze.

"I will ever be your companion," said Sorrow. "I just can't be your queen."

"Can't, or won't?" asked the king. "Thrice I have asked you."

"And thrice I have declined. You have my heart," Sorrow confessed, "but I cannot give you this." There was something familiar about this conversation.

"You shame me," said the king.

"How? What is 'queen' but another need of yours I have no notion to fulfill?"

There was a pause, and then heavy footsteps. Rumbold flattened himself against the cold stone. The shadow angel embraced him, cloaking him in her darkness. "I will toss her aside and take you instead." The king's tone was forceful, almost growling.

"You will grow old and wither and die, and when your bones are dust, no one will remember your name." There was a hitch in Sorrow's voice. "I would not have you go like that. I would not have you leave me."

"You would see me wed to yet another woman instead?"

"I have no choice," said Sorrow. "You will wed her and bind her fey soul to yours. You will steal her shadow and eat her flesh and survive another generation, and that is how it must be."

There was no name for this monster whose tainted blood ran through Rumbold's veins, this cannibal who had killed his own wife, and the wife before her. Rumbold was sick at the thought, gagging at the realization. He wanted to claw through his own skin, draw the blood, and coax the poison out. He reached for his dagger and opened his mouth to cry out his revenge, but the impish shadow stopped him. She trapped his arms at his sides and stopped his mouth with darkness so that he could not scream.

"She is powerful," said Sorrow, not referring to Wednesday by name or family connection. "You will not need to marry again for a very long time."

"How long?" asked the king.

"Long enough for your son and his sons to die, and for another world to forget you all over again," Sorrow answered. "Maybe even long enough for the pain of this match to fade from my mind."

There was another pause, this one without all the anger of the previous silence, it seemed. Rumbold could not stand to hear any more. The shadow angel released him. Lamps flared to life as he sped down the hall. He emptied his mind of everything but the wind in his mangy hair, the breath burning in his lungs, and his feet as they ran back from stone to carpet. He opened his mouth and screamed a silent scream.

If all of this was destined to happen, as Wednesday had said, then why had the shadow angel led him up those stairs? Rumbold beat the walls with his fists and cursed a few gods. He might not be able to save Wednesday from her fate, but he had to try. He could not in good conscience let Sunday's sister die. He could not knowingly allow his father to take one more innocent life.

Rumbold, Rumbold, his heart beat frantically in his ears.

Free me.

17

If You Believe

THE KING SENT two carriages that evening to collect the Woodcutter family. The carriages were confections on gilded wheels pulled by teams of white horses that marched in perfect step. The drivers and coachmen matched as well, as if someone had opened a set of dolls and ensorcelled them to height and life.

Mama and Papa took the first carriage along with Saturday, who whined and wailed and carried on. She wore her new dress only because Mama had told her she must, and Papa flatly refused to let her bring her ax to the wedding, so Saturday was loudly doing her best to make them both regret their actions. It took Papa and three footmen to get the injured girl inside the vehicle; one would have thought Saturday was being man-handled by the brute squad. Sunday mentioned as much to Trix.

"They should have sent the brute squad," said Trix. "She'd be too fascinated to have any objections, and too proud to show weakness."

Tonight was one of those times Trix looked like the older brother he really was. Sunday wasn't sure how Friday had managed to accommodate the extra length in the arms of his overcoat, or how Mama had managed to keep him so busy between dress-ing and leaving that he didn't have time to cover himself in mud or soot or some other unquestionably malodorous substance. His hair was short and neat, his posture straight, his head high. If it weren't for the white birds perched on each shoulder, Sun-day might have guessed her brother was royalty himself.

Aunt Joy did not join them on this journey. Sunday won-dered what good her aunt could do at home, but Joy had simply shrugged her off, said she was needed here, and that was that.

There was no riot this night. The courtyard fell to silence as the carriages approached, and the crowd parted for them. The soldiers edging the yard snapped to attention; the one with the copper hair and the barrel chest had the wheeled chair from the garden. Oh, to be in that quiet garden again with her head pillowed on the prince's shoulder, exchanging whispers. Sunday shivered and glowed at the memory. Her birds, having followed the carriages from the house, settled into the hedge behind the guard.

The people closest to the pathway curtseyed or bowed

their heads. Sunday recognized none of them. *That's right,* she thought. *Be glad I don't remember any of you who didn't stoop to help my sisters and me.*

The sky above them was ominous with cloud; the uppermost spires of the castle disappeared into the climes. Sunday could taste rain on the wind. There would be no moon peeking through this cover with curious rays so that the gods might bless this union. Sunday thought it fitting.

The sisters made a show of displaying their bare forearms to the guards at the Grand Entrance. Friday had modified the sleeves of all their garments, splitting the seams to the elbow so that the flesh of the lower arm, when displayed, would be framed by colorful layers of fabric. They knew the king's men would be examining the arms of all the young women that evening, to ensure that the branded Savage Seven did not make an appearance. Judging by the sound of rending fabric Sunday heard behind her, Friday's new fashion was already a trend.

"Fancy," Trix breathed. Sunday had forgotten that neither he nor Peter had ever seen the palace before. Papa might have chanced to visit back when Jack Junior had been in the king's employ, back when her brother had been alive, back when her feelings for Rumbold wouldn't have been such a burden.

Trix wasn't wrong: it *was* fancy, the decorations exceeding the extravagance of either of the nights before. Guards lined the path from the Grand Entrance all the way to the giant staircase. The ballroom still had heavens full of magical crystals, but the floor below was now covered in rows of chairs and benches and more flowers than Sunday had ever seen—red and blue and

yellow and violet—more flowers than were currently bloom-
ing in all of Arilland. They had to have come from Faerie. For
her shadow sister, Sunday expected nothing less.

Sunday and her family came to a halt at the top of the stair,
and when they were announced, the assembly bowed as one.
Sunday restrained herself and did not run down the red-
carpeted stairs to take the hand of her prince, who waited
expectantly below, but she had it soon enough.

"Isn't this is a bit much?" she whispered.

"No. You look beautiful."

He said she was beautiful and so she was, with words full
of no more magic than a sincere desire to compliment. She could
have been made of gold and not been happier. "Thank you."

The prince bowed to Papa, who did not look amused. Prince
Rumbold folded Sunday's hand into the bend of his elbow
and—without letting his skin part from hers—led the family
two by two to the rows of elaborate chairs situated at the front
of the assembly. The redheaded guard followed behind them
all, having come in through a side entrance with Saturday in the
wheeled chair. Just as Trix had foretold, Saturday's caterwaul-
ing had stopped as soon as there were soldiers present.

Rumbold dismissed himself to the dais beyond the small
orchestra where the minister stood patiently awaiting the arrival of the king. Sunday wrung her fingers together, wishing
she had her journal to calm her racing heart. The whispered
voices around her were an anonymous cloak of soft noise that
settled around her shoulders, echoing the manic thoughts in
her mind.

The ballroom filled; the wave of voice-noise crested and broke as the musicians began playing. From behind a curtained wall, the king emerged to stand by his son. The assembly stood as one and turned in anticipation of Wednesday's arrival. Sunday, her eyes still locked with the prince's, did not.

Wednesday floated up the aisle, a posy of indigo wildflowers clutched in her pale hands like ink come to blossom. Monday attended her, organizing the shimmering train of the dress as she stopped beside the king on the dais. The rest of the dress caught the magical light and shimmered, too, overpowering even Wednesday's haunting fey beauty.

No, wait. That couldn't be right.

Sunday stopped examining Rumbold from sash to shoes and concentrated on Wednesday's wedding gown. She glanced back at her family; no one else seemed blinded by the power radiating from the fabric. If some enchantment were embroidered into the elaborate patterns, wouldn't Friday have been the first to notice? But her moon-faced seamstress sister just smiled up at the couple while the minister began his speech and made his blessing. Friday would never grow out of being a romantic.

So Sunday was on her own. She blinked, took a deep breath, and then blinked again. She could make out lines of power covering the gown, crisscrossing over and under themselves around Wednesday from neck to toe and beyond, pooling around Monday with the rest of the train. Along the lines were markings in some strange alphabet Sunday did not know.

Wednesday was like a mermaid, her pale skin tangled in a magical net cast by a wayward fisherman.

Sunday blinked again and the net disappeared; now there was only the feathery white lace of the wedding gown. She blinked again and the net was back, its strange markings dancing in the air around her. Sunday turned once again to her hae-fairy siblings, amazed that none of them would notice such a thing. And then Peter blinked.

Sunday waited until he blinked again, and his dark brows knitted above his pale blue eyes. Peter? Of course! Sunday *had* seen those strange symbols before; they were the runes Aunt Joy had been teaching Peter to carve into his sculptures. Sensing her stare, Peter looked to Sunday, the same questions mirrored in his face.

Even if she had possessed the freedom to speak, Sunday could not have answered those questions. She knew only that Wednesday had to do this unstoppable thing. Somehow the gown must be as vital a part of the ceremony as Wednesday herself. That dress had been worn by Rumbold's mother and the queen before her: women both gone now, asleep forever in the dark of the Great Beyond.

Sunday's eyes burned at the thought of losing her sister. Wednesday was a great comfort to her, if only because her unique presence meant that Sunday was not the most extraordinary of the Woodcutter brood. Having her removed to the castle would be a difficult adjustment; having her removed from Sunday's life altogether was unfathomable.

Trix shifted to cover Sunday's hand with his and gave it a little squeeze. People were supposed to cry at weddings; they just weren't supposed to cry because they suspected that the bride was going to die. Sunday blinked again, willing away the disturbing vision of the magical dress that held her sister prisoner. Angrily, she blinked again. Again. And then Wednesday turned to her.

Only . . . Wednesday didn't turn to her. The service continued uninterrupted. The minister droned on, the bride and groom seemingly lost in each other before the warm sea of huddled masses below them. It was a ghost of Wednesday that she saw, a vision of her sister in the same body, in the same cursed gown, who turned in her place. Wednesday blew her little sister a kiss and then raised a ghostly unwed finger to her lips. Whatever Sunday saw, whatever distressed her, this inner, secret Wednesday urged her to keep it to herself.

Sunday nodded to the apparition of her shadow sister, and then shook her head cautiously at Peter, who was still staring at Sunday inquisitively. She took a deep breath, squeezed Trix's hand in hers, and waited for the torturous ceremony to be over.

Like mother like daughter: Wednesday said only the two words required of every bride in every wedding ceremony, and the deed was done. There was leaping and cheering, calls of congratulations and blessings of good fortune. Servants collected chairs and distributed wine to hungry hands; there was dancing even before the music started up again, even before the king and new queen had left the dais. It was a new day for the kingdom and hope for a better tomorrow. Trix grabbed Sunday's other hand, and they skipped wildly in circles through the crowd, just as they had around the monster beanstalk. Sunday was swept up in the excitement, toeing the line between exquisite happiness and hysteria.

As if she had summoned him, Rumbold appeared at her side once more. "Sunday, there's something I need to tell you."

"My sister just became your stepmother." She shook her head. "Please, don't speak, for my sake. Let's just dance."

"As you wish, my lady."

A dance was what Sunday needed to work out her troubles. Tuesday's silver and gold dress wanted to dance as well. The beat of the music was intoxicating, the tapping of toes and waving of arms, the polite bows and the swinging of skirts, the beads of sweat that curled the tendrils of hair by her ears. One dance led to another, and another, and Rumbold seemed happy to partner her for as long as she required. Couples beside them tired, and new couples took their places. The hours ticked by, and still Sunday and her prince danced on.

Rumbold pulled Sunday up onto his hip during one turn of the set, and in spinning her moved them both off the dance floor entirely. "Enough," he said when he sat her down, and she realized how much her frantic need for activity had exhausted him.

"I'm sorry. That was selfish of me. We should have taken a break long ago." How callous of her to wear out a man so obviously fresh from the sickbed!

"I am just as selfish," he said. "I don't want you to dance with anyone else."

"You honor me."

"It's really not honor I'm feeling right now." He straightened his sash and blotted the back of his neck with his sleeve. "Shall we get some air?" He led her onto a balcony that overlooked a very familiar garden. Perhaps now that Wednesday was queen, she would let Sunday visit this garden to relive the pleasant memories of Rumbold she had here. Sunday breathed deeply, catching the scent of lilacs on the cool night air. The generous display of fey flowers in the ballroom might have confused her senses, but spring was still very much at hand in the world.

A guard appeared, the redheaded man who had been tending to Saturday, the same guard who'd kept watch for them the night before. Sunday hadn't heard him approach.

"Erik, would you please have a servant fetch us some refreshment?"

"Of course, Highness." Erik bowed, which Sunday expected, and then he pointedly glared at the prince, which she did not.

Rumbold cleared his throat. Sunday wondered if she should fetch the water herself. The two men exchanged something understood but unsaid, and with a curt nod, Erik left them.

"I have to tell you," he said as soon as they were alone. "I . . ." He pulled at his sash again. "I hated letting you go last night. The party wasn't the same without you."

"I missed you, too." The truth hurt just as badly when spoken aloud. She'd hoped all the dancing would make a conversation with the prince less awkward. She needed to tell Rumbold about Papa's discontent and his expectations, which meant presuming on a relationship between them she wasn't even sure existed. It was time to find out. "Your Highness—"

"My friends call me Rumbold. Sunday," he asked softly, "will you be my friend?"

Sunday could not address him so familiarly. Not yet. But his request gave her hope. "Your Highness, we can't be anything. This pretense can't go on any longer. Surely you know who I am, what my family is."

"The past is past," he said. "Can't we put it behind us?"

How could he shrug off her brother's death so lightly? Jack Junior's fate had ruined her family. Rumbold had led a princely life, spoiled and pampered and locked away in his ivory tower, and Sunday could see that he was blissfully unaware of the exact situation. It was her duty to set him straight.

She held a hand to his mouth. "Please, let me finish." He began to kiss her fingers. She must be dreaming. Someone in the crowd had handed her a poisoned goblet of wine and she was having visions. That would explain the wedding dress, the ghost of Wednesday, and what the prince was now doing with his lips to the pad of her thumb. "I am a Woodcutter," she said, determined to make him understand. "Sunday Woodcutter."

"'. . . and you are doomed to a happy life,'" he finished. "I already know that part."

Sunday froze. All the familiar words hit her in the gut at once. His asking her to be his friend. The first words that she had spoken to a frog all those very long, very hard days ago.

The world spun around her and clicked—slammed—horribly into focus.

Grumble.

Rumbold.

The prince hadn't been sick or off on holiday. He'd been enchanted. That last kiss she had given the frog, the one filled with all her friendship and gratitude and . . . love, *that* had finally broken his spell. Grumble hadn't died in the thunderstorm. Or, rather, he had, and had been reborn into the man who stood before her. The trading of the golden bauble for royal tokens, the prince picking her out of the crowd only seconds after her arrival. How worried she had been, how torn, how miserable! She had tormented herself with first Grumble's absence and then Rumbold's presence. She had wondered if her feelings were unrequited. Only he'd been in love with her the whole time—and toying with her like a puppet on a string.

Prince Rumbold's eyes twinkled, and he kissed her fingers again. How much fun he must be having at her expense. How he and his friends must laugh at her. Her stomach roiled. Oh, she was such a fool.

A dog's faraway howl at the moonlight snapped her out of her shock, reminding her exactly how much royalty had already taken from her family. Jack Junior. Monday. Wednesday. He would not have her as well.

"I love you, Sunday," he confessed.

Wrenching her hand away, she turned and fled.

This time the hellion horde worked in her favor: the women of Arilland were all too eager to see her leave the festivities and all too happy to mob the prince in the ballroom and slow his pursuit. Sunday heard her sisters' voices calling after her, but she did not stop for them. She did not stop for anyone until she met Trix on the carriageway. He sat on the steps there, waiting for her.

"Come," he said. "I will run with you."

She didn't stop to tell him it was no use, that the prince would saddle his horse and overtake them, that his hunting hounds would nip at their heels until he arrived. They ran, her snow-white birds flying the path before them. They ran through the fields and the scrub woods, on and on, until her breath was knives in her throat and the baying and the hoofbeats were almost upon them. They stopped beside a small pond.

"We must keep going," Sunday said to Trix.

"You cannot run anymore." And he could?

"They will catch us," she said.

"Then we will hide," said Trix.

"How?"

"You have to believe," he told her. "Just like when you write or Mama speaks. Just like when the wool turned to gold and when the beans grew. Tell yourself the story, Sunday. Weave the words in your mind. If you believe we can hide, we will be hidden."

Sunday grabbed her brother's hands, closed her eyes, and believed with all her might. She believed so hard that when the prince slowed his horse by the pond, she believed he did not see a woman in a gold and silver dress and her wild brother, only a tree with gold and silver rosebuds on it and a rock at its foot. She believed that he sat on the rock and buried his head in his hands, and that when his shoulders shook, he was not laughing. She believed that he stood up, plucked a rose from the tree where two snow-white birds cooed lazily, and rode off back toward the palace. And when he was gone, she believed that Trix stood up and cracked his sore back, and that she ran beside him, half barefoot, all the way home and into her aunt's waiting arms.

18
Sight of Joy

T WAS VELIUS who found him first, stumbling along the riverbed, trying to lead his horse home. Erik might have been the first to see him leave and the first to respond to the alarm, but it was Velius who talked to horses. His fey cousin had crossed the county like a rumor.

"Rumbold! Rumbold, can you hear me?" Velius's face was right there. Violet eyes bored into the prince, but his cousin's voice called from miles away. "Cousin!" Rumbold didn't feel the first slap. The second one stung.

"Velius?"

"What are you doing out here? Why didn't you get back on your horse? He would have led you home."

His mouth was dry. It tasted like sand and salt and blood.

"I can't remember how," he said, "and I can't . . . I can't . . ."
Velius pried his fingers open and pulled the reins out of them.
In the other hand, the prince held a silver and gold rose, its petals smashed. There were lines of red dots where the thorns had bitten into his skin. It smelled of green and sunshine.

"What is that?" Before the last word left Velius's mouth, the rose transformed into one perfect, dainty, silver and gold dancing slipper.

"It's a recurring theme," Rumbold said, and then laughed as if his heart was breaking. "Gods, Velius, it's all I have left of her." He thought he had prepared himself for the worst. He put a hand to his chest. It hurt if he breathed too deeply. The air he took in to scream out his tragedy, long and loud, was excruciating.

"Should we continue on after her?" asked Velius. The dogs were upon them now, with other men and other horses.

"Please," Rumbold implored his cousin. "Ride back to the castle as quickly as you can and stop the Woodcutters from leaving. There is"—he clawed at buttons that choked him—"something I need to discuss with Sunday's father." He ripped his undershirt open at the neck to feel the air on his skin, never once letting go of the shoe in his hand. "He will hear me out."

"Yes, Your Highness." And Velius was gone.

Rumbold collapsed to his knees and let one of the men fetch him a drink from the stream. He stared at the perfect slipper in his hand, nudging his sadness over into anger. He let the madness fill him with energy, just as it had when he'd first fought Velius on the training grounds. After he guzzled one cup of water and dumped another over his head, a soldier helped him back onto his horse.

With each step of the horse, Rumbold's anger grew. He was mad at every minstrel who had ever sung a song about love. He hated every girl who had giggled in the hallways and every simpering fool who had picked wildflowers to garner her affection. He was furious with himself for having lived these last days on a wish. On a lie. A kiss does not make the future. Love alone does not make a life.

By the time he'd reached the edge of the castle proper, he despised prying families, busybody fey, and weddings . . . and he'd stayed on his horse. He'd had it with aunts and god-mothers. He was sick to death of fathers, both Sunday's and his own. Who were they to dictate in what manner his life should be lived? Why must everything he did be affected by the whims of a generation past?

He remembered now how to ride enough to kick his horse into full gallop. By the time he reached the courtyard, he hated all woodcutters, and remembered how to dismount without aid. By the time he reached the Grand Entrance, he hated Aril-land and every king who'd ever lived, and he remembered the way to the ballroom without a guide. By the time he marched through the library doors and right up to Jack Woodcutter, the anger that had kept him upright and flushed his cheeks spilled out over his tongue.

"She ran away because of you," said Rumbold. Silence fell over the ballroom. He sounded like his father, and he cringed at the feeling. The demon of energy inside him swallowed the sickness. The glass beads on the tiny slipper cut into in his hand. "She ran from me because she thought she was betraying her family. What have you told her?"

Sunday's father wiped the prince's spittle off his own cheek with hands that could easily have ground Rumbold's bones to make his bread. Those hands were attached to arms and a chest as big around as the trees in the Elder Wood. Woodcutter's hard face remained unreadable. "I've told her nothing."

"Then what *haven't* you told her?"

Woodcutter looked to the doors, beyond which the festivities could be heard down the hallway. Rumbold nodded to Erik; the guard closed the doors and stood before them, in case a wandering partyer should enter unbidden. Wednesday remained in the midst of post-wedding festivities; there would have been no way for her to steal away for this meeting. But Monday was here, and the rest of the Woodcutter family, save Trix. Velius stood beside the richly upholstered wing-backed chair where Monday sat.

"We call it the Forbidden Tale," said Woodcutter. "None of my family knows the full truth of it."

"The Forbidden Tale is about Jack and the harem," said Peter.

"And the Sultan's daughter," added Friday.

"The Sultan's *sister*," Saturday corrected her sister from her chair. Her eyes were bright and her cheeks were flushed; her terrible injury apparently hadn't dampened her spirits.

"No, my children. The Forbidden Tale is about Jack"—he looked to Rumbold—"and the prince."

"What?" asked Peter.

"Why haven't you told us?" asked Friday.

"Because it was forbidden," said Woodcutter.

"It was forbidden to us all," said Velius, "by your Fairy God-mother Joy."

"*Aunt* Joy," spat Saturday, and murmured something about an ax.

"The only way to keep a secret is not to repeat it," said Erik. "Those of us who were there still bear that burden."

"I think it is time we stop keeping secrets," Rumbold said. "The danger is over now, thanks to"—he could not bring himself to say her name—"your youngest daughter. There is no one left it can hurt."

"Naught but my pride," said Woodcutter.

"We are all family now," said Monday. "Family shouldn't keep secrets."

Seven Woodcutter sat beside Friday on the sofa. She was small in stature, like her youngest daughter, but with deep lines in her face from a life well-lived and a pinched mouth from words rarely spoken. In Rumbold's mind she belonged in the backyard of a ramshackle house on the edge of the Wood, tending to the drying laundry right before a storm. And yet here before him in her finery, she was the mother of princesses and queens, and even more of a force to be reckoned with. "Tell us" was all she said.

And because he could not deny his wife, Jack Woodcutter sat before the fire and spun the tale.

"I will tell you the story the way I lived it, so that you

might better understand," said Woodcutter. "About five years ago, a parcel came to me from the castle. In it was Jack Junior's medallion, the nameday gift from his fairy godmother, which he'd worn all his life. The one I wear now, in his honor." Woodcutter unbuttoned his shirt and pulled the medallion from under his cravat. "Inside the package was also a letter from the prince. He let me know the circumstances under which the medallion had come into his possession, and the details of Jack's . . ."

". . . death," Rumbold finished when it seemed that Woodcutter could not. "The hunting party I was leading killed a wolf, deep in the Wood. It was the largest wolf any of us had ever seen. When I sliced it open, that medallion was in its belly." Rumbold suddenly felt the hilt of the dagger in his hand, the beast's fur, the blood bubbling over his fingers. He wondered if every memory would revisit him in such sensate glory.

"How could Jack have been killed by a wolf?" asked Peter. "He died as a dog on the castle grounds."

"Jack did not die here," Rumbold answered. "I know, because the day he was cursed, I was cursed as well." He expected to hear gasps at the announcement, but only silence answered him. Here was a family for whom strangeness was an everyday event, whose adventures could fill as many books as the library shelves around them. This family also knew about stories: how to tell them and when to listen. "As you know, my godmother cursed Jack."

"Aunt Sorrow," said Saturday.

"Yes. Just after that happened, Jack's godmother appeared."

"Aunt Joy," said Friday.

"Indeed. Your Aunt Joy used her power to shorten Jack's term as a dog to only a year. She then cursed me. On my eighteenth birthday, I was to spend one year as a frog."

"Was?" Monday asked, for clearly Rumbold was no longer the youth he had been.

"In an effort to break the curse, Sorrow postponed it a year, a year that I do not remember, and one I'm not sure I'd be proud to recount if I did. Finally, several months ago, the curse took hold."

Peter was quickest with the math. "Several months? Why aren't you still a frog?"

Rumbold showed them the slightly crumpled shoe he'd been concealing behind his back. He ran his fingers lovingly along the silver and gold embroidery and over the shining glass beads. "A girl found my well while wandering the Wood one day, not long ago. We became friends. She came back every afternoon and told me stories of her amazing, magical family: from Tuesday's death and Monday's marriage to Thursday's trunk and Friday's needle. I fell in love with her, and I fell in love with all of you as well, for I did not remember my life before. You were the only family I knew."

"The golden ball," said Seven Woodcutter. "That was you."

"Yes, ma'am." Rumbold made a small bow. "I felt responsible for what happened, and I wanted to help. Sunday kissed me in gratitude that day and ran back to the house, so she did not see . . ." He stared at the shoe, afraid to meet anyone's eye. "She did not see that it was me."

"Oh, this is ridiculous. Why didn't you just tell her?" Saturday asked from her chair.

"That was my question," said Erik. Saturday seemed beyond grateful to have a champion at her side.

"Come now," Jack Woodcutter said to his almost-youngest daughter, "would you have welcomed the love of a man you thought your father despised?"

"Yes." There was no hesitation in Saturday's answer.

"Sunday is not you," said Friday.

"No, my warrior girl," said Woodcutter. "She does not wield an ax quite so well." The siblings chuckled at their father's ribbing, Saturday included. Rumbold envied Woodcutter his ability to sway the emotions of a room so well. But there was one person he could still not control.

"A year," Seven Woodcutter said to her husband. "My son did not die, and you did not tell me. How could you?"

"With respect, ma'am," said Rumbold. "When Joy cast the counterspell, she forbade us all from telling anyone. As time went on, I realized it was for both my own protection as well as the safety of the kingdom. I forbade your husband, in turn, for had he revealed the truth of Jack's tale, he would have revealed my fate as well."

"If it was known throughout the land that the heir to the throne of Arilland was about to be magicked into a frog, what uprisings there would have been," said Velius. "The kingdom might have fallen just to teach one young boy a lesson."

"You did not tell me," Seven repeated to her husband.

"You thought he was dead," Woodcutter told her. "Would you rather have known that he was alive and well, with no intention of ever returning home?"

"It would have made no difference," said Seven. "I thought that anyway, deep in my heart. Somewhere, I still do." Woodcutter stood and crossed the room to embrace his wife, who did not cry. Friday quietly shed her mother's tears for her.

"I found only the medallion in the wolf's belly," Rumbold pointed out, "nothing else. It is entirely possible that Jack might still be alive."

"He's a fighter, that one," said Erik.

"Don't go spreading false hope," Woodcutter warned.

"I met a girl like sunshine and lightning. Suddenly I'm optimistic about everything." Rumbold's cheeriness faded. "Except the fact that I will never see her again." He held the shoe out before him, offering it to anyone who would take it. "I would appreciate it if you would return this to her, with my sincerest . . . apologies."

"Do you love her?" It was Woodcutter who asked the question, but they all waited for his answer.

"Yes," he said immediately. Yes, he loved her. Yes, he yearned for her. *YES,* his heart screamed.

"Then you should return it to her yourself," he said. "With our blessing."

"But I can't." Sunday had made it perfectly clear she wanted nothing more to do with him.

"We were just leaving," said Seven. "Will you be joining us?"

"She needs her family right now," Rumbold said. "She doesn't need . . . She doesn't want . . ." Words once again felt stupid and inadequate. "You should go."

"When you're ready, then," said Woodcutter.

"Please convey our best wishes to your father and his new queen," said Seven, "as well as apologies for our hasty departure."

Rumbold bowed. Seven curtseyed. Her children all stood and dutifully followed suit. Velius showed them the way out of the library and back to the main hall. Saturday, languishing in her chair, was allowed the luxury of staring down Rumbold until Erik pushed her along. As Friday passed, she whispered, "Come soon!"

Rumbold watched them walk away. This family had been his once, in a dream. Gods willing, they would be his again. With the rest of his strength, he clutched that silly silver and gold shoe, the same size as the hole in his heart. Apart from Sunday, there was only one thing left missing: himself.

"I need my memories back," he said to the empty room. "Please."

"The question is: do you *want* them back?" Sorrow sat beside him on the sofa and sipped a cup of tea. But it was not Sorrow; this was her twin sister.

"Do you want to remember all the tragedy, the terror, the mess, the heartbreak?" A bubble lifted off the foam on the surface of the tea and burst before him into birdsong on a sunny day in the summer of his tenth year.

"So much death and destruction. That's an awfully big burden for anyone to carry. I want to make one thing perfectly clear: my 'curse' of change and rebirth included everything. Your past is past. Gone forever. You are a clean slate, my boy." Joy popped two bubbles stuck in tandem; his horse slipped in the rain and broke its leg, and there was the smell of Cook's freshly baked cherry pie. "But only if you want to be."

She crossed her ankles, calmly sipping her tea as though they were not surrounded by a fog two feet deep. Bubbles rose out of it everywhere, as far as his eye could see. The books of the library had disappeared, and with them the walls of the castle. It was just the two of them and the fog, the couch and the tea. A bubble floated by with a cannonball inside it; another held the lush red lips of a very beautiful, very naked woman. He did not touch them.

"Do you think I should? Do you think I'm ready?"

Joy laughed, a sound just like one he had often heard right before the world turned black. Amazing how two sisters in bodies so alike as Joy and Sorrow could be so different down to the core. This laugh was playful, not scheming; mischievous, not vengeful; *for* you, not *at* you.

"Child, no one is ever ready for anything. I would never doom you to that. What sort of adventureless life would that be?"

Rumbold thought perhaps he'd be perfectly content with a nice, boring, uneventful old age. *Blithe and bonny and good and gay.*

Joy popped the bubble that swam right before his eyes. Inside it was a frog and a freckle-nosed girl in the dappled sunshine of the Wood and a different kind of laughter. This wasn't something he'd forgotten; he remembered every detail of that moment, every color and sound and smell. This particular memory was simply one he was trying to hide from himself, and he was ashamed.

The scene faded and left him staring into Joy's eyes, deep violet like the last moment of dusk before the dark and endless night. He lost himself a moment there, and did not miss his aching soul.

"Did you never wonder how you ended up at that particular well?"

Another bubble popped of its own accord: Rollins handed him his mother's golden bauble after the funeral. He pushed it away. *That and a hundred more like it wouldn't get me what I want most in the world,* the young prince said to his manservant.

"You put me there on purpose. Why?" Why would she set him up to meet the love of his life and then break his heart so cruelly?

"I cannot heal all the wounds of this world," she said.

"Can we save Wednesday?" he asked.

"We can try," she said. "I can sometimes nudge the scales away from chaos." She threw her hands out to her sides. The tea was gone, the couch was gone, and her neat black boots hovered just above the strange bubbling fog. The rich colors of her power blinded him. The cameo at her throat smiled and winked. "But first, you must tell me. Do you want them back?"

His mind was still too fragile to hold all his old memories, his body even more so. There were bubbles everywhere now—

a lifetime's worth—so thick he almost lost sight of Joy in them. It would be so easy to let them float off and leave his poor tortured soul alone. But— "I need them," he told her. "I am not whole without them."

Just like Sunday.

"Good answer," she said, right before the world exploded.

When you wake up, stay still. Don't try to stand up. You don't want to be standing up when your mind comes back.

Rumbold rolled to the edge of the couch and emptied the contents of his stomach into the nearest potted plant.

"You be sure to send a thank-you note to Sir Jon Stafford," said Velius. "That was a wedding gift."

Rollins produced a handkerchief and a small glass of water. Rumbold rinsed out his mouth and spat again into the plant. "Take that to the back garden," he ordered the guard at the library door.

"Shouldn't have let you drink that last glass of wine," said Erik.

"It wasn't the wine," said Rumbold, swallowing again to keep his stomach silent. "How long was I out?"

"Long enough for me to see your family safely home," Velius said kindly.

"Long enough for the festivities to have degraded into . . . well, degraded," said Erik.

The prince nodded. "I got the memories back," he said

incredulously. And then, with more disgust, "I got them all back." He washed down the lingering bitter taste with more water. For once, neither of his witty companions had anything to say. *They* had not forgotten anything. They had always known what he was and who he had been. They had not abandoned him, as so many others had. When the time had come for Rumbold to ask for their help, they had given it. And still they stood by him. Rumbold tried to stand as well. "I need to go after her."

With one hand, Velius pushed him back down before he fell down. "You need to go to your bed," he said. "Or be carried there."

"I can put my hands on just the conveyance," Erik said. "But I'll be damned if I'm pushing you around the castle. You're not pretty enough."

Rumbold grasped Velius's elbow. "I *need* her."

"When she sees how pathetic you are, how miserable you look, and"—his nostrils flared—"how bad you smell, I'm sure she'll jump right into your arms and wonder why she ever ran away."

Rumbold should have known better than to turn to family for help. Surely Erik would be more understanding.

"You have vomit on your sash," said the guard.

Rumbold tore the offending sash from his breast. It tangled ungracefully around his ears, and one of the medals scratched his cheek as he removed it. The effort exhausted him. Rollins calmly took the sash away.

"All right," Rumbold said. "I'll bathe, at least. Will you be staying?"

"Your father and his bride departed several hours ago," said Velius. "It's only the dregs left." He pulled Rumbold off the couch and helped him find his footing, keeping pace beside the prince on the way to his chambers. Erik and Rollins followed dutifully behind.

The sounds from the ballroom fell away quickly. The halls were as empty as they might have been at any other time during the wee hours of the morning. The silence and the exercise cleared Rumbold's mind enough for what Velius had said to sink in. If Wednesday and his father had gone, it might already be too late. "Wait! We have to—" Rumbold started, when, two by two, the sconces winked out down the hallway. Whatever he was about to do, the shadows agreed with him. He only wished they could find a way to lend him the energy he was sorely lacking.

Rollins, Erik, and Velius all turned with their backs to the prince, surrounding him in a protective triangle. Erik unsheathed a wicked dagger. Rollins wrapped Rumbold's sash around one fist, the medals splayed across his knuckles.

Rumbold slipped his hand inside Velius's and clasped it tightly. His cousin took the silent hint and hurriedly pushed some of his own health and vigor through their magical link. The prince's palm burned as he took in the energy Velius passed to him. Rumbold knew it wasn't enough and that he'd pay for it come the morning, but he found himself considerably less exhausted than he had been a moment before. Velius's skin burned like a firebrand, and Rumbold caught the smell of singed flesh. All his senses instantly became more alert. The air felt electrified. He could hear the flames in the remaining lamps hungrily consuming their oil. He breathed deeper and stood taller. After the brimstone faded, he could even make out the faint undertone of lilacs and lavender.

"Does anyone else smell that?" asked Rollins.

"Spring," Erik whispered. If the others smelled it, too, perhaps Rumbold wasn't as insane as he'd originally thought.

"Madelyn," breathed Velius.

"You recognize my mother's scent?" Rumbold asked.

"No," said Velius. "I recognize *her*." He pointed to where their shadows fell in a cluster on the wall. Among them was a fifth shade, shorter and wraith-thin, with long, loose hair and a flowing robe or gown. Velius and Rumbold stepped aside to make room for the woman, though she did not physically stand among them. On the wall, they saw her unfurl remarkable wings and encompass them all. "She didn't have those before," Velius said.

"She's had them since I started seeing her ghost," said Rumbold. "Since I returned from the well."

"The nights I woke you up on the hearth," said Rollins.

"Yes."

"Any other brushes with insanity you haven't thought to mention?" Erik asked. It didn't matter if the ghost was friendly or not; he made no move to let down his guard.

"This happened last night," Rumbold said. "The lights led me up to the tower." To his father and Sorrow and their secret plotting behind closed doors. And . . . Wednesday! His mother was leading him to Wednesday!

"The sky tower?" asked Erik, and Rumbold nodded. The commoners called it that, for it hid among the clouds most days. It was said one could venture to the top and seek communion with the Lords of the Wind.

"I'm not a fan of heights," Rollins admitted in a whisper.

"You should go on to my rooms," said Rumbold. "Erik and Velius and I can take care of this." He tore his eyes away from his mother's impressive winged shadow long enough to place a hand on the shoulder of the man who had been far more of a father over the years than his own flesh and blood. "I'll be fine."

Rollins didn't seem to trust Rumbold's show of bravado.

"He'll be fine," said Erik.

Rollins obviously trusted the guard slightly less. "I'll tag along, if that's all right."

"The more the merrier," said Velius.

"Well, gentlemen," said Rumbold. "Shall we?"

This time he knew where they were going, so Rumbold and his men made short work of the distance to the tower. Shadow Madelyn also dispensed with the light show, merely accompanying their fleeting forms as they raced down the hall and up the stairs.

The higher they climbed, the colder it became. Wind whistled through the cracks in the mortar and sang them a mournful lullaby. It wasn't long before Rumbold could see his breath before his face. He was thankful he hadn't removed his smelly jacket along with the sash. He patted the lump at his breast where he kept Sunday's shoe tucked safely near his heart.

"*Really* not a fan of heights," Rollins muttered again. He flattened himself against the wall as they ascended.

"I've always hated this godsforsaken tower," Erik said as they passed another window blocked completely by cloud. "Nothing should be higher than heaven."

"Nothing in this world, anyway," said Velius. "Tell me, Cousin, what are we hoping to find at the end of this maze?"

"Wednesday," Rumbold said. "My father and Sorrow . . . I think they're going to do something to her."

Velius halted mid-step. "No. Not now. Not yet. I mean, I suspected, but the marriage bond wouldn't have set this quickly. There hasn't been enough time. They don't need her consent, granted, but it's so new, the pain would be unbearable. Unimaginable. The pain . . . Oh, gods." He snapped to attention. "Quickly, men! There isn't a moment to lose!"

So Velius knew, then. Rumbold wondered how long his cousin had been possessed of the knowledge that the king was a wife murderer. The prince was desperate to know exactly what had happened to his mother, what pain she had suffered, what agonies had bound her to her current ephemeral state, but it was a conversation for another time. Right now, he needed all his borrowed breath to get him up those stairs and spare Wednesday a similar fate.

Rumbold lifted his knees to keep up the pace behind his suddenly eager cousin, being careful not to slip on the damp stone steps. Madelyn's shadow flew steadily and beatifically above their heads.

The prince's thighs screamed louder than his feet. His

sweaty palm still burned from Velius's touch, and his lungs froze with every breath of the chill mist surrounding them, but he was determined to see this to the end. He owed it to Sunday for the hell he'd put her through. He owed her the life of her sister.

The screams reached them before they arrived at the top of the tower: both a man and a woman, and possibly all the angels in heaven.

Up this high, the clouds outside had become guests of the castle, decorating the aerie with fog. Several times, the men were almost blind, and it hampered their pace. Screams echoed through the mist, bounced off the bare walls, and rang in their ears. Luckily the pea soup layer was thin, and they soon passed through it. Rumbold bade good riddance to the damp, but the cold lingered. It was much harder to breathe now, and his eyeballs felt too big for their sockets. If it hadn't been for Velius's magic infusion, he never would have made it this far.

They emerged from the fog to find themselves at a thick, dark Elder Wood door banded with iron. Velius stopped Rumbold before he could approach. "We do not want to play our hand before we know what awaits us on the other side."

"Wednesday," said Rumbold.

"Blood," said Rollins.

"Death," said Erik.

Madelyn said nothing.

"Which is why we're going to assess the situation first," said Velius, and he leaned out a window.

If one has a castle with a tower (or several) that scrapes the heavens, one puts as many unshuttered windows as possible at the top so that one can look out over one's domain on a clear day. Rumbold wasn't sure which ancestor had constructed the sky tower, but he'd had a very big ego and very strong legs. The screams came to them not from behind the massive door, but from the windows—which meant there was also a window in the room behind that door.

Erik stuck his head out as well and scanned the outside wall of the tower. "There's no purchase," he said. "You don't expect one of us to climb around."

"No," said Velius. "We're going to walk." He held a hand out the window, parallel to the sea of cloud just below them, and closed his eyes.

"Wait!" said Rumbold. "They'll notice you doing magic."

Velius opened one eye to squint at him. "Right now, they wouldn't notice the castle walls falling."

Fair enough.

Velius shut his eye again and whispered something that sounded like *"Xalda."* For the briefest of moments, the moonlit cloudscape shimmered a violet blue. And then Velius jumped out the window.

Erik was slower to follow, but follow he did. Rumbold turned to Rollins. "You don't have to do this. You can stay right here."

The manservant looked out at the clouds and then back down the winding stair. "I've come this far," he said. As Rumbold straddled the sill, Rollins grabbed his hand. "If we encounter any breaks in the cloud cover, I'll trust you to lead me around them."

"Of course," said the prince.

The cloud floor was less resilient than Rumbold had expected: it was more like thick grass than solid wood. The bright moonlight enabled Madelyn's winged shadow-ghost to fly along the outside wall to the window of the room they sought.

"Would you mind, Your Highness?" Velius asked. Madelyn spread her wings wide so that her shadow hid them from view.

Not that they needed it—they could have stood there belled like jesters and no one in that room would have noticed them. There was a white and red triangle painted on the floor, with a star inside it. On one point of the triangle stood Wednesday in her wedding finery, arms splayed, head thrown back, and screaming to the stars. Sorrow was on her knees at another point of the triangle, bent by the weight of the obviously powerful spell she was performing. She seemed to have taken back what power she'd lent the king these last three days. He sat at the third point like a statue, thin and desiccated and still as a corpse.

A corpse with a crown.

Before their eyes, Wednesday began to wither and shrink. She curled into herself like a fern in an ice storm. Her mouth closed, but the screams echoed on. The wedding gown she wore enveloped her in white, swallowing her. The only bits of darkness that remained were her eyes, those haunting violet eyes that now stared out from the body of a pure white goose.

She spread her wings and flapped wildly. Her screams transformed to a succession of quick, desperate honks.

But while Wednesday's body had turned into a goose, her shadow had not. It remained poised, arms outstretched, head tilted back, voiceless throat crying impotent nothingness.

Sorrow collapsed.

The king, who was not as dead as he looked, reached a skinny arm out in front of him and grasped tightly onto nothing. His shadow grabbed shadow-Wednesday's dress and pulled her to him.

"No!" Rumbold lunged through the window. Velius and Erik clawed at him, but they could not stop him. He swept the frantic goose under one arm to keep her from injuring herself with flapping wings. She pecked at his belly with her sharp beak, but he did not let her go.

Unhindered by his son's presence, the king reached the hand not holding the invisible Wednesday out to a bowl filled with blood. Fey blood. Judging by the deep slashes down her forearms, all that blood was Sorrow's.

Rumbold gagged as he put the pieces together. The king had feasted on goose after Madelyn's funeral. He had stolen Madelyn's shadow and drained her power, her essence, until there was nothing left for her, while he had gone on to live his long, unnatural life.

"You will not kill this bird, father."

"You are no son of mine." The corpse spat the words at him in a raspy voice. Rumbold had said as much to himself many a time throughout his life, but they still hurt. "I will take that bird from you, and I will devour it, and her power will be mine forevermore."

The king pulled a long, wicked needle from the hem of his wedding doublet and dragged it through the blood. When he held it up again, it was threaded by a fine, dark red strand. Dumbly, Rumbold watched him make a stitch.

He was sewing Wednesday's shadow onto his own.

He made another stitch and sat up straighter. With each pull of the thread, the king absorbed more of Wednesday's youth and power. Erik threw a dagger at the king to stop him, but it fell to dust at his feet. Velius cast a lightning bolt that shattered into a shower of fairylight.

One more stitch, and the king's hair turned from gray to wheat again. He began to grow taller, as big as he was before, and then more.

"That's certainly never happened before," said Velius. "I would have remembered."

"We have to get out of here!" Rollins grabbed Rumbold's sleeve and pulled him out of his daze. "Quickly!"

The four men spilled out the tower window, back onto the immense stretch of cloud. Erik headed for the stair, but Velius stopped him. Madelyn's shadow blacked the path.

"Not that way," said Velius. "We must run."

Like fleethounds they sprinted over the bright cloudscape. True to his word, Rumbold watched for any breaks in the surface, but there were none. He wondered how long it would take the king to finish sewing, and exactly what kind of monster he'd become once he did. Wednesday was by far the most fey-blooded wife he'd ever had; there was no guessing . . . Then Rumbold heard his name bellowed behind them.

The furious call, while familiar, was deeper and louder than he'd ever heard it before. The men paused and turned their heads long enough to see one enormous arm emerge from the tower window, followed by an enormous crown on an enormous head. The casing cracked and crumbled around the king, as if he were a chick hatching from a stone egg the size of a house.

Wednesday's awesome power had transformed the king into a giant, a giant who was about to chase them across the very cloud cover on which they had escaped. His legs were long enough to cross the distance in half the time it had taken them. He would eat them all in one bite once he captured them.

Rumbold closed his eyes and tightened his grip on the goose. As one, the men turned and began running again, headlong toward the Wood.

19

Those Left Standing

SUNDAY AWOKE on the stones by the window in Wednesday's aerie. It was still dark. The birds were quiet. Clouds still obscured the moon, and the wind whipped through the trees. A storm approached, but it hadn't started raining yet. Thunder rumbled in the threatening sky, followed by the sound that had broken through her dreams and prodded her awake.

Trix was calling for her.

Sunday didn't stop to change out of her old nightgown. She didn't care if she woke Saturday or Peter as she fled down the tower steps, nor did she call out to whoever was still tending a fire in the kitchen at this hour. She left the front door wide open behind her in her haste. Trix called for her and no one else. Her brother needed her, so she ran.

"Sunday!" he cried. "They're coming!"

Sunday rounded the corner of the house to see Trix, dwarfed by the monstrous beanstalk, pointing toward the sky. She squinted up into the darkness until finally, against a paler swath of cloud cover, she made out several tiny figures climbing down the beanstalk. As they grew larger, she realized they were men. There were four of them: two made their way down quickly and one of the slower ones carried something under his arm that hampered his movements, something that dislodged itself and fluttered, then glided, slowly to the ground.

"No!" he cried, and she knew at once that it was Rumbold up there trying desperately not to fall from the beanstalk. The white goose he'd held in his arms landed at Sunday's feet and looked up at her with violet eyes. Wednesday's eyes.

What had happened at the castle after she'd left?

The dark figure in the lead made quick work of the distance from the heavens to the ground, until he had come far enough to leap the rest of the way. "Quick," Velius said breathlessly as he crouched at her feet. "We need to chop this thing down."

"Trix, go get Saturday's ax," she said, but Saturday was already running toward them, ax in hand, long golden hair streaming about her determined face. Her white gown billowed in the darkness as if she were a warrior ghost fresh from beyond the veil. Their avenger waited only long enough for the burly red-headed guard to jump clear of the base before she lifted her strong arms and swung. The polished blade of her small enchanted ax bit into the flesh of the beanstalk and sank deep, but it would not be quick enough to stop whatever was chasing them.

Sunday met Trix's eyes long enough for them to make the mutual decision not to discuss Saturday's miraculous recovery. "I'll get Papa," he said, and ran toward the house.

Velius looked down at the goose, who watched the scene with detached indifference. "Is she . . . ?"

"She's fine," said Sunday.

"Sunday, whatever you may think—"

"Not now," she said. "Please. Just help them."

Erik had already begun hacking at the mass of beanstalk with his dagger, pulling each smaller stalk back and away to get to the heart of the tree at its base. Papa raced past Sunday in a loose shirt and trousers and added his own ax to the effort. The guard stepped aside as Papa and Saturday fell into a cadence: one striking and then the other in a long-practiced rhythm.

Sunday had never witnessed her father and siblings at work in the Wood. Their skill was impressive. Papa blew out even breaths as the sweat began to bead on his forehead; her sister was a flurry of muscles and blade and hair. But fast as they chopped, Sunday knew that none of the Elder Wood they felled was as thick around as this beanstalk.

Trix rejoined her at the base of the tree with bow and arrows in hand and the rest of the family in tow, all in dressing gowns save Aunt Joy, who must have been the one keeping the fire in the kitchen company with her confounded tea. Mama and Friday were both swaddled in blankets. Sunday should have been cold in her ancient nightgown and bare feet, but she felt nothing. She looked up at the beanstalk, at the resolute face of the man whose dreams she shared, and she felt nothing. He had come, as she hadn't dared hope he would.

He had come, but he hadn't come for her.

Thunder rolled again as the clouds trembled and slowly broke apart.

"That's not thunder," said Velius.

The giant's foot burst through the clouds and sought purchase on the beanstalk. It swayed, but the monstrous pillar held the giant's weight. The giant took one step down, then another, and then another. The clouds parted enough to bring out the colors in his wedding clothes and reflect moonlight off his golden crown: the king.

He bellowed again for his son. He called for his head and threatened to crush his tiny body between his mighty teeth. Suddenly, Sunday did feel something. She felt very, very afraid.

"RUMBOLD!" yelled the giant, and shook the stalk in his arms.

Velius was close enough to reach the prince when he fell. Erik dropped his dagger and caught the other man—Rumbold's manservant? Who brings a servant along to run from a giant?

Once they had regained their footing, the men moved back to where the family gathered. The prince looked as if he'd been beaten and then dragged a few miles down the road. She yearned to ask him questions, but now was not the time. She ached to tuck herself under his weary arm and give him comfort, but he stood apart from them and did not meet her eyes. He had not come for her.

"I CAN TASTE YOUR BONES," said the giant. Sunday felt his voice booming deep in her chest.

"Do you have another ax?" the redheaded guard asked Sunday. "Perhaps I can help."

"No," said Peter. "You'd break up the rhythm. This is the fastest way."

"Could we set it on fire?" asked Friday.

Velius shook his head. "Too green. Wouldn't take."

Trix began shooting his arrows into the sky, but they fell short of his target. Even if they'd hit the monster, they'd have been little more than an annoyance.

Mama's fear got the best of her. She grabbed Velius's shirt in desperate fists. "You have to help them," she cried, and then slapped her hands over her mouth.

"Fool of a little sister!" yelled Joy. "You should know better by now." She waved a hand, and Mama clutched at her throat. "You can have your voice back when you've remembered how to use it. You"—she pointed at Velius—"must help them now. You have no choice. Give them what strength you can." She put a hand on his shoulder. "You will feel compelled to siphon it all away from yourself. Try not to." The duke's son nodded and joined Papa and Saturday at the tree.

Honking furiously, the white goose took flight.

"No!" the prince cried again. His throat was raw. The guard and the manservant lunged after the Wednesday goose, but it was too late. "If he should manage to eat her . . ." Rumbold said to Joy.

". . . then the spell will be set," finished Joy. "And if he dies, she dies, too." She knew. This was why she had stayed behind at the towerhouse. This was the danger, the future from which she had pledged to save them.

Having inadvertently doomed yet another child to possible destruction, Mama collapsed into a lump of silent sobs. Friday wrapped her arms around Mama's shaking shoulders. The rest of them watched the Wednesday goose soar heavenward. She was quickly joined by two small bundles of white feathers: Sunday's pigeons. Trix cheered them on, the tiny trio set on attacking a giant against all odds. They flew at his face. The giant swatted them away. They missed being caught by his enormous hands and flew around the stalk again to regroup.

All the while, the Wednesday goose never stopped her taunting, accusatory honking at the giant king. The honking was answered by the screech of an owl. The cry of a whippoorwill. The song of a nightingale. At the bark of a raven, masses of birds burst from the trees around them and flew headlong at the giant. The humans and haefairies below all joined Trix in his cheer.

The birds pecked at the giant king's arms, his legs, his neck, his eyes. He didn't have enough hands to swat them all away. He leaned backward and forward, trying to dodge the attacks. The beanstalk swayed mightily. Papa and Saturday never stopped chopping. Velius was on one knee between them, hands out to each side, and all three glowed a violet blue. The swaying stalk creaked, and then cracked.

Peter dove for Papa. The prince dove for Velius. Erik dove for Saturday and rolled her as far away from the base of the stalk as he could.

"Timber," Trix whispered.

Not the house, Sunday prayed. *Please, gods, not the house.*

The stalk swayed again over the towerhouse, and then fell away toward the Wood. The growling, howling giant king, still engulfed in nightbirds, plummeted. When they both hit the ground, the world shook. Those left standing fell and were covered over by a layer of debris.

Sunday was blind. She opened her mouth to breathe and was choked with dirt and grass and dust. The roar of the giant king mixed with the roar of the earth, and then she could hear nothing at all. No birds chirped. No leaves stirred. The dust settled.

Friday was the first to find her voice. "Is he dead?"

"No." Aunt Joy was the first to find her footing. She marched over to where Peter and Papa lay and yanked Peter's charmed knife out of its sheath. She whispered to the blade, and blue symbols glowed down its length. Joy stepped over the giant's crown, pulled his hair back, and neatly slit his throat.

A geyser of blood and a thick black smoke erupted from the wound. The stench of it made Sunday gag; she pinched her nose shut and swallowed several times in quick succession. As more and more of the inky darkness exited the giant, the king's body shrank.

"Go," Joy told the blackness. "You are not welcome here." The smoke reared up, hovered over Velius and the prince, and then disappeared in the direction of the Wood.

The Wednesday goose landed on the king's stomach; the two white pigeons settled onto the fallen beanstalk behind him.

Joy snatched the goose up by the neck and slit its belly with the still-glowing knife. "As your blood gave him power," said Joy, "may his return it to you." Another fog seeped down from the stained feathers, this one more violet than black. Wednesday's body took form in the shadow. Velius was there to hold her when she grew solid and collapsed in his arms.

Friday moved to cover Wednesday's naked form with her thin blanket and gingerly took the body of the goose from Aunt Joy's hands.

"Now then," said Joy. "About those shadows." She drew a line in the dirt around the corpse with the point of the dagger, and several shadows flew free of the king's. One hovered beside Friday and the goose, her huge wings spread.

"Peter, Trix," Aunt Joy called. "Get some bowls and gather up as much of this blood as you can before the ground drinks it. Friday, we're going to need your needle." Friday, still as silent as Mama, extracted her needle from where it slept at her shoulder, in the seam of her nightgown. "Rumbold, come here."

"You'll forgive me if I decline any more of your magic, my lady." He bowed to lessen the hatred in his words. Sunday wanted to laugh, as she'd said much the same to Aunt Joy.

Joy rolled her eyes in exasperation. "You are stubborn enough to stop a hurricane, young man. Just like your mother." Rumbold smiled slightly at that. "But if you continue to let Madelyn feed off your life force, that storm will run right over you."

"What?"

"You were transformed for only half as long as Jack," said Aunt Joy. "You should have recovered completely in a day or two. But when you helped your mother separate her shadow from your father's, she attached herself to you."

The shadow angel bowed her head in shame. She folded her great wings and lingered sadly beside Joy's own shadow in the moonlight.

"She's been protecting me," protested Rumbold.

"And in doing so, she's very nearly killed you," said Joy. "You must let her go." She knelt at Rumbold's feet and used the knife to draw another line in the earth, through his shadow. "She will remain until the moon sets and the sun rises, and then she will be gone. You have that long to say your goodbyes."

Sunday's breath hitched; tears streamed down her cheeks and streaked mud on her dirty old gown. Lost for so long and just found, and now he had only a few hours in which to sum up a lifetime of love and confusion. Sunday looked to where her parents sat on the grass, Mama's cap burrowed tightly in Papa's solid embrace. They had their imperfections, but they were still her parents. She would always love them, she would always forgive them, and she didn't know what she'd do on the day she had to live without them.

Friday wept, too, crouched over Wednesday's feet, sewing her sister's shadow to her body with a thread of blood on her silver needle. Trix held the bowl for her. Peter knelt in the pool of the king's life and scooped up what he could.

Rumbold addressed the shadow. "I—" He choked and turned to Joy. "I don't know what to say."

"Thank her for having you," Jack Woodcutter said.

"Thank her for protecting you," Peter suggested.

"Thank her for staying as long as she has." Friday hiccupped and caught her breath on a sob.

"Tell her you're proud of her!" shouted Saturday.

"Tell her you'll always remember her," said Trix.

Rumbold nodded at each suggestion but remained forcibly calm. He looked at the shadow of his mother and through that shadow to the beanstalk. He opened his mouth to speak and then clamped it shut again. The pain he felt began to show on his face, and he bowed his head. Sunday knew he did not want his mother's last sight of him to be as a weak man. But she also knew, deep in her heart, that his mother didn't care. Rumbold's mother would love her child now, just as much as she always had, and so on forever, until the end of time. Just as Sunday's own did.

Mama looked at her then and saw the sorrow in her daughter's eyes. She punched Joy in the shoulder. Joy waggled her fingers at Mama's throat. "Just tell her you love her," Mama said.

And because Mama had said it, Rumbold obeyed. "I love you," he cried to the shadow, and then covered his wretched face with his hands.

Sunday could be still no longer. Rumbold might not have come for her, but she could not let him stand alone. Sobbing freely now, she ran to him and flung her arms around his waist, wishing into him whatever strength she had in her meager body. He hugged her back, burying his face in her neck and letting her shed the tears he could not.

Sunday felt the night darken further around them as the

shadow angel encompassed them both with her wings. If nothing else, Rumbold's mother would leave this world knowing that her son was loved.

Wednesday began to stir in Velius's arms. Mama and Papa still clung together in relief. Rumbold's manservant whispered in Trix's ear and sent him scampering back to the towerhouse. Erik and Saturday retrieved the axes at the base of the beanstalk—but what Saturday held up to the sky was no longer an ax. It was a brilliantly shining longsword, its hilt decorated in lines of runes, like Peter's knife.

"That's more like it," said Sunday's warrior sister with the miraculous healing ability, not quite so normal after all. She practiced swinging it around wildly. The redheaded guard jumped to stop her from injuring herself again.

The madness was over. Wednesday was safe. The king was dead. Rumbold's mother would finally rest in sweet peace long deserved. Aunt Joy had overseen the healing of the world. There they all stood, Sunday in her old nightgown, in a pool of giant's blood by the ruins of a magic beanstalk, bathed in quiet moonlight and surrounded by the people she loved most in the world. They were going to survive, and in time, they were going to be all right. But not together. This was the end.

In that moment, Sunday felt utterly, completely alone.

She let go of Rumbold. Then she spun on a heel and began walking back to the towerhouse, one dirty bare foot in front of the other, back to the quiet insanity of her life before. Trix passed her on his way back, carrying one of Friday's embroidered sofa pillows in his hands.

"Sunday, wait."

Finally. Finally, Rumbold called for her. Finally, when she no longer had the will to turn back. She stared at her house, at the gaudy tower jutting out of it that had been her home and would remain so, always and forever. She kept walking. Maybe now that Wednesday was queen, Mama would let Sunday have the aerie.

"I'm sorry," he said.

She stopped and clutched her hands to her breast, wondering how a heart that had been broken so many times in the past week had any piece left large enough to shatter. *Don't do this,* she pleaded silently.

"Sunday, please," he cried. "Don't leave me again."

She refused to turn around; doing so would only smash her resolve. "Attend to your mother. You don't have much time," said Sunday. "And then go home. Go on without me."

"I don't know how."

She closed her eyes. There was so much joy in her, and so much sorrow. How aptly named their godmothers were. What a pair they made.

"It's late." She sighed. "I'm tired"—which was true—"and I'm filthy"—she didn't want to think about the contents of the grime that covered her from head to toe—"and . . ."

The air around her shimmered blue and filled with small bolts of lightning that made all the hair on her body stand on end. Her feet left the ground briefly, and her tears were washed away in a warm, invisible sunlight. Immense happiness filled her, and she *glowed,* from the inside out. When her feet touched the ground again and the blue fairydust dimmed, she found herself back in the silver and gold ball gown. Her hair was clean and pulled back with Thursday's fantastical pins. Even the dirt under her nails had vanished. She lifted her skirts to see that the blood had been washed from her feet, and that she wore only one shoe. With no excuses left, Sunday turned around.

Her family smiled back at her.

The glamour Joy had showered upon her enveloped them all: Mama, Papa, Peter, Friday, Saturday—even Trix—were similarly bedecked in their finery. Velius stood with an arm around Wednesday in the fairy-kissed gray dress she'd worn to the ball that first night.

Rumbold stood before Sunday, as handsome as she remembered, his servant dutifully beside him. In his outstretched hands was Friday's pillow. On that pillow was Sunday's missing shoe.

". . . And?" asked Rumbold.

". . . And we're both saddled with nosy godmothers who are too powerful for their own britches," Sunday finished.

"Agreed," he said.

"Something's not quite right, though," said Sunday, and Rumbold frowned. She walked back to him, reached up, and tousled his magically tamed hair back into the mess it always was. "Better," she said.

Sunday and her prince stared at each other for a very long time.

"I have something for you," he said finally.

"Do you?"

He nodded. "You seemed to have misplaced a recurring theme." He gestured to the shoe and the boot-shaped house behind her. If he only knew that it was Tuesday's dress she now wore. "I'm very glad I didn't take more than a bloom off that bush," he whispered. "I'd never have forgiven myself if you'd lost a leg."

"Are you sure it's mine?" she teased.

"This shoe belongs to the woman who holds my heart," he said. "It belongs to my soul mate. It belongs to my princess."

Sunday melted at his words. Hope blossomed inside her, and she felt alive once again. She reached for the shoe, but Saturday snatched it off the pillow before she could touch it.

"Fantastic!" her sister cried. "I thought I'd lost something back there. Thanks so much for returning it, dearie!" Saturday made a show of tossing her own shoe off and then trying to cram her statuesque foot into the delicate silver and gold creation. The faces she pulled while struggling to get the shoe on as she balanced herself with her new sword made Sunday laugh.

As terrible as they were sometimes, she was glad she had her sisters with her. She put a hand on Tuesday's gown, felt Thursday's pins in her hair and Monday's kiss on her cheek. *All* her sisters.

"You idiot." Friday jumped in, grabbed the shoe out of Saturday's hands, and pushed her just enough to send her toppling to the ground. "You'll destroy it with those great elephant feet of yours. It's obviously *my* shoe." She lifted her voluminous skirts. "I figure I may as well be a princess as anything."

Sunday was forced into action at this, since Friday was not much taller than she and her foot probably *would* fit in that shoe. She frowned and plucked it right out of Friday's hands. Friday smiled and kissed her playfully, then returned to where the shadow angel stretched against the beanstalk. She and Madelyn both raised their arms to the sky in victory.

Rumbold steadied Sunday while she pulled the shoe on. "I cannot promise you a happy ending," she admitted as she took his hand. "But I can promise you an interesting life."

"A man could not be doomed to a better future."

They smiled at each other.

"If I may be so bold, Miss Woodcutter . . ." he started.

"Please, call me Sunday."

"Sunday." He smiled again. "Do you think you could find it in your heart to kiss me?"

Sunday had wondered how long it would take before he got around to asking. And as the morning sun peeked over the horizon to greet them all, she did.

20
The Barefoot Princess

SHE'S UP THERE again."

Rumbold massaged his temples while Rollins settled a new sash over an old doublet. This one was violet, and bedecked with twice as many medals as the last one he'd worn. A week earlier, this much weight on his chest would have toppled him. He tried not to think about what he'd sacrificed to regain that strength.

"The queen is up in the Sky Tower again, writing on stones," Erik repeated. "You'll forgive me if I haven't gone after her."

Rollins shuddered visibly at the mention of the tower.

"We should seal it off," said Rumbold. "There's nothing up there but clouds and ruins and bad memories. What if she should fall?"

"She'd probably fly," muttered Rollins, before excusing himself. That theory seemed to be the general consensus regarding the fate of Rumbold's godmother as well; the whole top of the tower had crumbled and fallen after the wrath of the giant king, but no one had seen Sorrow in the aftermath, and no bodies had been found beneath the rubble.

"How do I look?" Rumbold asked Erik.

"Like a pompous ass with bad hair," said the guard.

"Perfect," said Rumbold. "The Woodcutters are coming by this morning. Will you be joining us?"

"I wouldn't miss it for the world," said Erik, this time without sarcasm.

"Excellent. Now if you'll excuse me, I need to check in with my wife."

Sunday was in "their garden," as she called it, the side garden off the ballroom and over the hedge from the courtyard, where they'd sat after the Savage Seven Riot and where she'd run from him on that fateful night she'd lost a shoe. Rumbold snickered at the thought; after he'd returned that little miracle of silver and gold and professed his love, it was as if she'd vowed to never wear shoes again. She'd only capitulated at his father's funeral, when Arilland mourned the loss of its long-lived ruler, King Hargath.

It was Joy who'd remembered his name; her link to Sorrow allowed her alone to hold on to it when no one else could. When the minister first heard it, his eyes grew a little wider, but he never let on that the name of Arilland's lord and master had slipped his mind. It took a moment more for the mental fog to lift and reveal the king's betrayal: exactly how long he'd been king, what he had done to get there, and how no one could have stopped him. When the minister repeated the name aloud again over the grave, Rumbold watched the eyes of the crowd go wide in waves. The breaking of the spell was thick in the air, and then the wind blew it away.

Sunday had run wild during their small private wedding ceremony in the Wood by the Fairy Well. She'd danced with him in that little clearing, her toes bare, wearing a homespun gown, a wreath of daisies encircling her golden head. They'd joined hands and shared a cup of water and together they'd thrown silver in the Well, thanking it for making a desperate dream come true. Rumbold had loved Sunday more on that sunny afternoon than he'd ever thought possible.

It was a rare thing to see his Sunday shod at all these days. He'd overheard her being referred to around the castle halls as the Barefoot Princess. But the courtiers always smiled when they said it, so Rumbold let them keep their silly nickname. He found it hard not to smile when he thought of Sunday, too.

This morning was no different. Rumbold stood on the balcony and watched as Sunday and Trix tried to convince a squirrel to pull a rope up the old oak tree and throw the knot over the other side so they could hang a swing. The squirrel seemed intent on thwarting them, and each of Sunday's blustery cries of frustration ended in giggles. Trix jumped up and down, waving his arms in a demonstration of what he expected the squirrel to do. Sunday stomped her foot on the path, and Rumbold caught a glimpse of dirty toes peeking beneath her long skirts. Her hair flowed loose down her back, sprinkled with leaves and tiny flowers, like a river turned gold by the sun. A butterfly perched by her ear, oblivious to Sunday's halfhearted rants. She would always be his girl in the Wood. He would have had it no other way.

Rumbold took a deep breath of spring and the wildflowers in the air. He was glad his mother's spirit had remained long enough to see the two of them together, to see him happy. He turned his face to the sky and smiled into the sun. If the gods were kind, perhaps she could still see.

~eeeee~

"How many times do I have to tell you? You cannot rush training!" Velius's command fairly echoed off the walls of the Grand Hall. Rumbold had never heard his cousin raise his voice as much as he had since the death of the king, since Saturday had shown up at the training grounds with her sword and demanded to be taught how to use it.

Saturday was hot on Velius's heels. "You insulted me by handing me a stick." She could only mean the practice swords the boys used on the grounds. Actual swords were forbidden to all but the most advanced students.

"You insulted *me* by refusing to be taught properly!"

"I've held an ax since I was a baby."

"That doesn't mean you know how to wield a sword."

"Only because you won't let me try and find out!" spat Saturday. "Did you use all your fancy magical powers when you first started training?"

"Yes," admitted Velius. "Which is why I don't advise using them as a crutch."

"But you've seen what I can do," said Saturday. "You know what I'm capable of."

"I have," Velius said, "and I do. I also know how quickly you overreact, and how easy it would be for you to get yourself hurt."

She shrugged. "I wouldn't be hurt for long."

Velius looked very much in danger of hurting her right then and there to test exactly how long it would be, when Erik put a hand on his shoulder. "Tap out," he said. They had been taking turns with Sunday's headstrong sister for several days now, and though the switches happened further and further apart, Saturday still possessed the necessary brazenness to wear both men down to the breaking point again and again.

It was a sight to be seen, one Rumbold alone had not yet tired of. He remembered the arrogance and frustration that came with being unbreakable. He considered offering Saturday her own rooms at the castle. Then again, she could always stay with her eldest sister, as Princess Monday had chosen to remain in residence.

"She's all yours," spat Velius.

Saturday opened her mouth as if to speak. Erik said nothing, only raised one finger. She shut her mouth again and glared at him balefully.

"Saturday," scolded Seven. "You're not going to wash up before joining us?"

Saturday adjusted her swordbelt and patted some of the dust off her sleeves. "I'm no dirtier than the princess's feet. If she gets to stay, then so do I."

Everyone turned to Sunday, who simply smiled and shrugged. Rumbold made a mental note to speak with his new warrior sister. Her being indestructible meant she had a destiny to fulfill, as he had. They should probably find out what that was before she drove his best friends to madness.

"Oh!" Friday gasped, and put a hand on her patchwork pocket. "I almost forgot." She reached in and drew out a perfect golden egg, only slightly smaller than the one Rumbold had visited in his father's collection of curiosities.

Trix hopped on his toes, eager to tell the story. "Friday sewed the goose back together, too," he said. "She lays golden eggs!" The ever-frugal Seven beamed at the news, and Sunday visibly relaxed in the knowledge that her family would be taken care of without anyone seeing it as charity.

Rumbold took the egg from Friday—it was much lighter than he'd imagined—and transferred it to the steady hands of a serving boy. "See that this gets to Cook," he said. "Tell her to keep the shell for herself." In a slightly lower voice, he added, "And send the butcher up if you would, please."

"They're good eating," said Jack Woodcutter, who was still ever so slowly opening up to him. "I had a golden omelet just this morning."

"Did it turn your tongue gold?" asked Sunday.

"It did," said her papa. "And your mother did everything I asked her to do for the next hour solid." Seven swatted her husband playfully on the backside.

"Ah, Friday, before I forget," said Rumbold. "Yarlitza Mitella was to have returned to the mountains today, but I made sure she heard of you and your deft needle before she finished packing. I took the liberty of arranging a tea with her this afternoon. I hope you don't mind. She's very interested in meeting you." He had braced himself for Friday's inevitable throwing of herself into his arms, but he had not been prepared for the ear-splitting squeal that came with it. "I'll take that as a yes."

"Thank you," Joy said to him. "I had not thought about pairing those two together."

"It seemed to make sense."

"Of course," she said, and welcomed Friday's embrace when she turned to express her happiness. "I could not have chosen a better apprenticeship for you, dearest," she said into her goddaughter's curly mane. "Mistress Mitella will teach you well." Friday chose her mother as her next hugging victim, and Joy straightened. "In fact, I shall be taking on an apprentice of my own."

The family turned as one to see Wednesday in the doorway with Monday at her arm, dark in her dress as a windblown shadow against Monday's shining light.

"You're leaving us?" Trix asked mournfully.

Wednesday put a gentle hand on his head. "None of us ever leaves," she said, "not really."

"I must take her into Faerie," said Joy. "She is far too powerful to remain here. Her continued presence will upset the balance." So *that* was why Wednesday spent all her time as close to the clouds as possible: to avoid causing chaos in the world below. What they had all perceived as borderline insanity for so long had been necessary for their protection.

Wednesday tilted her head at him in acknowledgment. "This evil has passed, and now I must go."

No one but Rumbold seemed to notice that she said "this" evil instead of "the" evil. He was sure the turn of phrase had something to do with Sorrow. If his godmother had fled back over the borders of Faerie to lick her wounds, then Joy was doubly obliged to follow.

"I knew you were never meant for this world," Seven told her daughter, "but you got to be mine for a time. May the gods watch over you, child."

"There is only one thing left to do," said Joy. "One wound left to heal. We need to give this country back its king."

Wednesday stepped forward, placed her hands on Rumbold's shoulders, and kissed both his cheeks. "I hereby cede the throne of Arilland to you," she said. "My stepson, my brother, my savior, my friend."

He was indeed all of those—as Wednesday herself had said, a man born four times. Sunday's hand slipped inside Rumbold's and she squeezed her support. The family and whatever servants were present to witness the event took to one knee.

"Long live the king," Wednesday whispered.

The phrase sent chills through his body. Sunday squeezed his hand again. Rumbold did hope to live a long and full life, but not one terribly longer than any other mortal man. He was comforted by the fact that Sunday would remain by his side for all of it.

"Long live the king!" a voice called from the far end of the Grand Hall in a deep bass: Jolicoeur had joined them. "Long live King Rumbold and Queen Sunday!"

The cry was echoed throughout the room and then slowly, increasingly, echoed throughout the castle. Within minutes, Rumbold heard it shouted from the ramparts and parapets to the streets below. He bowed his head again to Wednesday and noticed his wife's dainty—and yes, dirty—toes peeking from beneath her skirts again. The Frog Prince and the Barefoot Princess, now King and Queen. There had been worse rulers.

In the clamor, Rumbold saw Velius approach Wednesday. He took the hand she offered and kissed it. "To me, you will always be a queen."

"Once in this life, again in another," she said, "and I will always be sorry for it."

"We bid you all farewell," said Joy.

"Not just yet," said Rumbold. He beckoned for the butcher. "Dearheart, may I introduce you to Mister Jolicoeur?"

Jolicoeur put a hand over his heart and bowed to Sunday, who looked up at both of them curiously.

"Mister Jolicoeur is Captain Thursday's first mate."

Seven gasped. Trix cheered. Sunday dissolved in a fit of laughter that filled Rumbold to the brim once again with love for her.

Jack Woodcutter crossed the room and put his arm around

Rumbold, who tried his best to remain conscious through the pain of that fierce embrace. "When you're cursed with one Woodcutter, you're cursed with them all, eh?"

"It would seem so, sir."

"I won the heart of Sunday's mother with a goose of my own," Woodcutter said. "Did I ever tell you that story?"

"No, sir," said Rumbold, King of Arilland. "I don't believe I've heard that one."

"Have a seat," said Woodcutter. "I'll tell you all about it. And then you can tell me how you came to meet my daughter the Pirate Queen."

Rumbold settled into a chair large enough for Sunday to curl up beside him, and prepared to be entertained by a lifetime's worth of his new father's stories.

They had a lot to catch up on.

~elle~

I still wonder sometimes about Jack Junior. I walk the flower-lined paths through the garden—my garden—and I dance down the empty hallways of the castle—my castle—and I think back on the adventures that brought me here, all the magic and misery that led us to this place. What songs will be sung about me and my family? What tales do they already tell? Am I a silly girl who befriended a frog or a beautiful stranger in a ballroom full of pretty gowns? Am I a barefoot princess or a benevolent queen? Bean sower and gold spinner and giant slayer: I was all those things. I have lived a life full of love and pain, of Joy and Sorrow, and I live on still. I have many, many years ahead of me, each day with the potential to be filled to the brim with trials to face and challenges to overcome.

I made Rumbold tell me again last night the story of what had happened with Jack Junior and the wolf, when he had killed the beast and retrieved the gold medallion and sent it back to Papa. I questioned everything, reached in and pulled out every detail he could remember. He went over and over it until he'd had enough of me, and I fell asleep with my mind still mulling over one incontrovertible fact: Jack's body has never been found.

All those school chants and drinking songs about this man who slew dragons and saved worlds—now that I have slain and saved as well, I see an even better picture of what might be the truth . . . and what might be a lie. New songs pop up around the countryside every so often about our legendary Jack. What if they're really a message to us? Maybe they're saying, in their own secret, storytelling way: I live on still. How better to communicate to a family of taleswappers than with a story well told?

How indeed.

The minstrels had fled with their stories after the king's death. There were only six bards left on the castle grounds, and I called them all to me. My first official command. Sometimes it's fun being queen.

I gathered these craftsmen together to tell them my story, the whole story, the complete truth of everything that had happened in the past few weeks. Thus armed, I planned to send these songwriters and storytellers on their way with purses filled with silver and a mission to spread the tales of my adventurous family far and wide.

If Jack's tales can reach us here in Arilland, perhaps our tales will find him someday, wherever he may be. He will laugh to discover how, *even in his absence, he brought the oncoming storm as a stone brings an avalanche. He will know we are safe and well, and he will know that it's blood and booty and business as usual around the Woodcutter house-hold. And maybe one day, when one of his new tales comes back to us, he will, too.*

This novel could not have been possible without four unlikely muses: a frustrated mother, a South American president, a North Korean dictator, and an Internet celebrity author.

I am sure that Marcy Kontis had no idea when her eldest teenage daughter sat at her feet in the dining room and whined, "Mom, tell me what to write," that her daughter would take it quite this far.

I am sure that Eric James Stone had no idea that when he raised the bar in the Codex Writers group by including *every single* story trigger in "By the Hands of Juan Perón" (instead of just one from each column) for the Get the Creative Juices Flowing Contest that I would then take every single one of the Fairy Tale Contest suggestions and jump over that bar. (He beat me in both contests, but I got published first, so we both win.)

I am sure that Kim Jong-Il never heard a word I said when Ken Scholes made me scream a promise to him out over the Pacific Ocean that I would finally finish my manuscript once and for all. (The roses I received on Mr. Kim's behalf upon completion were gorgeous, though.)

I do know for a fact, however, that John Scalzi had no idea that seeing him at Millennicon was the reward I had planned to give myself if I finished the manuscript and sent it off to my agent before the weekend of the convention. I'm so glad I did. I believe Cincinnati still speaks of us all in hushed tones.

I would also like to thank, in some particular order:

Casey Cothran-Muldrew and Margo Appenzeller, who penned the original Princess Stories with me. Orson Scott Card, for being the teacher in the back of my head constantly telling me to "just write the novel." Andre Norton, for being my guardian angel. Fellow Codexian and Orson Scott Card Bootcamper Christine Amsden, for suggesting the Fairy Tale Contest in the first place. Brian Keene, who was with me in the first dance. (I am happy that our forbidden friendship has lasted far longer than my relationship to the pillock who forbade it in the first place). Luc Reid, founder of the Codex Writers group, who sat me down the day after my birthday party and told me to submit "Sunday" to *Realms of Fantasy*. Shawna McCarthy (with help from Doug Cohen), who accepted my ten-thousand-word "short" story for publication in *Realms of Fantasy*. Scott Grimando, for the most amazing centerfold illustration a girl could ever dream of, and the fantastic story of the bicycling adventure that went along with it.

Deborah Warren, my agent of sunshine and delight, a kindred spirit from that moment in that little café in Pasadena when she peered at me over her rhinestone-studded sunglasses and told me she liked my aura. Reka Simonsen, fairy godmother and dream editor, a kindred spirit from the moment when, out of the blue, she quoted my favorite Diana Wynne Jones character in an e-mail. The Starbucks on Old Fort Parkway in Murfreesboro, Tennessee, for making that last homestretch of writing physically possible.

Mary Robinette Kowal and her parents, Ken and Marilyn Harrison; Lillie and Chuck Rainey; Ken and Sherrilyn Kenyon (and the boys); Janet and Mike Lee; J.T. and Randy Ellison; Eddie Coulter, Edmund Schubert, and Leanna Renee Hieber for their love, support, inspiration, motivation, and solace.

Joe Branson, a.k.a. "The Fairy GodBoyfriend," who knew exactly what it would take to win the heart of a princess but went and did it anyway.

And, finally, to Adam, Josh, Turtle, Rob, and Chappy of the Adam Ezra Group, because I wrote most of these acknowledgments on a scrap of notebook paper while waiting for their show to start at the 8×10 club in Baltimore.

May we *all* be doomed to a happy life.